SERWA BOATENG'S GUIDE TO WITCHCRAFT AND MAYHEM

Also by Roseanne A. Brown

Serwa Boateng's Guide to Vampire Hunting

SERWA BOATENG'S
GUIDE TO
WITCHCRAFT AND MAYHEM

by Roseanne A. Brown

RICK RIORDAN PRESENTS

DISNEY • HYPERION   LOS ANGELES   NEW YORK

First Edition, September 2023
1 3 5 7 9 10 8 6 4 2
FAC-004510-23209
Printed in the United States of America

This book is set in Meridien LT Std/Adobe Systems
Designed by Zareen Johnson
Adinkra images © 2022 by El Carna
Stock images: additional adinkra and chapter borders 1831107325/Shutterstock

Library of Congress Cataloging-in-Publication Data

Names: Brown, Roseanne A., author.
Title: Serwa Boateng's guide to witchcraft and mayhem / by Roseanne A. Brown.
Description: First edition. • Los Angeles ; New York : Disney-Hyperion, 2023.
• Series: Rick Riordan Presents • Audience: Ages 8–12. • Audience: Grades 4–6. • Summary: In order to steal the Midnight Drum and free her powerful grandmother, twelve-year-old vampire Serwa deceptively collaborates with her rival Declan, a Slayer, but joining forces compels Serwa to confront truths about herself she has tried hard to deny.
Identifiers: LCCN 2022057259 • ISBN 9781368066464 (hardcover) • ISBN 9781368066778 (ebook)
Subjects: CYAC: Vampires—Fiction. • Magic—Fiction. • Mythology, African—Fiction. • Ghanaians—United States—Fiction. • Supernatural—Fiction. • Interpersonal relations—Fiction. • LCGFT: Paranormal fiction. • Novels.
Classification: LCC PZ7.1.B7967 Sf 2022 • DDC [Fic]—dc23
LC record available at https://lccn.loc.gov/2022057259

Reinforced binding
Follow @ReadRiordan
Visit www.DisneyBooks.com

SUSTAINABLE FORESTRY INITIATIVE
Certified Sourcing
www.forests.org
SFI-01681

Logo Applies to Text Stock Only

To every person who still walks into a museum
hoping maybe this time the paintings will come to life

CONTENTS

Prologue
(Aka: How to Recap Your Life as It's Falling Apart Around You)

"Draw a monster. Why is it a monster?"—Janice Lee

ONCE UPON A TIME, a girl grew up in a world filled with monsters.

And not your gotta catch 'em all, cutesy mascot-type monsters. I'm talking darkness come to life—creatures with fangs and claws that can burrow into your brain as easily as they suck the blood from your veins. These monsters lived in plain sight, masquerading as people's friends, children, and loved ones.

But was the young girl frightened by this terrifying truth of the world? Did she hide under her covers wetting her pants because if anybody around her could be a monster wearing a human's face, how then could she trust anyone?

No, because the girl's parents made sure she knew that while yes, monsters were everywhere, they could be defeated. *She* could defeat them.

So the young girl dedicated her life to the task of monster hunting. She traveled the land with her parents learning everything there was to know about evil and the vanquishing thereof. Together, the three of them saved lives, reunited families, and kicked some serious vampire butt.

Until one day, the young girl discovered that her parents hadn't been completely honest with her. Her own mother was a monster . . . and not only that, the girl was—*is*—one, too.

As you can expect, the girl reacted . . . well . . . to put it nicely, she freaked the flip out. Monsters were bad and evil. If she herself was one, didn't that make her all those things, too?

She ran away from her parents, from the people she loved more than anything and anyone in the whole entire world, deep into the forest. There, she found a witch with a voice like honey and fangs like knives. The witch promised to teach the girl about what it really means to be a monster.

The girl wasn't stupid. She knew from Disney movies and fairy tales. She knew what happens to girls foolish enough to trust witches.

But still, the girl let the witch lead her into the unknown.

And voilà, you are now officially caught up on the flaming carousel that is my life. And unlike in the storybooks, there are no singing animals or guaranteed happily-ever-afters here.

The only guarantee vampires get is blood.

I

How to Start Your Day
with a Knife Fight

*"A true warrior knows their enemy's stronghold even
better than their own."*

—from the *Nwoma*, a collection of
Abomofuo teachings and histories passed
down through the generations

YOU KNOW SOMETHING HAS gone horribly wrong
in your life when you wake up surrounded by three
vampires wearing bow ties, and that's not even the
third most craptacular thing that's happened to you in
the last twenty-four hours.

The trio are adze in their giant firefly form. They
have not only bow ties but also little jackets and hats,
and they're each holding a silver tray filled with bagels,
fruit, and other breakfast foods. A normal person's reaction to something like this would probably be:

A) Scream

B) Cry

C) Pee

D) All of the above

But my first groggy, sleep-addled thought is *Wow, I've
never seen an adze wear clothes while in monster form before!*

My second thought is *I need to get the heck out of
here* now.

I leap from the covers, wobbling only a second from the thick pounding in my skull. This isn't my cousin Roxy's bedroom. Why aren't I in Rocky Gorge? What's going on?

Doesn't matter. When there's an enemy in front of you, there's only one thing to do—attack.

I crouch low to sweep the first adze's feet out from under him. He goes down with a surprised screech, a glass bottle tumbling from the tray in his claws. I snatch the bottle before it hits the ground and smash it against the base of the bed. Sparkling grape juice flows everywhere as I point my makeshift weapon at the other two adze, the jagged neck of the bottle in my hands, my back flat against the wall.

"Back up!" I yell. "Twe wo ho!" I repeat the command in Twi just in case they don't understand English. The adze let out nervous titters, but they don't come any closer. Even though my instincts have my muscles battle ready, my head feels like it's been squeezed through a trash compactor. Where am I? Why does my body feel like someone shoved it into a Nutribullet on high?

I hear my parents' voices in my head whispering at me to orient myself. For some reason, thinking about them only makes the pain worse. But still, I take a moment to search my surroundings.

I'm in a hotel room, the fancy kind with a mini bar and towels fluffy enough to steal. Though my head's killing me and my body aches, I don't have any physical injuries. I'm wearing silk pajamas, and they feel so nice they've got to be the real deal and not the cheap knockoffs Mom used to buy at the beauty supply store. The room has two viable exits: the front door and the window.

Speaking of the window, from here I can make out a host of

gray buildings outside, traffic moving as a city wakes up for the day, and a white dome-shaped building in the distance.

Holy mmoatia dookie, that's the Capitol! I'm in a hotel in Washington, DC.

I'm in a hotel in Washington, DC, and surrounded by *vampires.*

But this doesn't make any sense. Rocky Gorge, Maryland, the town I've been living in for the last few weeks, is miles away from DC. How'd I get all the way here? My memories feel like dandelion fluff—the harder I try to catch them, the farther away they fly. I'm shaking in confusion, looking wildly around the room for something, *anything,* that might explain how I got here, when my eyes land on my reflection in the mirror across from the bed.

Specifically, on the crimson eyes wide in my face and the blade-sharp fangs jutting out of my mouth. The answer to my confusion hits me harder than a semitruck:

There are vampires in this room because I'm a vampire, too.

A floodgate opens in my mind, and the memories pour out faster than a tsunami. Defeating the adze that possessed my old bully Ashley on Back-to-School Night. Discovering that the infamous obayifo Boahinmaa is my mother's sister. Confronting my parents over lying about my heritage my entire life. Unleashing a wave of black magic that plunged all of Rocky Gorge into a blackout.

And maybe worst of all, erasing the memories of the only friends I've ever had.

Tears burn the back of my eyes as the echoes of my friends' desperate screams ring in my ears. No, no I can't think about Roxy, Mateo, Gavin, and Eunju now because if I start crying, I don't think I'll ever stop.

What happened next? Okay, I erased their memories and then ran into the forest, which is when my aunt—

As if my thoughts summoned her, Boahinmaa—no, my Auntie Effi—enters my room without knocking.

"I hope all the commotion in here means you're getting ready for breakfast, because I am famished."

Even though it's *too early to legally be considered a time humans should actually be awake* o'clock, my aunt looks like she's ready to step onto the red carpet with her waist-length silk-pressed black hair and sharp business suit. She takes a sweeping look at the adze on the ground, the other two quaking in the corner, me backed against the wall, and lifts a single eyebrow. "Did you make a shank out of a sparkling grape juice bottle?"

When I glare at her, she lets out an amused chuckle. "My sister certainly raised you well. But come eat breakfast. We have a lot of ground to cover today, and you shouldn't do it on an empty stomach."

I have spent the entirety of my twelve years on this planet training to be a Slayer of creatures of black magic. All my instincts are screaming at me to attack this woman before she attacks me. But a voice in my head that sounds like neither my mother nor my father but my own reminds me of a single crucial fact: I have nowhere else to go. The Abomofuo, the secret society of vampire hunters I was raised in, will never accept me after I broke the seal that kept my black magic at bay. Neither will my parents. I can't go back after I literally attacked them in an IHOP parking lot. That's one occasion Hallmark doesn't make an *I'm Sorry* card for.

Besides, I spent the entire night surrounded by several vampires and one of the most powerful witches who has ever existed, and nothing happened to me. If my aunt wanted to hurt me, she would've by now. Even though it goes against everything I've been taught, I'm safer right here than I would be anywhere else at the moment.

Then again, that might change if I don't put this shank down.

"One question before I follow you: Where am I?" I demand.

"Isn't it obvious, Serwa?" Auntie Effi's mouth curls up in an expression far too sharp to be a smile, her fangs gleaming over her bottom lip. "You're with the vampires now."

IF YOU'RE ANYTHING LIKE me, when you hear the words *vampire lair*, you probably imagine a decrepit haunted house on a hill with spiderwebs everywhere and creepy organ music playing in the background. Well, Auntie Effi's headquarters couldn't be more different. In fact, her lair isn't a house at all but an entire hotel.

"I would've given you a tour when we arrived, but you were so distraught that I thought it best to just put you to bed," says my aunt as she leads me out of her massive penthouse suite. Behind us the adze butlers mutter what sound like bug insults while they clean up the smashed breakfast I left behind. "Now that you're awake, let me be the first to officially welcome you to the Luciole Hotel."

Now, I've been in some fancy-schmancy places in my life, but what I see while the glass elevator carries us to the ground floor makes my mouth hang open. The center of the Luciole Hotel is a twelve-floor atrium of sparkling windows and gilded railings all centered around a bustling lobby filled with more creatures of black magic than I've ever seen in my life. Sasabonsam hang from the balcony railings, sunning their leathery wings in the warm light. Bonsam in little green bellhop hats and vests drop off food deliveries to the rooms. A whole group of red mmoatia—the evil kind, as opposed to white mmoatia and black mmoatia like my father's partner, Boulder—are managing the front desk, frantically yelling into phones that look comically oversized in their miniature hands. The whole place is like Disneyland for creatures of black magic, and it's so . . .

Peaceful.

I don't even realize I have my nose pressed to the glass until Auntie Effi says, "This must look so surprising to you after all the years of Abomofuo propaganda saying our kind is capable of nothing but chaos and destruction."

I shiver at the words *our kind*. Some tiny part of me still doesn't want to believe what I am . . . what I can do.

My mind fills with the wailing sirens and frantic screams that followed my black magic outburst in Rocky Gorge. My hands begin to shake, and Auntie Effi places one of hers on my shoulder. "No obayifo goes through her first blood frenzy without a few injuries," she says. "At least nobody died."

I feel like if the best thing you can say about a situation is "at least nobody died," then things aren't going so great for you. It's uncanny how easily she can guess my thoughts, but I nod and let her lead me through a tour of the hotel. The rest of the building is just as magnificent as the lobby, and my aunt is practically glowing with pride as she shows me the state-of-the-art conference rooms, restaurants, and other amenities. Everywhere we go, the creatures of black magic stop whatever they're doing to greet Auntie Effi like loyal subjects admiring their queen.

Me, on the other hand, they look at like the kind of monster who follows the fairy-tale queen home.

The feeling is very mutual.

"Is that owuo atwedeɛ?" I ask as we pass the sculpture at the center of the atrium's ground floor. It's an obsidian ladder with only four rungs. Offerings of libations and foodstuffs have been left out at the base of it.

Auntie Effi nods. "Death's ladder. One of the few Adinkra we beings of black magic aren't harmed by." She places a hand against the sculpture and gives a small prayer before continuing on our way. "It's always important to honor the source of our powers."

Whoa, the god of death is the source of black magic? That's news to me. But it makes sense. If divine wisdom comes from Nyame and the other gods, I get why its opposite would come from Owuo, the god of death.

I grimace. "Obayifo worship Owuo?"

"We do not worship him. We acknowledge that death is an inescapable and necessary part of life. Respecting its power allows us to live alongside it rather than be controlled by the fear of it."

I nod along slowly, though I still don't really get it. Owuo is one of the more mysterious members of the Akan pantheon. Among the Akan people, he's a farmer with a cutlass he uses to strike down human souls. They consider him evil—one of his first actions after being born was to try to kill his dad, Nyame, and he succeeded! (Don't worry—Nyame got better.) A craver of human flesh, he has been known to offer it to unsuspecting people. He commands the spirits of the afterlife to do his bidding and can send them in a giant whirlwind against his enemies.

But according to the Krachi people, another tribe in Ghana, Owuo is a cyclops who is just doing his job and isn't that bad. Either way, he's one god I'm glad I haven't had to deal with yet.

"I saw the Capitol from my window," I say as I follow my aunt into a private dining room with two more of the adze butlers standing outside the door. "How are you hiding this place right in the middle of DC?"

Without getting caught by the Abomofuo is the part I don't add, because reminding my aunt that up until about twenty-four hours ago I was allied with her mortal enemies seems like a bad idea. (And that's coming from someone who tried to fight off a bunch of vampires with a beverage bottle!)

"As far as non-magic entities are concerned, this building has lain abandoned for decades as it's at the center of a rather convoluted legal dispute that bars the city from renovating or selling the land," my aunt replies. "And as for your Abomofuo, our people would not have lasted as long as we have if we weren't able to camouflage our magic when we need to."

Several of the bonsam fly around our heads adjusting napkins and bringing out more cutlery. I duck to avoid one. "And how are you paying for all this?"

"You'd be amazed how much wealth one can amass with a bit of black magic unleashed on the right Wall Street banker at the right time."

Well, that opens more questions than it answers—and very possibly makes me an accomplice to insider trading—but the woman I once knew as Boahinmaa waves her hand toward the food in the universal auntie gesture for *Shut your pie hole and eat before I feed you myself.* A whole feast stretches out on the table between us. There are some Ghanaian dishes, like egusi stew with thick chunks of roasted goat; warm balls of kenkey; still-steaming tilapia; and a whole bowl of red red bean stew and rice. There are also fluffy blueberry pancakes, smoked salmon, and those little green pea things I can never remember the name of.

And there's blood. An entire crystal pitcher full of it. Nausea roils through my stomach as my aunt pours two glasses of the red liquid and places one in front of me.

"I wasn't sure if you'd prefer Ghanaian or American food, so I had my chefs prepare both." It must be clear from my face I'm ten seconds away from puking, because Auntie Effi calmly adds, "Relax. Today's meal comes courtesy of one of our informants in the local blood bank. Nobody was injured acquiring it."

That does make me feel a bit better, but it doesn't change the fact that my human side is physically recoiling at the thought of ingesting another person's bodily fluid.

But I'm not human . . . at least, not fully.

And the part of me that isn't human? The one I repressed for years, until I let it free in a wave of magic and destruction?

My vampire side craves that cup. Because I am an obayifo, just like my mother, my aunt, and my grandmother before me. My vision tunnels in on the blood as my tongue runs across my fangs.

One sip . . . Just one sip couldn't hurt . . .

No! I grip the edge of the table with both hands to stop myself from reaching for the glass. It feels like my human and vampire sides are playing tug-of-war with my brain. Drink or don't drink; blood or no blood. My aunt lifts her glass and swirls it around like someone appreciating a fine wine. "The more you fight the black magic, the harder it'll be to control." She takes a long swig from her own glass and lets out a satisfied sigh. "Ahh, O negative. My favorite."

Ew, ew, ew, ew, *ew*. "If we drink blood, what's with all the food?" I ask to keep myself from throwing up.

"Nutrition-wise, non-blood foodstuffs do to our bodies what junk food does to a human's. We can digest it, but if that's all you eat, you're going to feel really sick after a while."

"But I've been eating nothing but human food my whole life, and I've been fine."

Auntie Effi eyes me over the top of her glass. "I'd bet that has something to do with both the black magic seal your parents forced you to wear and the fact that you are half-Slayer. The amount of blood needed by the various kinds of vampiric beings is different. You likely need less than I do to survive."

The thought of having to drink blood for the rest of my life fills me with dread. Has Mom secretly been doing that behind my back my whole life? Does Dad know? He has to. If I'm being real, he's probably been her main food source, which is a gross line of thinking I'm choosing not to follow. How much do you have to love someone to let them use you like a walking fridge?

"Have you met any other half-obayifo?" I ask.

"Most obayifo have a human parent, almost always their father. But, Serwa, there are no other half-obayifo who have a *Slayer* for a parent. Our peoples have remained separate for as long as anyone can remember. Your mother could only become an official member of the Abomofuo and gain divine wisdom after sealing her black magic. But you, a being born with *both* divine wisdom and black magic? There has never been anybody like you."

Boahinmaa says this like it's a good thing, but all I hear is that I'm alone. If there is no one else like me, then there's no place for me. On instinct, my hand moves to rub the spot behind my right ear where the seal used to be. Touching it used to bring me peace, but now the tic is just another painful reminder of everything I've lost.

I quickly clutch the sides of my chair. "What day is it?"

"It's a quarter past ten o'clock on Tuesday morning."

The blackout happened on Monday morning, a whole day

ago. I've been missing for twenty-four hours. Oh gods, my parents must be worried sick. They probably have every Slayer, Middle Man, and amateur true-crime podcaster in America searching for me.

"You can't keep me here. The Abomofuo are going to come looking for me."

"Of the latter, I have no doubt. As for the former, I'm not keeping you anywhere." She nods toward the door. "You are free to leave at any time. I've already ordered my subordinates not to stop you if you choose to go."

That sounds like a trap if I've ever heard one. I eye my aunt warily. "You'd really just . . . let me go? Even though I know all about your secret hotel lair?"

"Unlike *some* people, I won't lie to you just because it's easier," she says.

Unlike your mother, she means. The implication hangs heavy. For twelve years—my entire life—my mother hid the fact that she and I are both obayifo, creatures of black magic. I trusted her more than anyone else in the world, and she'd lied to me from the moment I was born.

When I don't reply, my aunt pulls an object out of her purse and slides it across the table to me. It's one of those brick cell phones that's so old it doesn't even have a touchscreen or camera.

"Call them right now, if you'd like," she challenges.

My hand hovers over the phone. I have four numbers in the entire world memorized—Auntie Latricia's because she taught it to me in case there was an emergency while I was living with her; the number for the taco place near our old safe house because they made a mean carne asada; and, of course, each of my parents'. One little call, and we'd be together again. I could shove my face into one of Mom's scratchy cardigans and smell Dad's familiar sandalwood cologne as they pulled me into the world's tightest hug.

One little call, and I'd have to face the truth that blew apart our family all over again.

My hand curls back in my lap. Auntie Effi gives a knowing nod.

Tears burn in my eyes, but I'll throw myself in front of a hundred adze before I let another one fall. I believe my aunt when she says no one in this hotel would stop me if I ran screaming from it right now. If she didn't hurt me while I was sleeping and vulnerable, it's unlikely she'll do it when I can fight back. But even if I got out the front door, where would I go?

Rocky Gorge is the first place that comes to mind, home of my Auntie Latricia and my cousin Roxy. But the last time I saw Roxy, I was erasing her memories along with those of our friends Gavin, Eunju, and Mateo. Shortly before that, I'd unleashed a wave of black magic that plunged the entire town into chaos, so I'm pretty sure I'm not welcome there anymore.

Maybe I could find my way into the Compound, headquarters of the Abomofuo? But the Abomofuo only accepted me as a rookie member when I was wearing the seal on my black magic. There's no way they'd ever let me back into the organization without it. And though I don't want to drink anyone's blood, I don't want to reapply the seal, either. I can't go back to feeling like a part of me was always missing.

I can't go back to Rocky Gorge. I can't go back to the Abomofuo.

The truth is, I'm safer surrounded by dozens of bloodthirsty vampires than I would be with my family and former friends. That realization hurts worse than any adze bite ever could.

Ugh, all this wallowing is making me hungry. I try one of the bagels, but just like Auntie Effi said, I don't feel any fuller after eating it. My eye keeps wandering back to the pitcher of blood. "What does . . . What's going to happen to me now that both my divine wisdom and black magic are active?"

"Now? We find the Midnight Drum."

My aunt's lips curl up, revealing the tips of her gleaming fangs once again. Just like that, she goes from a friendly relative to the dangerous vampire the rest of the world knows her to be.

"And when we do, we save your grandmother."

2

How to Work Out, Vampire Style

*"Sometimes, the difference between a truth
and a lie is in who does the telling."*

—from the *Nwoma*

NANA BEKOE, MY MOM and Auntie Effi's mother, was the leader of the forces of black magic during the Third Great War between them and the Abomofuo. They say she was the most powerful obayifo in the history of the world, and she could do things with black magic no one had seen before. She was so strong that the Abomofuo had to seal her away in an object called the Midnight Drum, and ever since it's been hidden to prevent anyone from releasing her.

I also know my mom was so scared of Nana Bekoe that she defected to the other side of the war just to get away from her. But if I've learned anything, it's that I was only told half of the story.

And Auntie Effi is determined to make sure I hear the rest.

"What do you know about the Midnight Drum?" my aunt asks as she stretches her arms above her head like she's about to run a marathon. We've finished breakfast and are now in the hotel's fitness room, standing on yoga mats and surrounded by dozens of clay pots. There's a whole nest of bonsam rearranging the dumbbells on the wall and a sasabonsam running on a treadmill. I'm pretty sure I can hear Britney Spears blasting from its headphones. Bloodsucking creatures of the night enjoy pop workout playlists? Wow, who knew?

"It's an object made of both divine wisdom and black magic, which makes it impervious to both," I say. "Similar to the null zone that surrounded Rocky Gorge." My stomach rumbles in protest when I stretch into downward dog. Even though I ate several plates' worth of brunch, I'm still hungry. Now I get why the old folktales say a single vampire can eat through a village's entire food supply. A part of me keeps fantasizing about the glass of blood I left untouched back on the table, but that part of me doesn't know what it's talking about.

I'm not drinking anyone's blood. Not now. Not ever.

"Correct. As such, it's likely we're going to need both divine wisdom and black magic to free my mother from it. We never had access to divine wisdom before. However, now that you're here, we can finally rescue her and right an injustice twenty years long."

My aunt's so excited, but all I feel is this sinking dread in my stomach. I wish Gavin were here. He always knew what to say to ease an uncomfortable situation. I wish all my friends were here.

And I wish my parents— No. *No.* I'm mad at them. I shouldn't miss people I'm angry at. Since I'm not ready to go back to them yet, I may as well gather as much information as I can while I'm here.

"Adze hijack people against their will," I point out. "Working with them is messed up and you know it."

"What if I told you not every adze host is unwilling?" Auntie Effi shoots back. "Do you know how many people fantasize about gaining the abilities of a vampiric being? If the adze weren't constantly being hunted, it'd be easier for them to find those people instead of resorting to the first person available."

A bloodsucking firefly rooting around in my brain sounds like a nightmare, and my parents and I have saved enough adze victims to see the destruction they can cause firsthand. However, what if my aunt's right, and there was a way to get the adze fed with minimal harm?

Still, there's something else about the obayifo that's bothering me.

"Nana Bekoe—I mean, my grandmother—she hurt a lot of people." It still feels weird having a name to put to a person I've wondered about for so long. A vampire witch wasn't my first choice for a granny, but honestly, I'll take what I can get. "I'm not saying she deserved to be locked away, but . . . if we let her out, will she hurt others?"

My aunt sneers. "Ah yes, the Abomofuo brainwashing runs deep. Tell me, did your precious Slayers ever explain *why* Nana Bekoe started her war against your organization?"

Because vampires are bloodthirsty and evil and destruction is just what they do, no rhyme or reason to it is the answer, but I enjoy having all my limbs intact, so I just shake my head.

My aunt's eyes grow heavy. "Seeing as how Akosua never mentioned me to you, I'm assuming she never mentioned our sister, Abena, either?"

Hold on, I have an Auntie Abena, too?! Just how many secret relatives can a person learn about in a single week?

When I shake my head again, Auntie Effi continues. "When she was not much older than I am now, my mother lived in Northern Ghana with her eldest daughter, my and your mother's half sister, Abena. Neither Akosua nor I had been born yet. Though my mother and sister were both obayifo, they were determined to live quiet lives and not cause any trouble. They took jobs at the local hospital so they wouldn't have to hunt, and they invested time, energy, and money in their little village to offset any bad luck their presence might bring upon the community. They did everything we obayifo are told we must do to live in human society."

I've only had to ignore my full bloodlust for a few hours. Suppressing it without a seal for years sounds impossible.

"Then a young man in their village became smitten with Abena. He begged and begged for her hand in marriage, but she refused. Enraged by her rejection, he went to the town elders and accused my sister of being a witch." Auntie Effi lets out a dry snort. "The irony is, of course, that he was right. But he wasn't making the claim based on any solid evidence that she'd performed black magic. In parts of Ghana, if someone is found guilty of witchcraft, they often face panicked mob justice. He had decided that if he couldn't have Abena, he would ruin her."

Auntie Effi's voice begins to shake. Above us, the fluorescent lights start flickering on and off.

"He convinced a group of villagers to drag Abena from her home in the middle of the night, claiming they were taking her to a local witch camp. Despite knowing the risk they posed to our kind, my mother found a member of the Abomofuo and begged them to save her daughter. She had years of proof that neither she nor Abena had ever intentionally harmed a human and that any passive damage done by their black magic was outweighed by their contributions to their community."

Auntie Effi's hands ball into fists at her sides. "And do you know what your precious Abomofuo said to my mother? Do you know what they told a woman who was about to lose her only child?" The walls begin to rumble with her barely contained fury. "They told her, *'We aren't in the business of saving witches from witch camps.'* In fact, they tried to capture my mother as well, claiming that just because she hadn't harmed anyone yet didn't mean she never would. My mother miraculously escaped their attack and trekked through the jungle on her own for days, determined to save my sister. But when my mother reached the camp . . . Abena was already dead."

As quickly as the rumbling began, it stops. Auntie Effi takes a deep breath, and just like that she is calm and composed once more, like she hasn't been describing a grief that shaped my existence decades before I was born.

"The knowledge that she had done everything right, followed every rule she had been told, and she still lost her child is what made my mother realize your Abomofuo are corrupt frauds. They claim to serve everyone, but they're only interested in protecting the *right* kind of people. And to them, Serwa, you and I are not people."

I'm shaking now for reasons that have nothing to do with the AC blasting through the fitness room. My aunt could be lying, but I don't think even the world's best actor could fake the raw rage and sorrow that filled her story. Besides, I know firsthand how passionately the Okomfo—the priests who run the Abomofuo—teach that beings of black magic are inherently dangerous, that they—we—can't be left to our own devices. I can completely see them refusing to help a young mother and her child simply because they were obayifo.

All I've ever wanted was to be a Slayer, when this whole time I've been the thing they hate most in the world.

But as passionately told as my aunt's story was, I can't stop thinking of the memory she showed me back at the tot lot in Rocky Gorge a few days ago. I'd watched the training Nana Bekoe had put both Auntie Effi and my mom through as young obayifo; it had been grueling, with my grandmother even striking Mom across the face when she tried to talk to her about it. All that to avenge a sister neither of them had ever met. . . .

"In the memory you showed me, Nana Bekoe hurt you and my mom," I say softly.

A muscle twitches in my aunt's jaw. "My mother made me strong," she argues, but her voice wavers at the end, like she's trying to convince herself as much as me. "Do you understand now why we must free her? Your grandmother wasn't always the most . . . sentimental person, but when she led us, we had a chance of winning the war. Now our kind has been hunted to its last breaths and the Abomofuo are free to rewrite history as they wish. This cannot be allowed to stand."

With a flick of her wrists, Auntie Effi douses all the light in the room. The bonsam let out nervous chitters and there's a yelp as the sasabonsam crashes to the ground from the force of its treadmill shutting down. My aunt's eyes burn like crimson stars as she moves her arm in a precise slice that shatters the pots surrounding us. Each shard shimmers in a tiny pinprick of light, swirling through the black magic around us. She's turned the room into a miniature Milky Way, everything orbiting around with us as the heart. I've studied magic my entire life, and I've never seen anything like this.

"If you learn one thing from your time with me, my niece, learn this: These people hate us not because of what we do, but because of what we *are*. But what we can do is far beyond what we've been told is possible."

She sweeps her arms, and the darkness returns to her. Light floods the fitness room once again, and the clay shards fall to the ground in a harmless circle all around us. She nods at the single pot remaining untouched in the center of the room.

"But we already know how my powers work. Now it's time for you to demonstrate yours."

3

How to Have the World's Most Awkward Phone Call

"It is ill-advised for a Slayer to return to a town once their time there is done. Our impressions on the lives we protect must be minimal, for their safety and our own."

—from the *Nwoma*

YOU'D THINK THAT AFTER almost accidentally destroying a suburban Maryland town, I'd have this black magic thing on lock.

You would be wrong. Because no matter what I do, no matter how much I struggle and try, the stupid pot WILL. NOT. BREAK.

"Remember, you are a conduit *for* your magic, not a container *of* it," my aunt instructs as my sixth attempt to destroy the pot in as many minutes results in a broken elliptical machine. "Black magic is a moving current, not a stagnant pool."

"Yeah, yeah, be a river, not a bucket. Got it." I wipe the sweat from my brow, square my shoulders, and face the stubborn pot once again. *Come on, Serwa, you can do this. River, not bucket. River, not bucket. River, not bucket.*

I reach deep inside of myself into that molten lava I used to call the Big Feeling. My black magic crackles alive with glee, like a dog eager to greet its master after a long day apart. The power rushes out from my core and up through my veins, pulsing like a layer of fire simmering just beneath my skin. Yes, yes! I'm doing it!

But as I angle my focus toward the pot, the magic intensifies from a warm glow to a searing burn. I fall backward with a startled yelp. A bolt of black magic flies from my hands, and my aunt and I duck as it bounces around the room ping-pong style until it blasts directly onto the fan where the bonsam were resting. All but one of them fly off with offended shrieks, while the straggler falls to the ground in a pile of debris.

"Sorry!" I rush over to help the poor creature. Most bonsam are fully gray, but this one's coat is so light it's basically silver, with spots all over that remind me of a dalmatian. One of the bonsam's wings is smaller than the other, and it valiantly attempts to fly after its friends, only to crash back down again, ensnared in the mess I made. I free it from the wires, and it coos in my arms. Aww, the little guy is kind of cute—if you can get past the whole *gorging on human blood* thing.

Auntie Effi's eyes flick from the damaged ceiling to the unfortunately undamaged pot with a small frown. "To be completely honest, this lack of coordination from an obayifo of your power level is highly unusual."

I have to bite the inside of my cheek to keep my lip from quivering. Wielding magic is the one thing that has always, *always* come easily to me. If I'm no good at that anymore, what *am* I good at? Now I have a better idea how my friends felt when our first few Slayer training sessions ended in disaster— like a big, steaming lump of useless.

"Let me try again!" I cry, but Auntie Effi shakes her head.

She goes to her fitness bag, pulls out a pen, and offers it to me. "I want to test something. Try using your divine wisdom on the pot instead."

"But is that safe with all the black magic in this building?"

"A single Adinkra won't do any serious harm to anyone here. Besides, right now our priority is mapping out the balance between your two magics. Understanding exactly how your powers work in tandem will be tantamount to your ultimately being able to control them. If you can't, the consequences could be quite . . . unpleasant."

"Wow, no pressure, then," I mutter too low for my aunt to hear, because in Ghanaian culture, sassing an elder is the fastest way to get your butt sent straight to the underworld. I drop the baby bonsam, who wraps itself around my feet like a kitten, and grab the pen.

My black magic may be a dog waiting to prove itself, but my divine wisdom is a wolf, evolved and honed to perfection. I close my eyes, and the hundred and ten basic Adinkra all Slayers must learn circle through my mind—gye nyame, sankofa, mframadan, nsoromma and so on and so forth, the ancient language of my people filling my mind in a looping chant. One pushes to the forefront: fafanto, the butterfly symbol of gentleness and fragility. This should make the pot so brittle a single touch will dissolve it to dust.

I draw the Adinkra on the pot, taking care that every line and curve looks exactly like Dad taught me. I press my hand against the clay and reach deep inside myself, ignoring my obayifo magic to find the power I've had since before I knew my own name. Warmth rushes up through me and then . . .

Nothing.

Huh?

"What the—?" No, this isn't right. I've drawn fafanto like a million times during my Slayer training, and I've never messed it up even once. But the pot isn't any more breakable than it was before I drew the Adinkra, like the spell didn't even affect it.

A terrifying thought hits me: What if activating my black magic made my divine wisdom disappear?

"Serwa, it's all right. We can try again later," Auntie Effi tries to reassure me, but I shake my head.

"I can do this." I draw fafanto again, because doubling the symbols should double the strength of the spell. Still nothing. Why isn't this working? What's going on?

"Serwa."

I slam my hand against the pot again and again with frenzied desperation. No, no, no! I already lost my family and my friends; I can't lose my magic, too! I can't, *I can't*—

"SERWA!"

Auntie Effi grabs me by the shoulder and yanks me away from the pot. The object remains unbroken, but small spatters of blood cover the smooth surface. Even more of it drips from my nose, and a wicked ache pulses through my head. At my feet, the baby bonsam whines in fear, tail tucked tight between its legs.

"A vampire is supposed to drink blood, not lose it," jokes my aunt as she hands me a tissue from her purse. I can't laugh along. If my black magic is out of control and my divine wisdom is actively revolting against me, what do I have left?

"I'm sorry. I'll—I'll try harder," I plead. I don't know if I want to help my aunt find the Midnight Drum, but I do know if she kicks me out, I'll have nowhere to go.

Auntie Effi places a comforting hand on my shoulder. "I know you'll get it."

There's still so much I don't understand about my own powers. Not only do I have to worry about the black magic and the divine wisdom individually, but also the places where they intersect come with a bunch of new unknowns.

"When I broke my seal back in Rocky Gorge, it didn't just release my black magic. I teleported, which I've never done before." I try to grasp that feeling of starlight and endless sky I felt the moment before I transported myself to Sweetieville—nothing. "Is that also an obayifo thing?"

Now it's my aunt's turn to look surprised. "If it is, I've never heard of it," she says slowly. "But magic is an art, not a science. I wouldn't be surprised to learn of new powers growing out of the traditional ones."

That aligns with what my old art teacher, Mr. Riley, told me about his own variant healing abilities, which evolved from his ancestor's divine wisdom. But that took several generations to happen. . . . What does it mean that my powers are mutating within my lifetime?

Auntie Effi takes a look at my worn face and says, "Let's call it a day for now. We'll figure this out. Don't worry."

I nod along, even though everyone knows that people telling you not to worry is when you need to worry most.

SURPRISING ABSOLUTELY NO ONE, things don't get better. In fact, one week passes.

Then two.

Before I know it, the trees surrounding the hotel have all turned bright crimson, the back-to-school ads on TV are now spend-your-whole-life-savings-on-Halloween-candy ads, and there's a giant jack-o'-lantern sitting in the middle of the atrium next to Owuo's ladder. October's here, and I'm no closer to breaking the pot, though I did cause at least ten thousand dollars' worth of property damage to the hotel during my increasingly frustrated attempts to do so.

When I'm not training (read: failing) to use my black magic, I spend my time exploring the Luciole. Just like Auntie Effi promised, none of the other creatures try to stop me from learning the ins-and-outs of my new home. By my third day, I've checked out every floor. By the seventh, I've memorized every exit. The baby bonsam from the fitness room—whom I've taken to calling Biri, from the Twi word for *dizzy*, for the way he flies in circles when he gets excited—often comes with me. More than once we got in trouble for getting stuck in a laundry chute or interrupting an all-mmoatia Zumba class during our explorations. I even get my hair rebraided by some chatty sasabonsam at the on-site salon, since I'd taken out my old box braids the day before I left Rocky Gorge. Auntie Effi tried to get me to do something new with my hair—the woman sure loves her makeovers!—but my trusty ponytail makes me feel more like myself when little else does these days.

I play off my wandering like I'm just a bored kid with nothing to do until my aunt gets back from her super-secret obayifo missions I'm not allowed to go on. In reality, though, I'm mapping out the place. Some might say it's paranoia, but I say when you've spent your whole life on the run from monsters, you learn quick to always have an exit plan.

Old habits and all that.

The first reminder that there is a world outside my vampiric bubble comes about three weeks into my new normal. I'd snuck into the fitness room early to get in some black magic practice without Auntie Effi hovering over my shoulder. However, when the pot doesn't break—again—and my nose is bleeding—

AGAIN—I slide to the ground with a frustrated scream bubbling in my throat. Homesickness wraps around me tighter than a rattlesnake. Without really thinking about it, I slip out the burner phone for the first time since Auntie Effi gave it to me and quickly punch in my dad's cell number.

However, I pause with my finger over the Dial button. It's been almost a full month since I vanished from Rocky Gorge and there's still been no word from my parents. A quick Google search showed no missing alerts on me, either. I don't know if that's good or bad. In general, the Abomofuo try not to involve civilian law enforcement in our—their?—affairs on account of the whole *somewhat illegal secret international monster hunting* thing. However, just because Mom and Dad haven't publicly reported me missing doesn't mean there aren't people scouring the country for me right now.

If I called and they picked up, I don't even know what I'd say. It's just . . . I haven't heard their voices in so long. My hope wins over my common sense as I press the button with a shaking finger. Each ring pulses through my body, and by the third one, I feel ready to combust from all the nerves roaring through me.

On the very last ring, someone finally picks up. "Hi there! Uncle Edmund can't come to the phone right now, but I can take a message!"

My mouth opens and closes but no words come out because Roxy James is the last person I expected to pick up my dad's phone. The last time I saw my cousin, I had abandoned her in the woods outside Rocky Gorge after erasing her memories. What do you even say to someone after something like that?

"Hello? Anyone there?" Roxy asks again since I'm just breathing heavily into the phone like some kind of weirdo. What I want to do is tell her how sorry I am for leaving the way I did and how grateful I am that she reached out to me when I first got to Rocky Gorge and how scared and confused I am about this whole vampire side of myself that I still don't understand.

However, all I do is yell "Tell my parents I'm okay!" before hanging up, throwing the burner phone across the room, and curling up in a ball with my head on my knees. The outburst startles Biri from his nap on the yoga mat, and he flies over to me. I bury my face in the bonsam's soft fur as I struggle to piece together what just happened.

If Roxy answered Dad's phone, then he must be at her house right now. He and Mom are still in Rocky Gorge. My parents, Roxy, and Auntie Latricia must all be looking for me together. The idea of the four of them worrying themselves sick over me is both comforting and heartbreaking.

I want to go back to being a family again. I want to yell at Mom and Dad until my voice gives out. But I can't just waltz back into their lives when I left so dramatically.

There are so many things I want that the world has decided I don't get to have.

Doesn't the unfairness of the world make you rage, Serwa? Don't you wish you could burn it all down and start again?

What the—? I whip my head up, but the room's empty except for me and Biri. Great. Now I'm sad AND I'm going bananas.

The sound of Auntie Effi's footsteps approaching the fitness room pulls me from my wallowing. I jump to my feet, wiping my eyes to catch the few tears that slipped through. My aunt's face twists with worry, so before she can poke for an answer I don't want to give, I blurt out, "I'm fine. Let's get started."

I throw myself into the black magic, but my powers are even more haywire with my concentration shot. The pot remains unbroken. After a bleak thirty minutes, Auntie Effi starts to say that maybe we should take a break for now when she gets a call. At first it looks like she might ignore it, but then her eyes go wide when she reads the caller ID.

"One moment, Serwa. I need to answer this," she says before practically running out of the room.

So, given that super weird behavior, do I:

A) Go back to my practice, pretending that was completely normal and not suspicious at all?

Or do I:

B) Eavesdrop on a vampire witch with full knowledge it might result in my insides being turned to black mold if I'm caught?

I choose B. Obviously. Have you even met me?

Seconds after my aunt leaves, I poke my head out of the fitness room door, crouching low so I can claim I'm tying my shoe if anyone asks. She has walked to the end of the hallway, so I can only catch snippets of her conversation.

"You're sure this is it? . . . All right . . . All right . . . Nine-fifty Independence Avenue Southwest . . . All right. I'll head over right now . . . Yes . . . Yes . . . Understood. See you soon."

I practically trip over my feet to get back to the fitness room. Once there, I pretend to be surprised when Auntie Effi announces, "Something has come up and I'll be away the rest of the afternoon. We'll continue this when I return."

I nod along, but mentally, I'm already planning the fastest way out of this hotel. If my aunt is up to something, I want—no, I *need* to know about it. Besides, keeping myself busy will also keep away thoughts of the family I can't bring myself to talk to.

I might not know what's located at 950 Independence Avenue SW, but if it's what I think it might be, the quest to find the Midnight Drum just took a major turn.

4

How to Appreciate Modern Art

*"When treading through the world of mortals, do so as
silently as a shadow crossing a cloud."*

—From the *Nwoma*

THE THING MOST PEOPLE don't understand about
disguises is that the absolute best ones aren't really disguises at all. Walk around with a hoodie over your head
and sunglasses over your face and all the world sees
is *HELLO, I LOOK VERY SUSPICIOUS* even if all you're
doing is watering flowers. Double that if you're Black
or Brown.

No, the secret to a good disguise is making yourself so unremarkable that people forget your face the
moment they see it. That's why before I leave the hotel,
I change out of one of the nice outfits my aunt bought
me and into an I DC T-shirt, shorts, and fanny pack
I found in the penthouse's massive walk-in closet.
(Another fun fact about Auntie Effi: She is a die-hard
fashionista. These were shoved to the very, *very* back.)
The outfit is 100 percent tourist, and if there's one thing
I've learned from my years traversing the country, it's
that no one gets less attention from locals than a tourist.

I considered simply trailing my aunt to her rendezvous, but her heightened obayifo senses mean she can hear me coming from dozens of feet away. That's why I wait till after she's left to make my way to the location. As it turns out, 950 Independence Avenue SW is the address of the Smithsonian National Museum of African Art, which is only about ten blocks from the Luciole, in the heart of downtown DC. It's disgustingly gorgeous outside, the kind of October day where the weather tries to pretend it's still summer before the cold sets in for good. The museum is located not far from the National Mall, meaning I have the Capitol looming on one side and the Washington Monument towering on the other as I cross the wide green space leading up to the building.

It's my first excursion outside the hotel grounds since the blackout, and every hair on my body stands on edge. I keep looking over my shoulder, like any second a bunch of Slayers are going to jump out of the reflecting pool and haul me off in chains. I wish I could've brought Biri just for the company, but I couldn't take the risk. Little guy whined like the devil when I left, though.

My tongue runs frantically over my gums as my eyes squint in the harsh sunlight—unlike Western vampires, obayifo can walk outside during the daytime, but that doesn't mean it's easy for us. Now I get why Dracula sleeps in a coffin all day; waking up with coffin bedhead every day seems like a fair trade-off for not tearing up every time it's even a little bright out. And on that note, I'm also glad garlic doesn't bother obayifo, either. What kind of self-respecting master of the night can be taken down by a hunk of garlic bread? An adze could kick Dracula's butt any day.

The National Museum of African Art is one of the smaller

Smithsonian collections (also, did you know there are multiple Smithsonians and it's not all just one big super museum? Because I didn't. The more you know!), but the breath leaves my lungs as soon as I step inside. The interior is what you'd expect for a hotel lobby—a reception desk and signs directing patrons around—but there's an energy in the air that trails goose bumps over my skin. This can only mean one thing: magic.

Most humans—Slayers included—can't detect magic without the help of an Adinkra or a creature like a mmoatia to alert them to the presence of the supernatural. But I can feel the divine wisdom permeating this building like a blanket smothering all my senses. Finally, a perk of being an obayifo that doesn't make me want to hurl my guts out. After so many weeks with just black magic, being in the presence of divine wisdom once again feels like slipping on a pair of shoes I lost years ago and realizing they still fit.

In fact, the magic is so overwhelming that I don't even know where to start. Normally, I'd try a honing spell to see if I could sort through the noise and pinpoint the origin, but I still can't wield divine wisdom without getting a nosebleed. I'm pretty sure a geyser of blood suddenly gushing from my nose would definitely alert security.

All right, since magically investigating this place is out, the boring way it is. Auntie Effi had a twenty-minute head start on me, meaning she's probably deep in the museum by now. I shuffle into the back of a large group of field trippers as they make their way down the stairs. Hopefully, I can find her and figure out what she's doing here before she spots me.

The building is circular, with all four levels centered around a giant fountain at the bottom floor. Art from across the African continent and diaspora fills each room. There are traditional pieces, like Benin ivory masks and Makonde ebony sculptures. But there are also modern exhibits as well, some focused on comic books by African creators, others on photography and even video walls showcasing cinema from the mainland. I make a mental note to come here one day when I'm not investigating a bunch of shady vampire activities. The only place I've ever been with this many African things in one place is, well, Africa. I wish I could stop and really enjoy the experience, but there simply isn't time.

I make it all the way to the lowest level of the museum without finding my aunt. Here, there's only a room that's completely empty save for a giant statue of a two-headed crocodile and a sign that reads:

EXHIBIT UNDER CONSTRUCTION

FUTURE HOME OF THE GHANAIAN VISIONARY ARTISTS COLLECTION

SPONSORED BY DR. RICHARD AMANKWAH

AND THE MID-ATLANTIC GHANAIAN CULTURAL PRESERVATION SOCIETY

Oh, I know Dr. Richard Amankwah. He's a doctor, philanthropist, and your garden-variety rich dude who thinks throwing money at a problem will make it go away.

He's also a member of the Abomofuo who grew up alongside my father at the Compound. Whatever's going on with this room, it's Slayer related.

The magic buzzes in my ears louder than bees trapped in a jar, but a quick inspection of the walls, floors, and ceiling reveals nothing. Either I'm wrong, or someone—Dr. Amankwah, most likely—put a protective ward on whatever he's hiding here. I turn my attention back to the crocodile and— Wait. I recognize this reptile. It's a figure of the Adinkra Funtunfunefu-Denkyemfunefu.

They call this creature two-headed, but that's kind of misleading. Unlike Cerberus or Hydra, where all the heads share the same neck, Funtunfunefu-Denkyemfunefu are two crocodiles that connect at the stomach. The symbol is supposed to represent cooperation, because while crocodiles in the wild are usually independent, these two have no choice but to work together. I always felt really bad for it, because the idea of sharing my body with anyone else sounds like a nightmare. What if you hated Doritos but the other head ate them all the time, and your burps always tasted like nacho cheese dust? Ew.

After checking again there's no security guard coming, I start inspecting the statue, even running my hands over its legs and tail. If the Abomofuo put any enchantments on these two, they probably drew the Adinkra where they'd be hard to see, like—

"Didn't your parents ever teach you it's rude to touch someone's tail without asking first?"

I jump back, banging my head on the underside of the statue in the process. The head closest to me—whom I hereby dub Righty—gives me a wide grin, while the other one—Lefty—bursts into tears.

"Nice going, you fool. You killed it!" moans Lefty. "Now we're going to be arrested and charged with child homicide!"

"On the bright side, I heard the food in prison is great!" chirps Righty.

"Grandpa Amankwah gave us one job, and you already messed it up!" Lefty lets out a sob. "We can't go to prison! They don't even make jumpsuits in our size! Or for creatures with connected torsos!"

"So we'll start a trend! Who knows, maybe two-pronged orange jumpsuits will be all the rage this time next year."

"I'm fine! Nobody has to go to prison or wear a two-pronged

jumpsuit!" I scramble to my feet to put an end to this bickering, because something tells me once these two start, nothing will stop them. It says a lot about my childhood that a talking statue doesn't even ping my weirdness scale. "But what was that about Dr. Amankwah? What job did he give you?"

"Why, guarding the secret exhibit hidden right behind this wall, of course!" pipes up Righty.

"We're really good at it," adds Lefty. "We haven't told anyone at all, not even that really nice family of Japanese tourists that rubbed our noses for good luck last week."

". . . But you just told me . . . ?"

All four of its eyes go wide. Righty gasps. "Oh no! That means we have to kill you now. Sorry! It's nothing personal, really!"

"Nothing is personal in a universe as cold and unfeeling as ours," mumbles Lefty.

The sound of ripping metal fills the air as Funtunfunefu-Denkyemfunefu pulls itself off its base and lunges for me. I try to duck out of the way, but the creature is surprisingly fast for its size, and it easily pins me to the ground. Both sets of jaws open wide, and as razor-sharp teeth fill my vision, I scream out, "W-wait! I already know all about the magic exhibit!"

The heads pause. "You do?" they say in unison.

I don't. "I do! So, if I already knew, that means you didn't actually break any rules, did you?"

You can practically see a whirring beach ball spinning over both their lizard brains as they process this. After a couple of way too long seconds, the monster releases me and returns to its statue base.

Righty beams as much as a giant metal crocodile can. "If you already know about the room, that means we won't get in trouble. Oh, happy day! Everything works out all the time always!"

"Until entropy reaches its inevitable conclusion and the fiery heat death of the universe consumes us all," says Lefty.

"Heat death sounds toasty. Mmmm, toast. I could go for some right now . . . some nice, buttery, crispy—"

"I'm here because I'm doing a special project on the Mid-Atlantic Ghanaian Cultural Preservation Society," I interrupt, the lie coming to me quickly. Gavin would be so proud. "I need to write about what's in that room. Can you let me inside real quick so I can finish my assignment?"

There's no guarantee that whatever is in there has anything to do with the Midnight Drum, but now I'm too curious to leave it alone.

However, both crocodiles shake their heads.

"Not without the code," says Lefty.

"Grandpa Amankwah said we'd be in very, very, very, very, very, *very* big trouble if we let anyone in the room without the code."

I bite back a scream of frustration. Getting past Tweedledum and Tweedledummer here is going to be harder than I thought. "And who knows the code?"

"Only two people! In the whole entire world! Including Australia *and* New Zealand!"

"And let me guess, one of those people is Dr. Amankwah himself?"

"Correct! And the other is in there right now!"

"He should be out in ten . . . nine . . ."

Wait a minute, did that oversized gecko just say *now*? I practically trip over my shoes running from the restricted area and into the shadowed alcove near the bathroom. Just in time, too, because the second I round the corner, a crack brimming with light appears in the perfectly smooth wall. It widens into an Adinkra-covered door through which a single person steps.

"All right, I'm heading back now. Anything happen while I was in there?" the person asks.

"Nothing, boss!" reports Righty. "Well, nothing except this little reporter girl, but she just ran off!"

Lefty sighs. "Everyone we try to befriend always runs from us in the end."

"Aw, sorry to hear that. Well, keep me updated if anything happens. See you in a few days."

The figure goes the opposite direction from my hiding place, so I don't get a good look at him before he's climbing the stairs to leave this floor.

But I don't need to see his face because I'd know that voice anywhere.

It belongs to the bane of my existence.

The figurative thorn in my side.

The worst thing that has ever happened to this world since the invention of DIY bangs:

Declan Amankwah.

Which means my eternal nemesis is one of only two people in the entire world who have access to whatever the Abomofuo are hiding inside this museum.

5

How to Embarrass Yourself
in Front of a Boy

*"What has transpired has transpired for a reason.
Do not let the distractions of the past keep you
from the needs of the present."*

—From the *Nwoma*

FIVE YEARS AGO, WHEN I was seven and still full of youth and joy, my family went to a Kwahu Easter party thrown by the Abomofuo. (Kwahu Easter is a big deal in Ghana. They have hang gliders. It's incredible.)

Every year they held an Easter egg hunt just for the kids, and I was determined to win it. I drew maps of the venue. I had tactics. I made a spreadsheet! In the end, I collected sixty-four eggs in the span of a single hour at a rate of 1.07 eggs per minute.

But do you know who beat me by a SINGLE EGG to take home the crown?

Declan Amankwah.

Four years ago, at an outdooring party for one of the Okomfo's children, they had a mini tournament among the kids—just for fun, with foam weapons so no one would accidentally hack off a limb into the cake.

I made it all the way to the finals, even beating some

kids in high school to get there. But do you know who knocked me out in the very last round?

Declan.

Amankwah.

Do you know who is the second youngest person EVER— behind only my dad—to pass his Initiation Test, gain his abode santann tattoo, and become a full Slayer? Do you know the person I fantasize about whacking upside the head with a sock full of butter, the person who has been the pain in my butt, snake in my boot, annoying itch on my back I just can't reach but will never go away and every time I remember it I am filled with pure RAGE because that scratch has been the ONE THING I've always wanted but could never have?

DECLAN.

FREAKING.

AMANKWAH.

And right now, he is standing in my way of accessing the Abomofuo's secret exhibit.

So this is great. This is just stellar. Getting the Midnight Drum and freeing Nana Bekoe was already going to be difficult enough, but now my mortal enemy is involved? I'm so busy fuming over how much more complicated this entire situation has become that I'm not really paying attention to where I'm going . . . which is why I don't see the kid in front of me until I've already bumped into him by the fountain and spilled water all over his sweater.

"Oh my gosh," I cry. "I am so, so sorry!"

"D-d-don't . . . You're fine."

And for the second time in like ten minutes, I'm stunned speechless, because I know that voice even if the owner of it doesn't know me.

Mateo Alvarez was one of the members of the Good Citizens Committee (GCC for short), the community service initiative my school forced me to join all because I caused one teensy, tiiiny food fight on the first day of school. If the five of us in the group were the Avengers (with way less cool-looking costumes), then Mateo was our Coulson. He could be a scaredy-cat sometimes, but there's not a nicer person on the planet. I wouldn't put it past him to send a letter to the North Pole asking what Santa wants for Christmas.

Mateo's eyes go wide then narrow in the universal expression of someone trying to recall how they know the person standing in front of them. "You're Roxy's c-c-cousin, right?" he asks.

"Yeah, I am! I was staying with her until a few weeks ago, but my parents came back, so I had to switch schools, which is sooo annoying, but, like, what can you do?"

I let out a high-pitched laugh even though internally I want to throw myself into the museum's fountain. What is wrong with me? *Come on, Serwa, he's just a boy! There are literally billions of them on the planet—calm down!*

Mateo nods. "Yeah."

"Why are you here?"

"Remember that m-m-mural we did? Mr. Riley submitted it to some c-contest, and the museum invited us t-t-to the early p-p-p . . ." Mateo pauses, his face flushing red, and I give him an encouraging nod. Hard consonants are always most difficult for him. "P-preview gala tomorrow night. T-today we're visiting the main exhibits."

You always remember people as they were the last time you saw them, so it's jarring when you meet them again and realize their life kept moving forward even when your image of them didn't.

"No way, that's awesome!" I exclaim, only to cringe at my own enthusiasm. Gods, I feel like all I ever do is embarrass myself in front of this boy. Besides, he just revealed that the entire GCC plus our adviser, Mr. Riley, are at this museum *right now*. I have to get out of here ASAP, but I can't bring myself to move.

"Are you g-going tomorrow?"

"What? Me, at a gala? No way."

An awkward beat passes. I wait for Mateo to say something else before I realize he isn't going to. Because of years of being bullied for his stutter, Mateo has a hard time talking to strangers. When we first met, he couldn't even look me in the eye. But as we spent weeks training to hunt vampires, fighting immortal beings, and even turning a dog into a sword, he opened up bit by bit until he never hesitated to speak around me or our other friends.

A pang goes through my chest. Mateo and I used to be close enough to spend all night talking, or even just working side by side in comfortable silence. He always knew when I needed a nudge in the right direction and when I needed space to figure out stuff alone. He was the first member of the GCC I really connected to, yet here we are shifting awkwardly from foot to foot.

I'm the reason for the distance between us now. I'm the one who erased all his memories of spending time with me, Roxy, Gavin, and Eunju. The Mateo I befriended during my time in Rocky Gorge no longer exists, and I have no one to blame but myself.

Mateo glances up at me, startled. "Are you all right? You look . . . s-sad."

"What? Me? No? I'm just . . ."

I'm sad and I'm scared and I'm confused and I miss my parents and I'm so angry at them and I don't know how I can be both at the same time and you are one of the only people in the world I could've talked to about it but now you barely know who I am and it's all my fault.

"Hungry," I finish. "Haven't had lunch yet."

Mateo nods. Silence again. The smart thing to do would be to excuse myself and get back to the hotel, but for some reason I blurt out, "How's the café? How's Alicia doing?"

For just a second, an expression flashes across Mateo's face—Frustration? Disbelief? Whatever it is, it's so unlike him that I shudder. But then I know I said the wrong thing when he bites his lip in confusion. "How d-d-d . . . how d-d-d—you know my sister?"

Welp, I am just stepping in every kind of doo-doo today. The GCC and I hung out a lot at Mateo's family's cafe in between school and our training sessions, which is where I got to know his older sister, Alicia, and her love of all things K-pop and cinnamon-dusted. I don't have any siblings, so I thought it was pretty cool how friendly she was to a bunch of kids she barely knew. As much as it embarrassed Mateo, I liked listening to her rambling tales of boyfriend troubles and other high school trials and tribulations.

But I shouldn't know any of that, and Mateo's confusion is just going to raise more questions I cannot answer. "Oh, right, ha-ha. You mentioned her . . . during . . . homeroom . . . once . . . remember? Like a couple weeks ago?"

Mateo pushes his glasses up his nose, brows scrunching together as he tries to remember a conversation he definitely shouldn't. Heat courses through my body, and the room seems to get smaller and smaller. He doesn't believe me. Oh no, oh no, I've gotta get out of here. I start backing away, mumbling something about needing to get home to my parents, when my legs bump against the edge of the fountain. It's the smallest bit of contact, but that's all it takes for my black magic to zip free.

The ground rumbles beneath my feet, and seconds later, the fountain erupts. A jet of water shoots up in a geyser big enough to make Old Faithful weep with jealousy, soaking Mateo and me to the bone. We manage to get away from the worst of the deluge, which is when I notice the nyame dua wards drawn at the base of the stairs. The symbols are blinking on and off like little Christmas lights. Great. As if this situation weren't already bad enough, I've just triggered an Abomofuo black magic alarm. Slayers will be here within minutes to find out what set it off.

Aaaand that's my cue to dip.

"Greatseeingyougottagobye," I scream at Mateo, and I ignore his shouts of protest as I turn on my heel and hurtle out of the museum. The guards are so focused on the flooding that no one is worried about a young girl running in the opposite direction, and even if they caught me, what could they do? The only thing the security footage would show is me bumping against the fountain. From their point of view, I had nothing to do with the fact that hundreds of thousands of dollars' worth of irreplaceable art is now in danger of getting water damaged.

But the Slayers will figure out what happened immediately, which is why I gotta get out of here *now.*

I'm halfway across the National Mall when a small boy near me shrieks in delight and points his ice-cream-stained hand toward the squadron of food trucks lining the street near us. "Look at the weird bat, Daddy!"

Sure enough, a familiar batlike creature flits in and out of the food truck windows. Biri! Oh no, my black magic flare-up must have drawn him to the area. The food truck owners are in a tizzy trying to protect their wares from the bonsam. One of them is yelling in what sounds like Arabic as the creature attempts—and fails—to fly off with a whole rack of kebab skewers while another flails around uselessly with a broom to swat Biri away.

Everything I've ever been taught tells me to vacate the area before the Slayers arrive and leave Biri to fend for himself. Not long ago, I would've done just that—in fact, I would've been one of the Slayers trying to vaporize the darn creature! But that was before I spent weeks living and training alongside Biri, my aunt, and a whole other host of black magic creatures. So even though there's a voice in my head screaming *LEAVE THE CRIME SCENE. GET OUT OF THERE. DO YOU WANT TO BE ON THE WRONG END OF A CROSSBOW BOLT?*, I run toward the bonsam and let out a high-pitched whistle.

"Biri! This way! Here, boy!" I yell. The bonsam lets out an excited yelp, then goes back to attempting to carry off an entire carton of chocolate-chip cookie ice-cream sandwiches. (I don't blame him. Those things are *addictive*.) Abosom help me, I don't have time for this! Luckily, I'd squirreled away some food from breakfast since I didn't know how long trailing Auntie Effi might take. I take a meat pie from my bag and wave it over my head. "Over here!"

That gets his attention. The bonsam zips toward me, and I run away from the Mall, toward the bright red Smithsonian Castle, which seems way less crowded than the other buildings here. Behind it is a garden that connects the castle, the National Museum of African Art, and the National Museum of Asian Art. There, Biri overtakes me, snatches the meat pie from my fingers, and settles on the wrought iron fence facing the street as he greedily devours the treat.

I approach it slowly. "Come on, buddy, let's get back to the hotel. That's a good bonsam. Come with me now," I mutter soothingly.

I am inches away from reaching the bonsam and shoving him into my bag when an arrow zips past my face, and who else but my mortal enemy commands:

"Back up. This one's mine."

6

How to Engage in Blackmail and Falsehoods

"If you're going to lie, do it well."

—From the *Nwoma*

THE THING ABOUT ME and arrows is that I have a lot of experience in shooting them at stuff and very little in having them shot at me. My brain goes into full-on panic mode because the Abomofuo have found me and now I'm going to be tortured or experimented on or, even worse, I'm going to have to talk to my *parents*. It's all over, and it's Declan Amankwah's fault.

I freeze, but the second arrow whizzes past me and pierces Biri in the wing, pinning him to the gate. The bonsam thrashes and squeals, but he's stuck.

"Get away from my prize!" Declan yells.

Hang on . . . he's not shooting at me—he's shooting at Biri! Now's my chance to escape. I move to do just that, but then Biri lets out the most pitiful mewl. The bonsam may be a nuisance, and one day when he's fully grown he may hurt countless people, but I can't leave him to suffer just because of what he might become.

With a groan, I rush to the gate, my back to Declan so he can't see my hands removing the arrow from the Biri's torn wing.

"Get back to the hotel, quick," I hiss as the creature gives me those big ol' *did I do something wrong?* puppy eyes. I have no idea if bonsam are smart enough to follow commands, but as soon as he's free, the creature zips up into the sky. Declan releases another arrow that sails harmlessly past Biri as the bonsam races toward freedom.

"Why'd you let it get away?" he yells.

I leap back from the gate and cradle my hand against my chest with mock agony. "The little turd bit me!" I wail.

How weird is it that just a month ago I would've been the one shooting at that bonsam, and now here I am aiding and abetting his escape? Life, man.

Declan opens his mouth like he wants to yell again, but then his eyes go wide with recognition and his lips pull into the smarmiest, most mocking smile I've ever seen. "No way! Serwa Boateng? What brings you to my neck of the woods?"

I open my mouth to respond, then pause. Hang on . . . is Declan Amankwah *tall* now?! The last time I saw him was two years ago at the party his dad threw in honor of Declan passing the Initiation Test and becoming a full Slayer. Back then, we'd traded barbs and well-deserved glowers at nearly the same height. But now I have to lift my head to meet his gaze. It's like someone took the boy I knew and stretched him into something just at the edge of a full-grown man. He's also switched out his fluffy childhood Afro for a sleek haircut with fades at the sides and thicker coils on top, which really adds to the illusion of Declan not being horrible in every way. Between the height and the hair, I can almost understand how a person—who is not me!—could maybe possibly think he was kind of cute. (Which I DO NOT.)

Ugh, focus! Panic bubbles up in my chest, which is why I blurt out, "Don't tell anyone I was here!"

I mentally kick myself as Declan's eyes narrow. Why don't I go ahead and tattoo I AM UP TO SOMETHING VERY SUSPICIOUS across my forehead while I'm being the world's biggest idiot? This is all Declan's fault. Whenever I'm around him, I get so hung up on how much I hate him that there isn't any room in my head for anything else. Even the way he says my name—like he's taking his time with every syllable—makes me want to punch a baby. And I *like* babies!

Come on, Boateng, you've gotten yourself out of worse scrapes than this one against stronger enemies. Declan may be a full Slayer and the human embodiment of stepping on a LEGO, but he's only a year older than me. If I can outsmart full-grown adults and escape even fuller-grown monsters, I can get away from this jerk.

"What I mean is . . . my parents . . . they don't know I'm here right now."

I once asked Gavin, the GCC's resident water-bender and truth-stretcher extraordinaire, how he came up with convincing lies so quickly. *It's easy. Just tell the truth until you don't have to*, he'd replied, and even though this situation is seconds away from going belly-up, I bite back a smile thinking of my friend's antics.

Declan quirks an eyebrow—the left one, which has a little scar running through it, also new—in the universal expression of *Thank you, Captain Obvious*. "I figured. As an active Slayer, it's my job to keep track of every member of the Abomofuo who comes in and out of DC. If you were supposed to be here, I'd know. What super-secret scheme are you up to that your parents can't know about?"

It's been like five seconds, and he's already rubbing the whole *I passed the Initiation Test years ago and you haven't even taken it yet, nyah, nyah, nyah!* thing in my face. Declan passed the test at eleven, making him the second youngest person ever to gain their abode santann tattoo and become a full Slayer. (The youngest person ever was my dad at age nine, while the average age is about seventeen. Apparently my father's some kind of Slayer prodigy, though you wouldn't guess it from the way the man cries over videos of puppies with broken legs.) I'm not exactly happy with the Abomofuo at the moment, but being a full Slayer was, up until last month, the one thing I'd wanted my entire life. Having my old dream thrown in my face stings.

I take a deep breath, resisting the urge to tell Declan that my weekly Jerk Interaction Quota is full so he can drop the attitude, thanks. He was already on the premises when I triggered the black magic alarm, but I'm certain there are more Slayers incoming to locate the source. I need to get out of here before anyone else can recognize me, AND I need to make sure Declan doesn't snitch when I go. Which means that, right now, the only way to save my butt is to play nice with one of my least favorite people in the world.

But how much does Declan know about what happened in Rocky Gorge? Has he or his father been in contact with my parents? The fact that both my mother and I are obayifo was a secret within the Abomofuo—even to me—and no one saw me leave with Auntie Effi the day of the blackout. I can't give away too much, but if I play my cards right, I just might learn something from him instead.

"Remember back in August, when the red alert about Boahinmaa went through the mmoatia network? My parents said it wasn't safe for me to join the hunt for her, so they put me on ice." I don't have to fake my annoyance because that is how I actually felt when it all went down. Tell the truth until you don't have to, indeed. "I've been worried sick this whole time, so when I sensed the black magic alarm go off in the museum today, I knew I had to check it out."

"The safe house your parents sent you to is nearby? Where?"

"It wouldn't be a safe house if I told you that now, would it?"

Declan pulls a face that makes it clear he doesn't 100 percent believe me yet. All right, if defense doesn't work, time to play offense.

"Say, I know you're a full Slayer with your own patrol route and everything—"

"Two patrol routes, actually."

Gods, I hate him. "*Two* patrol routes, but what are you doing here on a school day?"

While minors are allowed to be Slayers, the Abomofuo take education very seriously. Underage members aren't supposed to conduct any Slayer business during school hours outside of an emergency. Declan squirms with guilt, and now it's my turn to grin. Got him.

"I just needed to check something before the gala tomorrow night. I was going to be in and out, but then the alarm went off. I was hoping if I caught whatever triggered it, my dad might not care that I left school early."

Which definitely won't happen now that I let the bonsam go.

"How about a deal?" I offer. "I won't tell anyone you were here if you don't tell anyone I was here."

After a tense second, Declan gives a tight nod. "Deal."

Ah, don't you just love the sweet, sweet smell of blackmail in the morning?

Declan rolls his shoulders, then plucks the string of his bow like it's a violin. It transforms into a SmarTrip card for the DC metro, which he smoothly slides into the pocket of his green-and-gold varsity jacket. Even I've gotta admit that's a pretty genius disguise for the weapon.

"So, how long you in town for, rookie?" he asks.

I take it back. Declan Amankwah saying my name is bad, but hearing him call me rookie has to be one of the seven worst things that's ever happened. And yes, I'm including the eruption of Mount Vesuvius in that estimation.

"Till my parents come back for me." Again, technically, not a lie. It's moments like this I wish I had a phone. At least then I'd know what time it was. Something tells me I've been away from the hotel a little too long.

I'm racking my brain for an excuse to get out of this conversation when a woman standing on the sidewalk not far from the garden catches my attention. She lifts the brim of her wide sun hat, and my Auntie Effi stares back at me. Uh-oh. Time's up.

"Hey, uh, it's been great talking to you," I say to Declan, "but I really gotta get going now. You know, safe house, not supposed to be outside because vampires might abduct me, yada yada yada."

"Going already? But we've barely caught up." If I didn't know Declan was committed to my downfall in every way possible, I'd almost say he sounds disappointed. "Well, hit me up through the mmoatia network if you want to hang out while you're here. Tonight I have soccer practice and patrol, but I should be free after school until five."

"After school, before five, got it. Gotta go, bye!"

Before Declan can stop me, I race from the garden to the street veering away from the National Mall. I round the corner and there's a red-and-silver taxi waiting with Auntie Effi's distinctive sun hat in the backseat window. It's amazing she evaded me in the museum while wearing that thing.

I slide into the taxi and we're off, just another one of the hundreds of cars honking and screeching through the streets of DC. As soon as I have my seat belt buckled, my mother's sister levels me a look that would give the average person a heart attack.

"Someone's had quite the morning, hasn't she?"

1

How to Join a Witch's Coven

*"Obayifo are malicious, chaotic, unstable creatures.
Do not let their human likeness fool you—only
destruction lives within them."*

—From the *Nwoma*

"I CAN EXPLAIN," I blurt out, but my aunt holds up a hand before jerking her head toward the driver. Her message is crystal clear: *It's not safe to talk here.*

I'm practically buzzing with adrenaline the whole ride back to the hotel, but it's not until we're secure in our penthouse suite that my aunt takes off her hat, then turns to me and demands, "Now, can you please enlighten me as to why you launched a black magic assault on hundreds of works of priceless art?"

It all comes out in a jumble of words. "I overheard you talking when we were in the fitness room so I looked up the address and then I went to the museum where I found this talking statue but then Declan came out from behind the statue because there's actually a whole *secret exhibit* back there and the Abomofuo are hiding something in it and Declan knows what it is and my black magic flared and—"

"Hold on! Slower, please!"

I take a deep breath, then restart the story from the beginning. By the time I'm done, several lines crinkle my aunt's forehead. She looks so much like my mother with that bemused expression that I want to both laugh and cry. I brace myself for my punishment, but instead she just asks, "Serwa, if you wanted to know what I was talking about on the phone, why didn't you just ask me?"

Whoa, that is . . . not the reaction I expected. "I didn't think you'd tell me," I mumble, and even though I don't say it out loud, the implied lack of trust is clear.

Hurt flashes across my aunt's face, but it quickly smooths out to her usual calm, almost disdainful expression. "Well, in the future, give me a heads-up the next time you decide to flood a federally protected building."

I'm both relieved and a little disappointed at my aunt's reaction. If I'd pulled something like this with my mom, she would have grounded me until the next millennium, and only after lecturing me on how my recklessness endangered myself and others. I never thought I'd miss her monologues but— No, I need to stop thinking like that. Auntie Effi might be Mom's sister, but she's not my mother. I shouldn't expect her to act like it.

"B-but I found something interesting while I was there!" I add quickly. The last thing I need is my aunt thinking I might've triggered the alarm on purpose. I need her to know I'm not playing double agent. "Apparently there's some kind of gala happening at the museum tomorrow night, and I think the Abomofuo have something to do with it. Declan skipped school to check on something in the secret exhibit."

I'm not sure why I don't mention running into Mateo, too. Even after all that's happened, I feel protective of the GCC.

They're my team—my responsibility. Besides, them being at the museum today has to be a coincidence; no need to get them any more involved in the mess that is my life.

Auntie Effi taps a finger against her chin, deep in thought. "Flood aside, that is good information to have. Zuri called me to the museum because she'd accessed a secret encrypted email between the museum employees and members of the Abomofuo. She needed me to translate it and didn't want to risk copying or photographing. It confirmed that the Slayers are up to something, but I never would've thought the younger Amankwah was involved."

It's hard not to feel some pride at that. After feeling like a burden so long, it's good to know today's ill-advised sleuthing led to something useful. My brain rewinds to my encounters with Mateo and Declan. Each was different, but the same thing came up in both . . .

"We need to learn more about this gala the museum's hosting," I say. "It's come up too many times now to be a coincidence."

A quick Google search on Auntie Effi's phone brings up a press release about the event.

"'The Smithsonian National Museum of African Art and the Mid-Atlantic Ghanaian Cultural Preservation Society cordially invite you to a gala featuring a special early preview of the upcoming Ghanaian Visionary Artists Collection,'" I read aloud. Then I say to Auntie Effi, "The Mid-Atlantic Ghanaian Cultural Preservation Society was on the sign outside the hidden exhibit."

"It's possible the GCPS is one of the Abomofuo's many shell organizations," muses my aunt. "Working under the guise of an arts nonprofit would be a good cover for their dealings with the Smithsonian, with Dr. Amankwah heading up this particular branch. But I'm still not convinced they'd make themselves the face of something so public. Slayers prefer to move in the shadows, uncontested by and accountable to no one."

Whoa, I knew the Abomofuo had some reach, but shell companies? The scale of what we're dealing with is making my head spin. "Maybe what they're trying to pull off is too big to do in secret," I guess. "It needs to be semipublic, but in a way that can't be traced back to them."

I skim the rest of the press release until a particular line jumps out at me: *To make room for the new collection, the museum will be working closely with the Mid-Atlantic Ghanaian Cultural Preservation Society to send back to Africa dozens of pieces that were obtained by dubious and unethical means.*

Dubious and unethical means is just fancy grown-up talk for *stolen.* It's nine layers of messed up to hear people patting themselves on the back for returning things they never should've taken in the first place.

I slot in this new piece of information with all I've learned today, and everything clicks together. "What if the Midnight Drum is one of the objects the Abomofuo are trying to move out of the museum, and they're using this new exhibit and the gala as an excuse to do it?"

Auntie Effi's eyes shine bright with the primal glee of a predator that's just figured out their prey's hiding spot. "Serwa, that is brilliant!" She starts to pace around the room, muttering to herself like she's forgotten I'm even there. "If that's the case . . . it's very possible . . . Call Zuri and assemble the coven . . . We'll need to act fast to acquire the drum for ourselves."

It takes a second for my aunt's meaning to sink in. When it does, my eyes practically bug out of my head. "You want to steal the Midnight Drum? From the freaking *Smithsonian*?!"

Auntie Effi lets out a laugh that's exactly like my mother's, though I don't think either of them would be happy to hear that.

"Now you're thinking like a witch."

CHARGING INTO BATTLE AGAINST a horde of bloodsucking fiends? Easy.

Going toe-to-toe with a flying sword literally designed to never stop fighting? Sign me up.

Hand-to-hand combat with an adze that has possessed the meanest girl at my old school? Been there, done that, got the T-shirt.

But a *heist*? From one of the most famous museums in the world?

Look, *National Treasure* might be one of the single best movies ever made in the history of cinema, but I'm no Nicolas Cage. Stealing the Midnight Drum right under the nose of the Abomofuo—and again, from the SMITHSONIAN!!!—is ridiculous. It's impossible. It's . . . it's . . . some other word I can't think of right now!

But my aunt doesn't agree. In less than an hour, she has a whiteboard covered in bullet points and printed-out pictures of everything we know about the upcoming gala. Not only that, there's now a literal war council of black magic creatures sitting/crouching/hanging on various structures around the living room and munching on Thai delivery while Auntie Effi goes over the plan. They call themselves the coven, and together these four creatures of black magic—two obayifo, including my aunt; a red mmoatia; and a sasabonsam—have taken up Nana

Bekoe's torch to protect as many black magic creatures from the Abomofuo as they can.

"Are you sure the object in question here is the Midnight Drum?" asks the creature closest to me, a red mmoatia my aunt introduced as Fern. She's the largest of her kind I've ever seen—the size of a well-fed toddler—and she smells vaguely of cinnamon.

"Zuri's certain of it." My aunt nods to a woman stretched out on the couch with her legs dangling over the sofa arm. Zuri is a stocky Black woman with a head of long locs save for one shaved side, and from the casual way she and my aunt interact, they clearly go way back. Zuri has been eyeing me since the moment she arrived, and I shrink back farther in the couch when she throws me a withering glance.

"Today, when Boahinmaa came to the museum, she was able to decipher a secret Abomofuo document, which revealed this," Zuri says as she rises from the couch to hand us each a print-out. On it is an inventory of items—art pieces specifically, like the ones I saw this morning. One entry has been highlighted in yellow. The words are similar to Twi, but I can't understand them. "What language is this?"

"Ga," she says. That's another language in Ghana, one that I don't speak but my aunt and mom do. "And even though the metadata lists this object as being of Akan origin, it's the only one with a Ga name—nyorntein ban. Three guesses on what that translates to?"

My heart practically stops beating. "The Midnight Drum."

"Exactly. Putting this information together with what you discovered, Serwa, it's likely that the Midnight Drum is one of the objects the Abomofuo is hiding within the museum's collection."

"But the drum is moved every few years, and only a few

Slayers can know where it is, to keep its location secret," I say. "If right now those people are my parents, why would Dr. Amankwah and the others be involved?"

"That's usually the case, but the talk of transferring these particular items began in the last week of August. The same week your parents and I had our . . . altercation."

She's referring to when she destroyed our lake house, the catalyst that sent me to Rocky Gorge in the first place. One day I'm going to have to spend a long time unpacking the fact that there isn't a single member of my family who hasn't severely screwed up my life in some way, shape, or form. My aunt at least looks a little remorseful about it, though not enough to actually apologize.

"But the past is the past, Serwa, and all that matters right now is that the Abomofuo are scrambling," she continues. "They want to move the drum again without drawing any attention to themselves. And, though we've been looking, we can't find any record of where the drum will go once it leaves the museum. That means we have to retrieve it before it reaches its new location."

"The gala is happening tomorrow night," Zuri adds. "The museum is closed to the public during the day in preparation for the event, but once it begins, the building will be full of staff, donors, local students, and press. Until we can figure out where the drum is being taken, our best chance to intercept it will be tomorrow afternoon before the event starts."

All that matches everything Mateo told me. It's wild how my friends somehow manage to get mixed up in magic shenanigans even when I'm not around.

The same sasabonsam I saw in the fitness room lets out several low, guttural gurgles before shoving eight sticks of chicken satay in its mouth at once. Fern nods along as she says, "Agreed. How are we going to get the drum if we don't have the password to get past the giant crocodile statue?"

Silence falls over the table as they contemplate this dilemma. I poke at my food, still as hungry as I was before I ate three bowls of massaman curry. I carefully ignore the several pitchers of blood on the table.

Part of me feels bad about trying to come up with a way to steal something the Abomofuo have been working so hard to protect. But then again, my anger swells every time I think about what the organization did to my family. I know Nana Bekoe hurt a lot of people, but it's hard not to sympathize with someone who was trying to get justice for her dead child. What the Abomofuo did to her and to my Auntie Abena was wrong, which means we have to make it right. Besides, twenty years in the Midnight Drum has to be enough punishment. No one deserves to be locked up indefinitely.

I turn the pieces of this puzzle over and over in my mind, twisting them for any angle that might show a clearer picture. The museum, the enchanted statue, the two people with the password to get past it . . .

Wait! That's it!

"Declan's our way in," I say. "If we want access to the secret exhibit, we need to get him to give us the code."

Zuri rolls her eyes and snorts. "And how exactly are we supposed to do that? Just walk up to him and go, 'Excuse me, young man, I know we're the vampiric creatures of the night you've been training your whole life to destroy, but before you beat our brains to a bloody pulp, would you mind giving us the password to the secret exhibit hall we're not even supposed to know about?'"

I bristle. She might not be wrong, but there's nothing I

hate more than being treated like an idiot just because I'm the youngest person in the room. "I mean, he obviously wouldn't give the code to *you* . . . But he might give it to another Slayer, like me. He and I go way back. I'm our best chance of getting it out of him."

"But you're not a Slayer," Zuri challenges, and I can't tell if she means that as a statement or a question.

"I'm not," I spit out. Gods, even saying it out loud hurts. "But he doesn't know that. The truth of my heritage is a secret in the Abomofuo. As long as he thinks I'm still one of them, this could work. He has no reason not to trust me."

"But the gala is in twenty-four hours," Fern points out. "When would you even have time to get it out of him?"

"When I saw Declan at the museum, he invited me to hang out with him before he and his mmoatia go on patrol tonight," I say. "If I join him on his rounds, I might be able to convince him to give me the code."

"And what if you can't?" demands Zuri. "What if you take this monumental risk and you can't get him to budge?"

"Then we're back where we started, with no Midnight Drum and no idea where it could possibly be."

Auntie Effi has been surprisingly silent during this argument. As much as I'd like her to back me up, my gut tells me I need to stand up for myself if I want any chance of Zuri and the rest of the coven taking me seriously.

Fern bites her lip and digs through her piles of notes until she pulls one out and squints at it. According to my aunt, she's the one who keeps up with the network of black magic creatures, sending messages back and forth the way Boulder and the other mmoatia partners do for the Abomofuo. "I agree that it's risky, but Serwa has a point. Plus, our scouts report that

Dr. Amankwah will be out of town on business until the gala starts, meaning that Declan is the only person in the area with access to the hall until his father returns."

Zuri throws her hands in the air. "You can't be serious. Until a few weeks ago, she was one of them! How do we know the second our backs are turned, Serwa won't go running to the Abomofuo and rat us all out?"

"I wouldn't do that!" I cry.

"But we don't *know* that." She flips her locs over her shoulder in a brisk motion. "Sorry, but I don't want to put my safety and that of everyone I care about in the hands of a child I've known for less than a month."

I'm practically shaking with rage. I figured I'd always have to defend my obayifo side to the Slayers, but now I have to defend my Slayer side to the vampires? Is there anyone on this flipping planet I *don't* have to justify my existence to?

"If you don't like my plan, what's yours, then?" I shoot back.

"Honestly? I say we forget this entire museum business. There are just too many unknown variables involved, and something about the whole thing feels off, even by Abomofuo standards." Zuri turns her attention toward my aunt like I'm not even there. "The answer here is obvious. The Abomofuo have something we want, and we have someone they want. Let's propose a trade: We'll return your niece in exchange for the Midnight Drum. Simple, clean, easy, and best of all, it doesn't rely on one child being able to outsmart another."

Bullseye, the adze who was possessing Ashley back in Rocky Gorge, had suggested the same thing during the Back-to-School-Night battle, and the idea of being used as a hostage fills me with as much dread now as it did back then. But before I can make my case for why I shouldn't be traded away like a fistful of Monopoly money, Auntie Effi goes, "Zuri, do you remember the day we met?"

When Zuri looks at my aunt, her face gets all soft like my mom's used to do sometimes when she looked at my dad. "Like I could ever forget. It was only five years ago."

"And in that time, have I ever said or done anything to make you think that I am not always acting in the best interest of our people and our cause?"

"Not even once."

My aunt's eyes narrow. "So why, then, would you dare insult my judgment by even suggesting that I'd bring someone into our circle who means to betray us?"

Just like that, Auntie Effi is gone and Boahinmaa stands in her place. Her voice is cold steel, and while Zuri might be actively campaigning to punt me out of this hotel, even I feel bad watching the woman's expression crumple.

Auntie Effi continues. "I'd think that you, of all people, would understand how painful it is to be cast out from a place simply because of where you were born or who your parents are. Serwa has just as much right to be here as any of us. I won't even consider trading her for the drum—for the same reason I'd never trade any of you."

Zuri recoils as if she's been slapped in the face, but my aunt's not done. "I hear your concerns, but I think Serwa's plan is our best course of action. We'll move our forces into position in case she succeeds in securing the password for the exhibit hall. And if she doesn't, the time she spends with the Amankwah boy might still reveal other useful information that could come in handy."

Zuri is clearly not happy with the decision, but there's nothing she can say to my aunt's decisive tone. You'd think that would be the end of it, except Auntie Effi smiles and goes, "And one more thing?"

She slams her hand down on the table, sending the lights flickering on and off. Shadows leap from her fingertips, wrapping themselves around Zuri's throat.

"If anyone ever *dares* to suggest selling Serwa again, I don't care how long they've been with us . . . they will learn what happens to those who threaten my family."

Everyone in the room freezes, clearly aware that in a one-on-one black magic battle, no one here can beat my aunt. Zuri's eyes shine with an emotion I can't read. She finally looks away from Boahinmaa, muttering something too low for me to hear. But as the meeting wraps up, the look of loathing she shoots my way is impossible to ignore.

8

How to Fight Off a
Spork-Wielding Faerie

"The bond between a mmoatia and a Slayer is for life.
Underestimate the strength of it at your own peril."

—From the *Nwoma*

"SO EXACTLY WHAT IS your deal with the Amankwah boy?" Auntie Effi asks. It's early evening now, several hours after the coven meeting back at the hotel, and we're one of what feels like every car on the planet stuck in the very special kind of torture that is Washington, DC's rush hour. Auntie Effi's driving me to my mission in a car I'm very much hoping isn't stolen. (I straight up asked her if it was. All she did was laugh. Someone out there is going to have a hard time explaining to their boss they're late for work because vampires stole their SUV.)

"Deal? What deal? There's no deal," I say quickly.

On the dashboard, Siri cheerfully announces we're only ten minutes away from our destination. Figuring out where Declan went to school was easy; the only school with the same colors as the green-and-gold varsity jacket he was wearing this morning is this fancy-schmancy all-boys academy called Cunningham Prep.

He'd mentioned he had soccer practice today at five, so Auntie Effi and I are on our way there now. Hopefully I can intercept Declan and convince him to let me join his Slayer rounds tonight.

"I heard the way you talked about him during the meeting," says my aunt. "There's history there."

Wow, I really don't like the smug lilt in her voice right now.

"The only history between Declan and me is the fact that he's the biggest jerkface to have ever jerkfaced," I declare, "and I've had the misfortune of spending time with him because our dads grew up together and there aren't many Slayer kids our age."

Auntie Effi is about to answer when someone cuts her off on a left turn. After a colorful string of curses that my parents would launch me into orbit for repeating, she goes, "I understand that part, but what has he actually done to earn this level of vitriol?"

What has Declan Amankwah done? What *hasn't* he done?! "Anytime we're at an event together, he always goes out of his way to remind me that he's sooo much better than I am and he's doing things that are sooooo much cooler than what I'm doing. And . . . and . . . and today, when I saw him, he had this *smile* plastered on his face, and he's just . . . ugh!"

And because no one on this planet understands loyalty, my aunt actually laughs. "Let me make sure I understand this correctly. You detest this boy because he has feelings for you?"

If we were in a sitcom, this would be the part where I spit water all over the dashboard. "WHAT?!"

"In my experience, someone going out of their way to talk to and smile at someone is usually a sign of a crush."

"No!"

"Ah. So, *you* have a crush on *him*?"

"Nuh-uh. No way. We could be the last two people in the entire universe, and said universe could be getting sucked into a black hole, and I still wouldn't have a crush on Declan."

"Have you ever had a crush on anyone before?"

My mind immediately wanders back to the night I walked home with Mateo that (first) time I broke onto the Rocky Gorge Middle School grounds. Heat rushing to my face, I wave the thought away. "What does any of this have to do with my mission?"

"More than you might think." We finally pull out of traffic and onto a much calmer residential street near Georgetown. Auntie Effi parks behind a hedge a few blocks away from the school and turns to me. "Because black magic does not have a conduit to stabilize it the way divine wisdom does with the Adinkra, an obayifo's powers are particularly volatile during periods of emotional instability. I still remember the first time I kissed a girl. I got so excited I accidentally blasted a hole into the side of the local church." Auntie Effi gives a wistful chuckle before slipping back into serious mode. "Call your feelings for the Amankwah boy whatever you want, but it's clear he evokes a strong reaction in you, which means you need to be all the more careful not to reveal your true nature to him."

I swear, all the adults in my life think I'm an idiot. "Don't worry, I'm not stupid enough to tell a boy trained to hunt vampires that I'm actually part vampire."

I start to climb out of the car, but Auntie Effi stops me with a hand around my arm. "You haven't fed in weeks." It's an accusation, not a question.

"I'm not hungry," I lie, even though I can practically feel my stomach twisting in on itself. I've kept my promise to myself to not drink blood even though it's offered with every meal at the hotel. Aside from some minor dizziness when I stand up too fast, and every now and then I get so hungry I fantasize that everyone around me is a talking blood Popsicle, I've been doing great. Everyone was wrong about me. I can be a vampire without hurting anyone.

"You're not wearing the seal anymore, Serwa. Sooner or later, you will need to feed, and if you slip up in front of the Amankwahs, more lives than yours are on the line." Her voice simmers with that icy danger that signals I'm talking to Boahinmaa now, not my kind aunt. This is the woman who was ready to fight her own sister to the death if it meant freeing her mother. "Do you know that when I first met Zuri, she was so injured she couldn't even walk?"

My eyes go wide. "I didn't."

"She had been masking her powers for years, and when her partner at the time discovered the truth, she called their local Slayer, who attacked Zuri and held her captive for days. Zuri had no combat experience. She was a graphic designer before all this. Now she's nearly as deadly as I am in a fight, but I don't think she ever fully recovered from that attack."

My aunt's voice is softer when she continues. "The majority of the obayifo in my care aren't warriors. They weren't trained to fight like Slayers. They're women like you and me, all of them persecuted for something they can't control. The hotel is the only shelter most of them have, and all of them will be in danger if anything goes wrong tonight. So, no matter what happens with this Declan Amankwah, never forget whose side you're on. And remember, for an obayifo, there's often not much difference between a first kiss and a first bite."

I'm too stunned to speak, so I just nod. After reminding me that I can call her from my burner phone if anything goes wrong, Auntie Effi finally lets me get out of the car and speeds off into the evening. Now I'm alone in the middle of DC with the weight of my mission heavy on my shoulders.

But as scary as my aunt's warning was, it makes me feel a bit better about what I have to do. Vampires or no, the way obayifo have been treated isn't fair. I know we can't be allowed to suck blood whenever we want, but there has to be a better way for us to exist peacefully without being hunted to extinction. Freeing my grandmother will be the first step in changing things.

Okay, enough dilly-dallying. Dad always told me the first thing you need to do when entering enemy territory is reconnaissance. I survey my surroundings, eyes peeled for any vantage points or potential liabilities on the grounds. Rocky Gorge Middle School was pretty nice for a public school, but Cunningham Prep is the kind of place where the kids of ambassadors rub elbows with the kids of presidents. Honest-to-gods ivy crawls up the school's dark gray walls, and the whole building is surrounded by a tall brick fence that even I wouldn't attempt to climb over.

But luckily, the school's sports fields border a public park with a giant playground (or tot lot, as the people of a certain corner of Maryland would call it, because they're all weirdos). After shooing a couple kindergartners away from the top of the slide—they take one look at my *Do not mess with me right now* face and scatter—I camp up there to learn as much as I can about how Declan acts in his natural habitat before I make my move.

Okay, so one benefit of this whole *suddenly discovering I'm secretly a vampire* thing? Heightened senses. I can see and hear everything happening on the soccer field as if I were standing right on it, which makes it easy to pick Declan out of the pack of screaming boys charging down the pitch. Though he's taller than the average boy my age—not that I noticed or anything!—he's actually one of the shortest players on the team. But he keeps up effortlessly, swerving in and out of his larger team-mates with expert maneuvers that would impress even a veteran Slayer. I hate to admit it, but the boy's good, and that's without any of the magic he's hiding from his fellow athletes.

I let out a small yell of delight when Declan plows through the other team's defenders to score the winning goal. Okay, he's not just good—he's *incredible*. And not only that, but the other players clearly adore him; his teammates hoist him in the air as they cheer his victory. It took me weeks to get the members of the GCC not to hate my guts, and that only happened because we'd survived a couple of life-threatening incidents together, which really accelerates the bonding process. But look at how many friends Declan has. Everything is just so . . . easy for him.

Is that what my life would've looked like if my mother hadn't been an obayifo? Would I have lived in one town my whole life like Declan, gone to the same school with the same friends for years, been able to proudly call myself a Slayer without anyone questioning my motives or my heritage? I squeeze my Grandma Awurama's pendant, the familiar bite of the metal a balm to the swirl of emotions in me.

Almost like they're reacting to my thoughts, my fangs start to poke up from under my gums as my stomach lets out a low rumble. Oh no, not now. Gotta think not-hungry thoughts, not-hungry thoughts. Poopy diaper butts; landfills full of nasty, rotting food; Boulder's crusty mmoatia bunions—

"I've got you now, stalker!"

Something knocks me in the back of the head, sending me tumbling head over heels down the slide. When the world stops spinning, I look up to see a mmoatia hovering inches in front of my face and brandishing a plastic spork like a weapon. She's smaller and slighter than Boulder, with streaks of fiery red woven through her ankle-length braids. (The length of her ankles, that is. Each one is like a fraction of the length of my braids.) Her pearly iridescent beetle-like wings flap ominously as she slashes the spork as menacingly as one can with a tool meant for salads and soups. Whoa, so there *are* mmoatia that can fly! And to think that for years Boulder threatened anyone who dared to call him a fairy.

"You stay away from Deckie-poo, creep!" she yells.

I bite back a laugh. Deckie-poo? This must be Declan's mmoatia partner. I think I might have seen her at the party Dr. Amankwah threw two years ago when Declan passed his Initiation Test, but I was too busy seething with jealousy to remember her name.

"Calm down, Tinker Bell. I'm not here to hurt Declan," I say, which only earns me more spork jabs to the face. "Ow, quit that!"

The black magic in me flares along with my irritation, and a thought hits me: *I could snap this mmoatia in two with a single bite.* This creature is so much smaller than me. Why should I let her poke me and prod me and—

You are not some common creature to be ordered about, are you, Oseiwa?

—I . . . Huh? That was weird. Since when do I think of myself in the second person or with the alternate form of my own name? Maybe Auntie Effi is right, I gotta be careful about not overexerting myself if it's going to lead to all sorts of weird thoughts.

But before I can throw hands with a creature that's, like, a twentieth of my size, who else but Declan Amankwah jogs over, wiping sweat from his face with a towel.

"You good, Pepper?" he asks. "I sensed your agitation through our bond."

"I found this vagrant spying on you!" shrieks Pepper, and that *stupid smirk* returns to Declan's face when his eyes land on me.

"Long time no see, rookie," he says with a laugh.

This was a mistake. Forget the Midnight Drum and saving Nana Bekoe. Nothing on earth is worth dealing with this.

But I think about Zuri, and Biri, and my aunt, and all the other people hiding in the hotel because the Abomofuo made the world too dangerous for them to go anywhere else, and that gives me the strength to say, "I'm here to take you up on your earlier offer."

"Offer? What offer?" demands Pepper. "What's she talking about?" She motions like she's going to stab me again, likely out of pure spite, but Declan scoops her out of the air and plops her on his shoulder in one fluid motion. Luckily for us, the playground's empty now, so there's no one around to see the mmoatia and upload the truth of supernatural creatures all over social media.

"Serwa texted me that she'd be in the area, and I told her to hit me up if she wanted to hang out." Dang, he even lies well. And, apparently, he didn't even tell his mmoatia about his visit to the museum today. A Slayer is supposed to share everything with their partner. If he's already keeping secrets from her, maybe convincing him not to rat me out to the Abomofuo will be easier than I thought.

"But I meant right after school, before practice started. Pepper and I need to start our rounds soon, so I can't hang out right now," he adds while the mmoatia nods along on his shoulder like the world's tiniest bodyguard. I jump to my feet, hoping my expression is way calmer than I feel.

"That's no problem. I can come with you."

Oh no, he's frowning. Slayers aren't supposed to bring along anyone who hasn't been authorized to join them on patrol. If I can't twist his arm, Auntie Effi's dreams of entering the secret exhibit hall are over.

Earlier I channeled Gavin when I lied, but this time I'm recalling how Mateo could always wheedle the teachers into doing whatever he wanted by being sweet. "I mean, it's just that I haven't had a lot of chances to train while I've been in deep cover, you know?" I say. "I thought it'd be good for me to go on patrol and learn the ropes from a full Slayer since I'm, you know . . . not one."

It costs me everything to say those words without gagging, but Declan's suspicion immediately clears up. However, Pepper cuts in, "You know that's against the rules. She's trying to get us in trouble!"

"I wouldn't use any magic!" I add quickly. Look at that, the fact that my divine wisdom is AWOL at the moment is actually working in my favor. "I'd just observe, maybe take some notes. I'll be so quiet you won't even know I'm there."

Declan tilts his head and studies me slowly. Suddenly all I'm aware of are the scuffs on my sneakers and the frizzed-up baby hairs on my forehead. What does he see when he looks at me? I know it shouldn't matter at all but . . . it does. A lot.

UGH.

I'm dead sure Declan's going to say no and I'm about to have my butt hauled off to the Okomfo when he goes, "How about this? Let's spar. If you win, you can come with Pepper and me on our rounds."

I narrow my eyes at him. "And if *you* win . . . ?"

"*When* I win, I get to ask you whatever I want, and you have to answer. No lying or chickening out."

If that isn't the single most suspicious request I've ever heard in my entire life. I look around us. The playground and field might be empty now, but there are still cars passing by and people walking up and down the street. "You want to spar right out here in the open?"

"Yes, and after that, I want to call the UN and give them a detailed presentation about the existence of vampires, witches, and ghosts, plus reveal the international organization of Ghana-ian monster hunters working right under their noses." Declan rolls his eyes. "I'll set up an invisibility ward before we start. You know how to make one of those, right? It's a combina-tion of—"

"I know which three Adinkra you use to make an invisibility ward, thanks," I snap before he can Slayer-splain any further. If Boulder were here, he'd probably have a list of one hun-dred and one reasons why sparring Declan is a bad idea, along with some long-winded story involving Alexander the Great or something. But if I don't beat Declan, I won't get to go on patrol with him. And if I don't get that password tonight, then we're never getting into the secret exhibit.

Plus, seeing Declan's smug smirk vanish when I wipe the floor with his butt won't hurt, either.

"You're on, Amankwah."

STANDING BACK AND LETTING Declan draw the Adinkra was harder than I'd thought it'd be. Eban, the fence, to mark the enclosure; and fihankra, the symbol of security, to make us invisible to anyone walking by. The Adinkra are more than just drawings—they're the foundation of how I understand the world. Not being able to use them right now stings in the deepest part of me, but I'd never admit it out loud and have the other obayifo doubt my loyalty.

Once the invisible barrier is in place, Pepper explains the rules while Declan turns two sticks he found into makeshift akrafena for us to use.

"This is just a combat practice, so no drawing blood, no fatal blows, and no divine wisdom," says the mmoatia from her perch on top of Declan's backpack. "The first one to disarm the other wins, no time limit. Do you agree?"

We both nod. Declan tosses me my sword, and I can't suppress my grin as my fingers wrap around the wooden hilt. This is the first time I've held a weapon since leaving Rocky Gorge; having a sword in my hands feels so familiar—so *right*—like hearing your old favorite song for the first time in years and realizing you still know every word.

We position ourselves about ten feet apart in the center of the soccer field. My focus narrows to Declan shifting into an attack stance that mirrors my own. Everything else in my life fades away—I forget all about my wonky powers, my fight with my parents, even my mission for Auntie Effi. Nothing matters right now except the weapon in front of me and the boy wielding it.

Pepper lets out a high-pitched whistle. "Go!"

Declan and I launch forward in unison, our swords meeting and pulling back and meeting again almost too quickly for me to see. It's a good thing these aren't real akrafena, because the force we're using would cause limbs to fly if they were.

The sweat beading down Declan's face makes it clear he's taking this just as seriously as I am. Good. I'd never forgive him for holding back just because he's a full Slayer and I'm not.

Duck, swipe, stab, guard, parry, roll—my body moves through the movements from a place deeper than instinct. When I was training with the GCC, I always had to go easy because they were all beginners, and I didn't want to hurt them. But Declan was raised by Slayers just like I was. The warrior spirit is in his blood, same as mine. He knows what it's like to be in the midst of a battle and feel like your head, your body, and your heart are all moving as one even though—or maybe because—your life is on the line.

We lock weapons at a standstill with our faces inches apart. Our eyes meet, and there's an intensity in his that goes beyond a mere practice match. My breath catches as my aunt's words ring through my ears.

So, you have a crush on him?

What the—? Why am I remembering that now?! The stupid memory breaks my concentration, and I stagger forward instead of backing away. Declan takes advantage of my mistake to get in even closer, and now all I can notice is that scar on his eyebrow and how he somehow still smells good even after soccer practice, like grass and apples and some . . . other . . . boy smell.

With one move, Declan knocks my sword out of my hands, and with another, he has his blade up against my chin. The smirk returns as Pepper cheers her head off from the sideline. "Match point! Go, Declan! That's my partner!"

Declan steps back, lazily swinging the sword behind his neck and holding on to it with both hands. "Not bad, rookie," he admits. "Too bad I'm better."

I've never cried over losing a match before, but my eyes are definitely burning in a way I don't like. How is it after everything I've gone through and even with my heightened obayifo senses, I still can't beat this boy? I'm not a good enough Slayer or a good enough vampire or a good enough anything, I guess.

"Fine, you win," I say flatly, because I might hate losing, but I'm not a sore loser. Oh gods, how am I going to explain to Auntie Effi that I failed the one task she's given me since joining her? "What's your question?"

This time Declan looks at me with an unreadable expression. It's almost like how my parents used to get when they were unraveling a mystery during a hunt—full of frustration at having all the pieces in front of them but no clue how they fit together.

He shakes his head. "Come on, the night isn't getting any younger. You can keep the sword—it might come in handy while we're out on rounds."

Both Pepper and I blink at Declan in shock. "You're letting me come with you? But I lost!" I exclaim.

"I only said that if I won, you'd have to answer a question, which I'm choosing to save for another time because it's getting late. I never said I wouldn't let you join me," he explains, ignoring Pepper's shrill shrieks of protest.

Why do I feel like I just took a test, and even though I passed, I somehow failed? Is this Declan's way of being nice? I swallow back my confusion and say, "I meant what I said earlier. I'll be quieter than a ghost on their way to Asamando. You can pretend I'm not even there at all."

"Trust me, rookie. You're pretty hard to not notice."

And before I can figure out what *that* means, he turns his back to me and starts walking off the field. "And who knows? Maybe after a few hours watching a full Slayer at work, you'll be begging to become my apprentice for real."

I take it all back. Auntie Effi is never going to get into the exhibit hall because I'm going to murder Declan Amankwah with my bare hands before this night is through.

9

How to Break into Your Local Zoo

"Treat all animals you encounter with the proper respect.
Every creature on Nyame's earth has a part to play,
no matter how small."

—From the *Nwoma*

"YOU ACTUALLY PICKED A great night to play side-kick," says Declan.

"Okay, number one, I'm not your sidekick," I snap back. "I'm shadowing you. Very different. Number two, why?"

After our duel, Declan and I took the bus from Cunningham Prep and are now back in the hustle and bustle of the main part of DC near Foggy Bottom metro station. On the outside, we look like two ordinary kids strolling the street, but I know Declan's backpack is full of enchanted weapons and armor (and, of course, Pepper) to help him on his patrol, while my practice sword has been turned into a pen for the time being. (By the way, a sword disguised as a pen is a genius idea. Someone needs to write that down!)

"Tonight's patrol is different than usual," says Declan. "Instead of normal rounds, I've got a special task related to the gala tomorrow. You know how to make a nyame dua?"

I roll my eyes. As if I couldn't draw every Adinkra in my sleep. "Nyame dua is four interlocking heartlike shapes that resemble a clover—"

"Not the symbol, the thing the symbol is based on," Declan corrects. "Wait, you speak Twi, right? *Dua* means—"

"*Dua* means *tree*, so the phrase literally means *God's tree*," I interject before asking, through gritted teeth, "So, how do you make the actual tree?"

"With these." We stop at an intersection, and Declan discreetly opens his backpack to reveal three little clay pots packed to the brim with soil and a fragrant mixture of herbs. Divine wisdom buzzes off them from the nyame dua Adinkra drawn on the side of each pot. Immediately, pain starts thudding at my temples. "Plant one of these in the ground, and you'll grow a mystical tree with ten times as much black-magic-repelling ability as an Adinkra on its own."

Ugh, no wonder these pots make me feel like someone is playing Bop It with my skull. I'm just the kind of creature they're meant to repel. "Why do you have three of them?"

"A single nyame dua is powerful on its own, but when a trio is triangulated around a specific location and blessed in the name of the three celestial children of Nyame—Owia, Osrane, and Esum—it creates a barrier that amplifies their abilities. The Okomfo asked me to set one up ahead of the gala tomorrow as an extra safety precaution since Boahinmaa is still at large."

Whoa, using literal nyame dua as a supercharged protective ward? Now, that's a technique I've never heard of before. I try not to look too impressed, because I know that's exactly what Declan wants. "And where are you going to plant them?"

"Traditionally, a nyame dua was placed in a spot where sacred rituals were done. These have to be put in three spots of immense magical power, even more than a liminal space would have."

After that big speech, I was expecting a supercool and awe-inspiring location like, I don't know, the Washington Monument, or Barack Obama's favorite toilet or something. So imagine my surprise when Declan leads me down a musty flight of stairs into one of DC's many metro stations. I cover my nose as the pungent combination of pee, vomit, and rusting metal assaults my heightened obayifo senses. "Ugh, you're going to plant the first nyame dua down here?"

"Wrong again, rookie. We're going to ride the train to our real location."

Declan pulls out the SmarTrip Card I saw earlier and taps himself through, then pauses when I don't immediately follow. "Forgot your card?" He shakes his head. "A good Slayer is always prepared."

Now he's quoting the Nwoma at me, like my own ancestor didn't help write the darn book! (Okay, technically, so did his, BUT THAT'S NOT THE POINT!) "I don't have a metro card. I'm not from here, remember?"

"Right." He digs through his pockets until he finds a spare card and tosses it to me over the turnstile. "Consider it a welcome gift. You can't get anywhere around the city without one."

If there's one thing I hate more than needing help, it's needing help from Declan Amankwah. But since Auntie Effi hasn't included an allowance in the mountain of gifts she's given me, I begrudgingly use the card to tap through the turnstile then shove it in my back jeans pocket.

If you've ever ridden the DC metro, then you understand what I mean when I say that it is basically its own dimension. Not only are the stations home to smells that no nose was ever meant to smell, but every kind of person you can possibly imagine mills around the concrete tunnels. Declan and I squeeze onto a train between an entire girls' lacrosse team and what looks like at least half a dozen professional bagpipe players. Since it's still rush hour, there are no seats, so Declan and I have to pretend like we're not smooshed right up against each other.

"Um, your schedule must be pretty packed between Slayer stuff and eighth grade," I say before the silence can stretch on long enough to grow awkward.

"Ninth grade," he corrects. "My guidance counselor suggested I skip a year since I was above grade level last year."

So that's why everyone on the soccer team looked older than Declan—they were. Even I've got to admit it's pretty impressive that at thirteen he can keep up with high schoolers.

"You're juggling freshman courses, your Slayer duties, and a sports team? When do you sleep?" I ask only half-jokingly.

Declan gives an easy shrug. "It's not so hard. Plus, I can sleep when I'm dead."

Okay, I've been to the land of the dead, and that place had one of the wildest ragers I've ever seen. If ghosts sleep, they're not doing it there. "And this museum assignment? How has that been coming?" I straight up want to ask about Funtunfunefu-Denkyemfunefu, because it's a pretty cool use of magic to bring a statue that big to life (even if said statue has a single brain cell between its two heads) but mentioning it would be way too obvious.

"A mission's a mission. You know how it is." Declan's phone vibrates. He pulls it out, reads his latest text, then pulls a face.

"Everything okay?"

"Yeah, it's just that the nurse who usually stays with my daa during the evening is asking if I can be home by ten tonight so she can go take care of her sick kid." *Daa* is one of the affectionate ways to refer to you grandfather in Ghana, kind of like *Pops* in English. I've never used it because I never knew either of my grandfathers. "I'll have to go get him ready for bed tonight. That's less time than I would've liked for the mission, but I'll make it work."

It's about 7 p.m. right now, so that gives me roughly three hours to get the password out of Declan. Anyone else hear a clock ticking the seconds away, or is that just me?

I'm not sure how much more I can pry from him before he gets suspicious. The train stops and someone pushes me on their way out the door, shoving my face straight into Declan's chest. We're so close I can literally *hear* the blood rushing through his veins, pumping from heart to lungs and back again in an endless cycle. My fangs push at the edges of my gums, and an image of my teeth sinking into Declan's neck flashes through my mind as my stomach rumbles.

"You okay?" he asks, snapping me out of the fantasy of feasting on his blood.

I clumsily pull back, running my tongue over my teeth to double-check that they're normal and human and definitely not a vampire's. "Yeah, just a little hungry." We're nearing the end of the line, but Declan hasn't made any move toward the door. "Shouldn't we get off? The next stop is the last one."

"Just wait for it."

Minutes later, the conductor yells over the loudspeaker that we've reached the end of the line and everyone needs to get their butts off his train. I start to leave, but Declan motions for me to sit down. Passengers file out until it's just Declan and me sitting on one of the uncomfortably sticky seats we'd moved to.

The train lurches forward into the tunnel, and one by one, the lights shut off, leaving us in total darkness.

I let out a yelp of surprise, but then the lights flicker back on, and all around us the train begins to transform. The seats morph, some becoming wide enough to accommodate eight people sitting shoulder to shoulder, others shrinking so small that even a mmoatia would have a hard time fitting into one. The map on the wall rearranges itself before my eyes, and what's left is still an outline of DC but with metro lines and stations I've never heard of. Even the ads shift. A much-graffitied poster reminding people to visit the DC Public Library has been replaced by a photo of a pink-skinned spirit woman with a megawatt smile holding up a sports drink. The speech bubble next to her promises that the new and improved Ghostade can fix all manner of spectral worries and woes.

"Welcome to the Undertrain, rookie," says Declan, and I'm so amazed by the train's transformation that I can't even be mad at the smugness in his voice. "Fastest way for denizens of the magic world to move from their side of the veil to ours, and vice versa."

My parents had taught me that the human world and the magic one are like two sides of a single page. The words on each side could be completely different, but they still occupy the same space. Sometimes the distance between the two is so thin you can even see through the page, like in liminal spaces.

I slink down in my seat as all manner of spirits and magical creatures start boarding the train—mmoatia families, eerie floating wisplike lights, and even several hovering wooden masks engraved with traditional markings arguing loudly among themselves about the Washington Commanders' chances of making it to the Super Bowl next year.

I don't see any Slayers, but I can't be too careful. Overhead, the conductor is now speaking in Twi, and he lets us know we'll be arriving at the Boulevard of Not-So-Broken Dreams in approximately the time it takes a leopard's grin to go from one side of its mouth to the other. (Look, I don't know what that means, either. If there's one thing Ghanaians love, it's metaphors. I just go with it.)

"Why have I never heard about this?" I ask Declan. An entire train populated by magical creatures sounds like something that should be covered on the very first day of Slayer 101.

"Accessing the train requires a form of portal magic, which is highly regulated, so only active Slayers are allowed," explains Pepper. Now that we've crossed the veil, she pulls herself out of Declan's bag to sit on his shoulder and analyze the moving map on the wall across from us. "Plus, the points where the supernatural locations match up to the real-world ones are always shifting. A few decades ago, a trainee accidentally sent themselves to Antarctica while trying to access the train, and it was a bureaucratic nightmare trying to get them back. I'm talking mountains of paperwork and several meetings with the Antarctic Treaty. What a headache." To Declan, she adds, "Zoo's at the intersection of Good Intentions and Ill-Formed Plans today."

"Thanks, Pep." He pats his mmoatia on the head, and her wings do a happy little flutter.

"But this place is completely undefended," I ask. "Isn't anyone here worried about adze?"

"Creatures of black magic are banned from the Undertrain, and even if they weren't, since mortals can't access it, there's no source of food for them here. If one ever wandered in, the Slayers could have people here in minutes to apprehend it."

Welp, time to add trespassing on a magic train to the

worryingly long list of crimes I've committed since turning twelve. I slide down even farther in my chair and pull the collar of my T-shirt up over my nose just in case there are any hidden cameras. An obayifo's black magic is only detectable when it's actively being used, so I'm safe from Pepper or any of the other creatures here sensing me as long as I don't use my powers. But that doesn't mean I can't be recognized the plain old non-magical way.

We finally disembark into a completely new version of Washington, DC. It's nighttime now, and there are more stars on this side of the veil, as if the sky decided to give the finger to light pollution by shining even brighter over here. All the buildings and monuments look like they usually do, but the people are faded and washed out, like a shirt that's gone through the laundry one too many times. The magical creatures, on the other hand, are in full-on funky Technicolor. We pass a group of human tourists waiting for Ubers next to a giant elephant spirit waiting for the same, and a man who doesn't realize there's a mmoatia riding his head as he crosses the street. Part of me just wants to stop and take it all in, because I've never been this deep on the other side of the veil before. But since Declan isn't ogling, I don't, either.

We finally reach our destination—the Smithsonian National Zoological Park, or the National Zoo, as non-nerds know it. During the day, this place is filled with aimless tourists and sticky children heckling zebras, but now that it's after dark, it has become something else entirely. On this side of the veil, the zoo comes alive.

One of the rhinos gets up on two legs, stretches, and starts talking to himself about how he doesn't get paid enough to have children screaming in his ears 24/7. The monkeys somehow acquired a foldable table and are playing a spirited game of poker filled with both figurative *and* literal mudslinging. The talking animals part of the night is the least surprising thing that's happened so far. Ghanaian folktales make it clear that all animals can talk and carry on just as humans do—they just rarely do it when we can see it. It's only because we are looking from the other side of the veil that we can see all these creatures for what they truly are, because the old stories teach that all animals—from the mightiest lion to the tiniest fruit fly—are magic in their own right.

We pause outside the tortoise enclosure—they're engaged in the world's slowest game of pickup sticks—so Declan can pull a marker and one of the nyame dua pots out of his bag. He draws an Adinkra that looks like a diamond with four round circles branching off it—agyin dawuru, the symbol of alertness. Once he's done drawing, Declan squeezes the pot, and it begins to glow. "I picked the zoo for the first location because the presence of so many animals makes divine wisdom stronger. This Adinkra will attune the pot to the magical energy and lead us to the best spot to put it in."

We wander around for at least thirty minutes, the light from the nyame dua ebbing and flowing as we look for the place where it glows the brightest. Internally, I'm screaming with boredom. I understand the importance of our people's rituals and practices, but this is the part of being a Slayer I always found the dullest. I'd take a vampire battle any day over playing with the magic equivalent of a metal detector.

We make it to the Reptile Discovery Center, and I'm watching Declan try to climb the side of the building to follow the pot's light when a voice behind me says, "My oh my. Don't you have quite the peculiar perfume about you?"

I whirl around, my hand wrapped around the pen sword in my pocket. In the tree behind me rests a giant cobra wearing one of those green-and-white poker visors. Its massive black-and-cream body is wrapped protectively around a pile of poker chips. I try to keep my voice even as I reply, "Perfume? I'm not wearing perfume."

"Your natural odor. The flavor I'm recognizing in it . . ." The snake pauses to flick a black forked tongue in the air around my face. "Not quite human."

A shiver runs down my spine. The snake can smell I'm an obayifo. Okay, time to stall while I figure a way out of this.

"Hey, aren't snakes supposed to hiss everything they say?" I ask.

The cobra's hood flares in annoyance. "I will not adhere to that horrible pigeonholing! Why, I'll have you know that I have learned to communicate without ever utilizing that letter which will not be named."

"You mean the letter *S*?"

"Do not even utter it around me!" the snake snaps angrily.

Huh, a snake that refuses to hiss. Weird.

Then again, I'm a vampire who refuses to drink blood, so maybe I have no right to talk.

It flicks its tongue again, and then its eyes brighten. "You're an obayifo, aren't you?" At the shocked look on my face, the cobra lets out a laugh, and then starts counting through its poker winnings with the tip of its tail. "Do not fret, little witch. We with fanged teeth ought to look out for one another." It tips its head toward the building next to us. "Out of unity among our people, I am here to provide you with a warning. Be wary of the caretaker of our domain. If he were to find you here, you would not be welcomed with a greeting."

Caretaker of their domain? Like the zoo's owner? I follow

the snake's gaze to the window of the reptile building. Inside, a figure I know all too well is trying to extract a tuatara's head from inside a tiny VR headset. Even though the person is wearing the same rugged khaki shirt and pants that most zookeepers wear, the unnatural light in his eyes makes it impossible to mistake him for a human.

Of course, *of course*, Bia, the Akan god of animals, would be at the zoo the same night I am!

"But why is he even here?" I cry.

"Nyame charged Bia with the protection of all . . . of all . . ." The snake spits in frustration, clearly unable to figure out a way to end its sentence without using a plural.

"Bia is the god of the bush, so his thing is beasts, animals, fauna, yeah, I get the idea. But why is he here *tonight*?"

"Anywhere fauna can be, Bia can be."

That doesn't answer my question, but I clearly have bigger problems than arguing with a creature that has an aversion to sibilance. Bia's brother Tegare, god of hunters, is the official patron god of the Abomofuo, and Bia along with his war god twin brother, Tano, often helps to train and organize Slayers. Bia and I met face-to-face the day Boahinmaa attacked my lake house. He'd looked at me strangely then, and now I know it was because he was searching for any signs of my vampire side coming out. If he catches me here, forget being hauled back to my parents—he might vaporize me on the spot, or send rabid hyenas to eat my kidneys or something, just because he thinks I could be a threat.

I frantically wave down Declan and gesture toward Bia though the window. "God sighting, six o'clock. We have to get out of here, now!"

Declan's brow furrows. "But why do we have to avoid him? We're here on official Abomofuo business."

"You are, but I'm not. I'm supposed to be in deep cover, remember? I can't let him see me!"

Pepper narrows her eyes. Declan looks ready to argue more, but just then, the door to the reptile house opens. I grab Declan's arm and drag him into the hedges while overhead the snake continues to sift through its chips. Bia wanders out with the tuatara—VR goggles still stuck to its face—cradled in his arms. Compared to his twin, the god of war, who is built like a tank on steroids, Bia is thinner and lankier, like a Ghanaian Robert Irwin. He pauses, brow scrunched.

"I heard voices. Is something going on out here?" he asks the snake, who shrugs (and by *shrugs*, I mean wiggles from side to side in, like, a noncommittal way.) Bia turns toward our hiding spot, and my heart pounds harder and harder in my throat with each step he takes.

He is only a foot away when the snake says, "Hey, do I hear your twin lumbering around the Africa habitat?"

"Tano?! I told him never to show his face around here again! Those poor meerkats are still in therapy after what he did to them!"

Bia whirls around and charges for the meerkat enclosure. The snake winks at me from its branch, and I give it a nod of thanks back. Declan tries to follow the nyame dua back toward the direction Bia went, but I pull him deeper into the bush toward a rusted chain-link fence.

"The dua says we need to go that way," he argues.

I shake my head. "Can't risk it. Let's just go to the second location now and come back here later."

"But we're so close to planting this one! What happened to you being like a shadow and I wouldn't even know you're here?" He yanks his arm from my grasp and turns toward me, scowling. "Might I remind you, this is still *my* mission, rookie. I decide where we go and when."

Pressure builds up beneath my skin. My hands squeeze into fists so tight I can feel my nails pushing into my palms. No, I need to stay calm. Now is not the time for a black magic flare-up.

Declan advances on me, Pepper scowling on his shoulder like a tiny bodyguard. "Besides, why are you being so paranoid, anyway? Is there something you're not telling me?"

It's too hard to think, too hard to speak, with the black magic clawing up my throat. "What?! Me? No, I—"

Declan steps forward again, and my back hits the fence. That tiny bit of contact is all it takes for my black magic to zip free. I yelp as the metal behind me gives way with a snap, and in a panic I pull Declan with me as I go tumbling down a slope. We land in a heap at the bottom of a deep pit, one that wasn't listed on the map we filched at the zoo entrance. Fallen rainforest-like trees cover the ground, and high above us, I can just make out thick iron bars jutting from the fence and meeting in the center of the sky. Kind of like . . . a bird cage?

With a groan, I rub my head and look up to see a giant sign hanging above us:

WARNING: EXHIBIT CLOSED

(UNTIL WE GET THE MAIMING PROBLEM UNDER CONTROL)

Declan and I swap alarmed looks.

"Maybe that's left over from the last animal that was here, and the current occupant is a really fluffy bunny?" I joke.

Behind us, a high-pitched squawk slices through the air, so shrill that my eardrums rattle.

Oh, that is *definitely* not a fluffy bunny.

10

How to Throw Hands with a Bird

"When you find yourself in an unexpected battle, be ready to utilize unexpected tactics."

—From the *Nwoma*

I'VE ALWAYS BEEN PRETTY good with heights, but nothing will give you a fear of them faster than being abducted by a giant bird.

"SERWA!" yells Declan as a sharp beak grabs me by the waist and yanks me into the air. The ground falls away in a sickening *swoosh* of brown-and-gray wings as I twist my neck to see my attacker. I'm in the beak of a hornbill, one easily twice the size of a full-grown man. My brain scrambles to make sense of the situation until an old tale from the *Nwoma* jumps out at me. The Krachi people of Ghana had a legend about Animabri, the giant flesh-eating hornbill that killed so many people that their creator god, Wulbari, had to convene a court of every creature on earth to deal with him. The Abomofuo must be holding him within this zoo to keep an eye on him. But clearly, a millennium of confinement has only heightened his love of human flesh. If I don't do something quick, I'm next up on the menu.

"Let me go!" I click the pen into its wooden akrafena

form and whack it at the bird's beak, which achieves absolutely nothing. Seconds later, Animabri drops me into a giant nest at the top of one of the trees in the enclosure. He lets out another caw before flying off into the night.

"That's certainly no way to treat a guest in your home!" I yell at the bird's retreating figure. You'd think that'd be the end of it, except behind me there comes a cracking sound. I slowly turn around to see two ginormous eggs, each about a foot taller than I am, bursting open.

I want you to do something for me. Go ahead and Google *hornbill chick* really quick, and then tell me that isn't the single most horrifying baby creature you've ever seen in your entire life. If you don't have a phone, laptop, or tablet handy, then imagine a chicken if chickens had absolutely no feathers, corpse-gray slimy skin, ridiculously long beaks, and beady eyes filled with nothing but malice because their souls are made of nightmares and baby tears. That is what a hornbill chick looks like, and I've got two of them freshly hatched and very eager to enjoy their first meal ever, i.e., me.

"DECLAN!" I scream, because I know when I'm outmatched. I might stand a chance if I had a real weapon, like my mom's old akrafena, Nokware, or if I could use either of my magics. But right now I'm as useless as a bag of bird feed—which is exactly what I'll be if I don't get out of this nest. The chicks are too young to fly like Animabri, but that doesn't stop them from climbing out of their eggs and wobbling toward me, trailing the remnants of their yolk sacs behind them. I scramble up the side of the nest, but the ground below is a good thirty, maybe forty, feet down. No way I'm making that drop without ending up a Serwa-sized pancake.

The bigger of the birds, Chick 1, reaches me first and grabs my ankle, but I kick it off while swinging my sword toward Chick 2. The babies stumble backward with pained cries, and I feel a quick jolt of pity for them. They're only attacking out of a base hunger instinct, not because they actually want to hurt me. I know what that's like.

But that pity quickly disappears when Chick 2 retaliates my sword slap by grabbing the hood of my sweatshirt and pulling hard. Its sibling grabs my foot, and that's how I find myself gasping for breath while two mutant Tweety Birds pull me apart like Laffy Taffy. Black spots dance in my vision from the combined lack of oxygen and the pain in my foot, when a shimmering greenish light flits into the nest.

"EAT MY SPORK!" screams Pepper, and she jabs the utensil into Chick 1's eye. It lets out a bloodcurdling cry and releases my foot. Luckily, I don't think it's broken, but these shoes will definitely be unwearable after tonight. With my foot free, I brace myself against the wall of the nest and yank the hoodie from Chick 2's mouth. Then I slide out between its slimy legs as Pepper moves to engage both birds.

"Serwa!" Declan calls from below. I climb up the side of the nest again and look below. He's shimmied about halfway up the tree trunk and is waving frantically. "Jump! I've got you!"

I've honestly never felt less "got" in my life, but between a fall and the carnivorous birds, I'll take the fall. I leap from the nest, once again experiencing that lighter-than-air swooshing feeling but in reverse. Declan leaps from the tree right as I'm passing him and catches me in his arms. I squeeze my eyes shut and brace myself for the inevitable impact, but it never comes. I open my eyes to see we're not falling but floating down. For a fraction of a second, it's actually beautiful watching the world flow by in no hurry.

Declan lands gently on the ground, and explains, "I drew an antigravity spell on my shoes. Thought it'd be better than us breaking our necks."

"That's genius!"

I beam up at him, and he gives me this excited little smile back, and you know what? I think I like his *Isn't having magic powers cool as heck?* smile over his *I'm so awesome all the time* smirk. Then we both realize at the exact same moment that not only is he still holding me, I have my hands wrapped around his neck the way people do in a bridal carry. We disentangle quickly.

"I'm so sorry. I didn't mean—"

"No, you didn't do anything. It's my fault—"

Just when I feel like I'm going to combust from embarrassment, Animabri swoops back down into the pit and lands with a ground-shaking *thud* right in front of us.

But this time, when the giant hornbill shrieks in our faces, Declan and I are ready. Since it's clear the practice sword is useless against an enemy this big, Declan slips a leather bracelet off his wrist and tosses it to me. In midair, it transforms into an akrafena with both a golden blade and hilt. Dwennimmen, the Adinkra symbol of strength, has been carved into the shining metal, and my arm buzzes with the energy when I catch it. Declan pulls out his metro card and instead of a bow like before, this time it transforms into two machetes with furred tassels on the handles. We shift into attack position side by side, opposite Animabri. My brain feels like an engine roaring at full horsepower, all pistons firing on high.

"I go low, you go high?" I call out.

"Sounds like a plan, rookie."

I fought alongside the GCC when we were battling Bullseye and its army of black magic creatures on Back-to-School Night, but fighting with Declan is different. My friends were combat beginners, so I spent every battle half focused on my own opponent, half focused on making sure they didn't die horrifically. But just like me, Declan learned how to hold a sword before he learned how to tie his shoes. Just like me, battle is in his blood. That's why, when we rush forward, our efforts are coordinated in a way that needs no words. He has my back just as much as I have his.

I go for Animabri's legs while Declan goes for the head. The whole time I'm fighting, there is this voice in the back of my head urging me to push harder, move faster, *go, go, go*.

But our feathery friend here didn't get his reputation as one of the most dangerous beasts ever to walk the earth by being easy to take down. He's annoyingly fast, dodging both of our attacks with unusual quickness for a creature his size. Even Pepper, who has left the nest to aid our assault, can't get close enough to damage his weak points with her spork.

"This isn't working!" I yell out, and Declan grunts in response. I look around the enclosure until my eyes land on the tree holding the nest. I sprint over to it while Declan and Pepper have Animabri distracted and begin hacking away at the trunk with my sword. Sweat pours into my eyes, blurring my vision, but I keep sawing and sawing until I hear the sweet, sweet sound of splintering wood.

"FORE!" I scream as the tree begins to fall. At my warning, Declan snatches Pepper from the air and leaps out of the tree's way. Animabri isn't so lucky, and he lets out one last hideous caw as the tree slams down onto him.

Coughing from the cloud of dust that puffed up on impact, I run over to Declan and Pepper. "Everyone okay?"

"Yeah, I'm good," replies Declan, Pepper nodding along. "You think he's . . . dead?"

"He better not be," Pepper moans, "because the Okomfo will have us up to our butts in paperwork if you killed a legendary creature. Wulbari will never let us hear the end of it!"

Legendary creature, huh? Why is it that the Abomofuo think Animabri is valuable when his claim to fame is literally eating people, but obayifo deserve extinction? The hypocrisy burns. Just another way Auntie Effi is right that the Okomfo pick and choose who they consider worth protecting. Besides, if Animabri could speak, I bet he'd have something to say about being kept here against his will. The Slayers could've found a way to communicate with him if they really wanted to. But they didn't.

Luckily for us and our butts—not to mention the newly hatched chicks whose nest is still snug in a branch—Animabri's wings flap wildly from beneath the felled trunk, and he lets out several angry squawks. Phew, okay, he's not dead, but he's definitely not going to be chomping on more kids anytime soon.

Declan extends a hand to me, and I don't even hesitate to grab it. With one leap, he's cleared the edge of the pit and we pull ourselves through the tear in the fence I accidentally created. Once we're on safe ground again, Pepper flits around in a confused blur.

"Right before you guys fell in the cage, I *swear* I sensed a flash of black magic," she says, darting this way and that. Sweat starts dripping down my back. "But it just vanished!"

"Do you think it was an adze? An obayifo?" Declan's hands fly to the hilts of his machetes, and now he's looking around, too. I join them, feeling both terrified and extremely ridiculous pretending to look for a creature I know for a fact isn't here because I'm the true culprit.

"Th-that is so scary! I thought it was weird how the fence just broke like that!" I lie. "Maybe it was a bonsam playing a trick on us?"

We survey the whole perimeter of the cage before Pepper finally accepts that she won't find the source of the black magic. Phew, that was a close one. I need to keep better control over my powers. I doubt Pepper will miss them flaring up a second time tonight.

While the mmoatia angrily mumbles to herself about how the world's playing tricks on her, Declan seems to relax. He turns to me, and says, "You know you're supposed to say *timber*, not *fore*, when you cut down a tree?"

"I'm pretty sure you can say either."

"No, it's definitely— Bia! Hide, quick!"

I lock myself in a restroom near the path and peer through the little slats at the bottom of the door to watch what I assume to be Bia's feet join Declan's. (Yes, I'm lying flat on the floor of a public bathroom. Yes, I'm trying very hard not to think about that.)

"Young Slayer Amankwah," booms the god of the bush, and even through the door I can hear he is *peeved*. "Do you care to explain to me why poor Animabri is trapped beneath a fallen tree, and why there is a young girl currently hiding in the bathroom?"

So much for getting out of the zoo unseen.

"Apologies, Nana Bia. The Okomfo sent me to do a triple protection ward before the gala at the African Art Museum tomorrow. I came here to plant one of the nyame dua but got into a little scuffle with Animabri."

"I can see that. And what of the girl?"

By this point, I'm sweating more than a cactus trapped in a balloon factory. Tricking Declan into letting me join him on patrol was one thing, but lying directly to a god is something even Slayers with decades of experience don't dare do.

"Oh, her," Declan says, and my stomach sinks at being reduced to just some random *her*. His voice takes on a sheepish edge. "Okay, this is really embarrassing, but, um, she's this girl I know from training, and she asked me if I wanted to hang out, and I thought it'd be, you know, cool if I could show her around the city during patrol. . . . She already knows about magic, of course—her parents are in the Abomofuo! And I know it's against the rules, but she's never asked me for something before, so I thought . . . you know."

That is . . . not what I'd expected him to say. Much to my surprise, Bia lets out an amused laugh. "Ah, to be young. Fine, I won't report this incident to your higher-ups, but you and your little girlfriend better not cause any more trouble."

Now I'm sweating and my face is heating up. But instead of making it 100 percent, *no room for misinterpretation, Windex sparkling glass* clear to the god that we are very much NOT dating, Declan just goes, "Of course, and thank you, Nana Bia. We won't. And if I may make one more request, do you happen to know where the best place to plant this nyame dua might be?"

"Try in front of the panda exhibit. If there's any place with extraordinary magical power in a zoo, it's wherever the pandas are. Now, if you'll excuse me, I have a tutara to surgically extract from a VR headset. Don't bother any more of my animals, or our next conversation will not be so pleasant."

Bia's feet start to move away, but then he stops. "And one more thing, Young Slayer Amankwah. The gods see that you have been given a difficult task to fulfill. Never lose sight of what we're fighting for, lest you lose yourself in turn."

"I—I understand, Nana Bia," says Declan, but there's a waver in his voice that makes me doubt that he does. *A difficult task? Is the god referring to the nyame dua plantings?*

I wait until Bia's footsteps have faded before I burst out of the bathroom. I'm not sure what expression I should make after that embarrassing encounter, so I settle for a *ha-ha-ha let's pretend this isn't awkward at all* grin that probably makes me look like a serial killer. "Good job coming up with such a convincing lie on the spot."

Declan blinks. "You think I—?" He shakes his head, then turns on heel and begins stalking up the path to the pandas. "Whatever. Come on, rookie, we've wasted enough time here already."

Whoa, who peed in his jollof rice? We make the trek to the pandas in tense silence. Sure enough, the moment the enclosure comes into view, the nyame dua starts shining brighter than a beacon. I stand back as Declan kneels on the ground, digs a hole, plants the pot in it, and begins covering its roots with soil. Then he pulls out a small bottle of what smells like palm wine, a common drink offered as libations to the gods. He pours it over the mound of soil before he begins to speak.

"Nyame mefrɛ wo; Asaase Yaa mefrɛ wo; Nsaman mefrɛ wo, merefrɛ sɛ merebɛda ase. Yɛda wo ase wɔ ɔdɔ ho. Yɛda woyinaɔ nkwa ho. Yɛda mo ase wɔ asomdwoe ho.

"Osrane, yinarɛn yɛn so saa, obiara a ɔpɛ sɛ ɛyɛ yɛn bɔne no, mompam wɔn!"

Nyame, I call you; Asaase Yaa, I call you; my ancestors, I call you. I am calling to give you thanks. Thank you for love. Thank you for life. Thank you for peace.

To Osrane, the moon, who shines brightly upon us, whoever wishes to cause us harm, drive them out!

Even Declan's Twi is better than mine, the words coming

out strong and confident, without any hint of an American accent. But it's hard to stay jealous as the power of his invocation comes to life. With each word, the golden light coming from the nyame dua grows and grows until it explodes in a pulse of divine wisdom that blankets past us to encompass this whole area. None of the humans in the neighborhood will feel it, but all the animals in the zoo sense the shift in the air and they bleat/whinny/chirp/scream/roar in a frenzy at the sensation of their home becoming imbued with power. The black magic in me shies away from it, sending a dull pain thudding in my skull, but the corner where my own divine wisdom lays dormant seems to stir toward the power, like moving toward like.

Declan and I both watch in wonder as the golden light coalesces into a tree taller even than the one Animabri built his nest on. Within the branches, I see the outline of a figure dancing, her face shining impossibly bright, her arms twisting up, up, up toward the heavens. Osrane, the incarnation of the moon, drawing power from her celestial body. She nods at us, and her smile feels like being bathed in moonlight after an endless cloudy night. Even after she vanishes, the tree remains on this side of the veil, both a promise and a warning to any being of black magic that this place is now under the protection of the gods.

Declan, Pepper, and I look at one another in wonder. We've grown up in the world of Slayers and adze and obayifo, but it's moments like these we realize how much bigger than us it all really is. We're silent for a long moment before Declan stands up, dusting the dirt from his hands and checking his phone.

"All right, one down, two to go. It's only eight, so if we hurry, we can definitely be home by ten."

I shake my head to bring my focus back to the task at hand. That gives me two hours to get the password. The clock is ticking, and there's a nervous feeling in my gut telling me it's not ticking in my favor.

II

How to Go on NOT a Date!

"Though romantic relationships are permitted, a good Slayer should never let one get in the way of the mission at hand."

—From the *Nwoma*

I SPEND THE UNDERTRAIN ride to our next destination mulling over everything that happened at the zoo. All in all, I'd give the whole endeavor a seven out of ten on the grounds that neither of us lost any limbs. But the thing that sticks out the most is the interaction I had with the snake.

In Ghanaian folktales, the line between humans and animals is blurry at best. That's how Anansi can somehow be a regular human, a human with eight arms, a literal spider, a human with eight legs, a creature with a spider body and a human's head, and any other bizarre human/spider combo all at the same time. (I've seen people get into fistfights over which one is Anansi's true form. This is serious business to my people.)

The Abomofuo taught me that every creature hates the obayifo because we cause pain and destruction everywhere we go. But the snake didn't just welcome me—it helped me, claiming we were kin because we both have fangs. I mean, I don't exactly plan on getting all buddy-buddy with every reptile I meet from now on, but that is at least one creature that doesn't hate me for what I am. Maybe, if it can accept me, others can, too.

Maybe even Declan could . . .

"Serwa?" I snap to attention as Declan nods for the door. "We're here."

Here is U Street, and the first thing I notice about this neighborhood is the music. Muffled strains of jazz and other upbeat, bass-heavy sounds pour out of the windows as laughing people dressed in their finest walk up and down the glittering streets. There are more Black people here than I've seen in DC so far—though to be fair, I haven't explored most of the city. The spirits on this side of the veil are livelier, too, gathering where the music is strongest to float amid the joy radiating from this neighborhood.

"They used to call U Street Black Broadway," says Declan, and I can tell from his voice that he enjoys playing tour guide. "Howard University is right up the road, so there's always all sorts of cool events happening here." He points at a brick building with a vertical marquee spelling LINCOLN on one side. "That's the Lincoln Theatre. My dad took me to a really cool all-Black production of *Hamlet* there."

I've never stayed in one place long enough to have a hometown. Just from the way he talks, I can tell how proud Declan is of his. Honestly, the way he loves DC makes me love it a little more, too.

The dua brings us to a statue of four Black men holding guns and dressed in old-timey soldier uniforms. There's a figure in the metal above them with its hands crossed over its chest, almost like it's in prayer or even mourning. "Welcome to the

African American Civil War Memorial," says Declan, and just like in the zoo, I can feel the magical power radiating off this place. "This monument isn't as famous as the Washington or Lincoln ones, but divine wisdom is stronger here than at either of those."

Reading the descriptions of the Black soldiers who fought for their freedom makes me think again about George and Agnes, the enslaved ancestors of Rocky Gorge who used their divine wisdom and black magic, respectively, to protect the town. The descendants of those with magic stolen from Ghana still carry that magic now, though it's taken a different form here in America. They call themselves the Keepers, and both my art teacher, Mr. Riley, and my cousin Roxy belong to the group, though my cousin only found out about it around the same time I learned I'm a vampire. Even though they're descended from an obayifo, neither Roxy nor her mother, my Aunt Latricia, has ever displayed any vampiric tendencies. But just because they didn't inherit the bloodsucking gene doesn't mean others didn't.

I wish I'd stayed in Rocky Gorge long enough to learn more about the Keepers and what happened to all the other American-born descendants of Ghanaian magic.

I wish I'd done a lot of things differently.

But instead of sharing these thoughts out loud, I play lookout while Declan plants the second nyame dua in the grass near the memorial. He recites the same incantation as before, except he switches out *Osrane* for *Owia*—the sun—in the last line. This time, I'm ready for the wave of divine wisdom that pulses out from the pot, and I'm able to keep my discomfort to a minimum even though my black magic struggles under the assault. The second tree blooms just as brightly as the first, and this time the figure is a man with a halo of golden rays blooming out from around his head like a crown. Owia winks at us before disappearing in a snap of sunlight. Declan turns to me with a grin, the golden shine of the sacred tree dancing off his dark skin, but all I feel is dread.

Now there's only one nyame dua left to plant before Declan and I go our separate ways for the night, and I still don't have the password to the secret exhibit.

Okay, now seems like a good time to start panicking.

"What's that face for?" Declan asks when he returns to my side.

"That just felt so . . . easy." I wrinkle my nose. "Where was the flesh-eating hornbill? The meddling gods?"

"Not everything has to be a battle, rookie."

"In my experience, a mission isn't fully complete unless half a dozen things go wrong and at least one supernatural being threatens me with bodily harm."

Declan laughs at that, and my mouth pulls into the cheesiest grin. The laugh makes him sound like any other kid our age and almost makes me forget my sworn vendetta against him. "You gotta tell me about one of those missions sometime," he says.

My smile vanishes. "Sometime" is never going to come, because there's no way Declan will ever trust me again when he learns I helped the obayifo steal the Midnight Drum. This is just like what happened with the GCC all over again. I don't know how to stop myself from getting close to people I'm destined to leave.

"Right . . . some other time."

Declan frowns. "You okay?"

"Oh no, I'm fine. I just—" A rumbling growl from my stomach cuts me off.

Declan checks the time on his phone. "We're running ahead

of schedule now. If you're hungry, I know a place not far from here that you're going to love."

"**BUT WHAT *IS* MUMBO** sauce?" I press, eyeing the reddish-brown cup of sauce Declan triumphantly plunked down on the table.

Across from me in the red leather booth we're sharing, he lets out a scoff. "Mumbo sauce defies explanation. Mumbo sauce sneers at your desire for easy categorization. Mumbo sauce is love. Mumbo sauce is life. Mumbo sauce is the nectar of the gods."

"Amazing. I don't think I've ever heard anybody use that many words to not answer a question before."

"Be as skeptical as you wish, O ye of so little faith, but one bite and you will be converted just like the rest of us."

Declan slides the basket of chili cheese fries and the slightly ominous container of mumbo sauce my way. Around us, back on the human side of the veil, Ben's Chili Bowl roars with life, filled to the brim with all manner of DCers and tourists trying to get their late-night grub on at the iconic restaurant. Upon discovering that I had never even heard of Washington DC's (supposedly) World Famous, Completely Life-Changing Mumbo Sauce (his words), Declan Amankwah has now made it his life's mission to turn me into a fan.

Admittedly, the fries do smell amazing. But I can't tell him that he could put filet mignon and lobster in front of me and it wouldn't quiet my stomach rumbles because the only thing my body will accept right now is blood. I make a big show of grabbing a fry, dipping it in the sauce, and slowly raising it to my mouth while Declan quite literally holds his breath in anticipation. (Pepper is hiding in his backpack—and playing Candy Crush on his tablet, from the sounds of it—but she was just as adamant about the marvels of mumbo sauce as her partner.)

I take a bite and . . . "Oh my gods."

"Right? What did I tell you?"

I inhale my portion of the food while Declan launches into a spiel about the history of Ben's Chili Bowl and how there are lots of knockoffs but nothing will ever beat the real deal. He wasn't lying—these fries are to *die* for. But even half a basket of fries and an entire maple Oreo milkshake later, my stomach isn't any fuller than when I started eating. Auntie Effi wasn't exaggerating—human food tastes just as good as it always has, but it's like after I swallow, it all goes into a black hole, while the blood craving roars on.

Despite the tremors still panging my stomach, I grin at the boy across from me. "I can't believe I'm saying this—and you'd better get this on video because I'm never admitting it ever again—but . . . you were right. That was amazing."

Declan's smile is brighter than the fluorescent lights overhead. "See, was that so hard?"

Somehow even the teasing in his voice doesn't bother me like it did just a few hours ago. I give an exaggerated sigh. "Actually, it was excruciatingly painful. Getting all my teeth pulled at once would've hurt less."

Declan rolls his eyes, and then we're both laughing. In that moment I forget that he's a Slayer and I'm an obayifo. Right now, he's just a boy, and I'm just a girl, and we're laughing so hard there are tears in my eyes.

But then my stomach rumbles again, and this time, my fangs push up against my gums in time with the tremors. I swallow thickly, taking quick breaths in and out until the canines recede. I can't keep losing focus of my main objective here. I don't *deserve* to act like this is just another hangout because Declan isn't just another kid.

Declan is the enemy. I need to treat him like one, even when we're having fun.

"So, hey, about the gala, do you have to do any more prep after all the nyame dua are planted?" I ask with genuine curiosity.

Declan shakes his head. "No, everything's done. And I'm so glad, too. The Okomfo don't have me scheduled for any other missions for weeks after this one, so once the gala's over, I can leave for my trip in peace. My mom and I are going down to Harper's Ferry so I can try whitewater kayaking for the first time."

And once the Abomofuo are gone from the museum, the Midnight Drum will be, too. Once again, I get the sensation of a clock tick-tick-ticking just out of my view, and each second feels heavier than the last.

Before I can ask another question, Declan's phone begins to vibrate. The word *Mom* flashes across the screen, and if Declan was excited before, he's practically beaming now. "Hey, Ma, what's up?" he answers in an excited rush. "No, you didn't wake me up. I'm just finishing some stuff for the night . . . Yeah . . . Y-yeah . . . Okay . . ."

Then comes an awkward, tense silence from his end punctuated with a whole bunch of "uh-huh" and "no, it's cool, really." The conversation lasts two, maybe three, minutes tops, but once it's done, Declan slams his phone onto the table so hard that I flinch. A few of the servers give us the evil eye reserved for kids who cause a ruckus in an adult establishment.

"Everything okay?" I ask tentatively.

Declan let's out a sound that can't decide if it's a laugh or a scream. "Everything's fine! Never better! That was just my mom telling me that, *apparently,* my stepsister's recital got pushed up to this Friday because her piano teacher is leaving town for a wedding next week or whatever, so she's sooooooo sorry but needs to reschedule our kayaking trip *for the fourth freaking time*!"

Declan runs his hands through his hair, muttering something too low for me to hear. I know that expression on his face because I've worn it all too often these past few weeks. It's the face of someone who's doing everything they can to not show how much they're hurting.

My friend Eunju also had issues with her parents. I learned from comforting her that most of the time, people don't want a solution to their problem as much as they want someone who'll sit there with them and let them know they're not weak for being upset.

"I'm sorry. That really sucks," I say softly.

Declan takes an angry swig of his Coke. "Why are you apologizing when she didn't? After all, it's not like the river's going anywhere, but a fourth-grade recital is 'a onceinalifetime event' and 'really important' to my sister," he spits out darkly.

The black magic in me spikes, keenly aware of Declan's growing distress. If I were an adze, this would be the perfect moment to climb inside his head. People are most vulnerable to possession when they're emotionally compromised, and right now, Declan looks two seconds away from breaking down. He puts his head in his arms on the table, taking deep, ragged breaths. Something tells me that the source of his anger is far deeper than just kayaking.

I rack my head to remember what I know about Declan's family situation. His parents were never married, but now that

I think about it, they hadn't even sat together during his official Slayer induction ceremony. I guess I've always been so busy being envious of his life that I never really stopped to wonder what it was like.

"You know, a couple weeks ago, I found out my parents lied to me about something really big. Something about my mom's childhood and the truth of why our family left Ghana." A voice in my head screams at me to shut up before I give everything away, but I can't stop the words from pouring out. "I know it's not the same as what you're going through, like, at all, but I get how it feels to be just so . . . so . . . angry with your parents and then feel bad you feel angry because you know they love you and you know they mean well, but the anger just won't go away."

Declan doesn't move and oh gods, I'm completely messing this up, aren't I? "S-so, um, I won't say I get it, but . . . you shouldn't be upset about being upset."

Seconds pass. I'm pretty sure the universe is reconsidering letting me speak to anyone about anything ever again when Declan lifts his head and fixes me with that same look from the soccer field, the mystery piecing-together one that makes me feel cut open and raw.

"Has anyone ever told you you'd make a good therapist?"

I give him a small smile. "I get an email from Dr. Phil at least once a week begging me to intern for him."

That gets a weak laugh from him, which is a far cry from our previous hysterics but way better than nothing. He rubs at his face, and when he sits up again, he's more like the Declan I've been hanging out with all night. "All right, I'm ready to go whenever you are. Let's get this last tree planted so we can all finally go home."

By the time we leave the restaurant, the temperature

has dropped considerably. We're reaching that part of the year where fall has kicked summer to the curb for good, and winter is peeking its head around the corner with small reminders of what true cold really feels like. Declan rubs his hands together and blows on them. "Okay, I think the metro is down this stree—"

"Declan, I'm sensing black magic again" comes Pepper's muffled voice from inside his backpack. "Let me out!"

I stop in my tracks, a deer caught in headlights. Did my black magic slip out? But I didn't even do anything! My head's spinning with ways out of this mess—lie; deflect; run screaming down the street like my hair's on fire—as we duck into the shadowed stoop of a hookah store so Declan can discreetly pull his mmoatia from his bag. Pepper vibrates harder than a washing machine stuck on high.

"Which direction is it coming from?" asks Declan.

My heart thuds somewhere around my shoes. The mmoatia's wings flutter and her face scrunches up tight in concentration.

Then she lifts a tiny brown finger and points it . . .

Directly at me.

12

How to Appreciate the Performing Arts

*"There is no shame in retreat when all other options
have failed."*

—From the *Nwoma*

YOU KNOW THAT MOMENT when you're at the
very top of a roller coaster and you can see absolutely
everything for dozens of miles around? And then a split
second later you're falling faster than you knew it was
possible to fall, and you can't do anything but upchuck
all over yourself and the screaming family in the row
behind you?

Imagine that feeling multiplied by a hundred. That's
how far my heart drops when Pepper points at me.

"I d-don't—" I begin sputtering, but it turns out I
don't have to say anything at all, because Declan follows
Pepper's finger from me to the Lincoln Theatre across
the street, visible directly over my shoulder. Now that
my focus is turned that way, I can feel an undeniable
undercurrent of black magic pulsing from the building.
Yeah, that definitely wasn't there when we first got to
U Street.

"You're sure it's coming from there?" he asks, and
Pepper nods. The dizziness of my relief is almost as

disorienting as the sudden panic was. They're not onto me. My secret is still safe . . . for now.

But another problem has reared its ugly head, and that is whatever black magic shenanigans are going on inside that theater. Could it be my aunt or something related to her? No way. She would've told me if they had something going on at U Street . . . right? If that *is* Auntie Effi in there, how am I possibly going to get out of fighting her without making Declan suspicious?

"Maybe we should come back during the day," I suggest. "Creatures of black magic tend to be stronger at night."

Declan shakes his head. "What's the very first rule in the *Nwoma*?" he asks me.

"Nkwa nti, bere nyinaa." *For life, always.* That phrase is more than just some dusty words in an ancient book that kind of smells like an old lady's couch—they're the Abomofuo's oath to the world that everything we do, everything we are, is always centered on protecting those who cannot protect themselves.

If there are any adze in the theater and they have taken any victims, we are duty bound to do everything in our power to help them. I can feel Declan's disappointment that I'd even suggest going back on that sacred promise. I'm disappointed in myself, too. The old me would've run into that theater sword swinging, no matter how many vampires might have been inside. Is the new me someone who's willing to let innocent people suffer if it means saving my own skin?

My fingers find the familiar edges of my Grandma Awurama's pendant. I know what she'd do if she were here.

"All right," I say, even though a voice that sounds suspiciously like my aunt's is whispering in my mind that this is a horrible idea. "Let's check it out."

AFTER A QUICK SURVEY of the building, we find an unmarked side entrance where no one can see us breaking like at least six different trespassing laws. A few Adinkra later, Declan and I are inside what seems to be a costume closet. The black magic is stronger inside the building, and my own is pulsing in time with it. I grit my teeth, tongue frantically running over my gums to make sure my fangs stay in. I'm not sure what'd be worse: if I recognize whoever we're about to find in here . . . or if I don't.

"What're the odds that the source of the black magic is just a bunch of mostly harmless bonsam who've suddenly developed an interest in the performing arts?" I say to cut the tension.

In front of me, Declan steps around a box labeled MRS. POTTS COSTUME (BATB 2016)—REMEMBER TO FUMIGATE!!! "Somewhere between no way and never happening."

I'd hoped my joke might lighten his mood, but there's a hard edge to his voice. That's the sound of a Slayer slipping into battle mode. Once a Slayer sets their sights on a goal, gods help anyone who tries to get in their way. "I know you didn't want to use any magic tonight, but if things get ugly, I'm going to need you to provide backup."

"I've got you," I lie. The last thing I need is for Declan to see my nose gush blood all over a beloved DC landmark when I try and fail to use divine wisdom.

Our footsteps echo as Pepper leads us out of the costume closet into the theater's interior passageways, the ones that go behind backstage. Her wings cast an eerie green glow on the stark concrete walls.

"How close are we to the source?" Declan asks the mmoatia, his metro card clasped so tightly in his hand it's a wonder his palm doesn't split open.

"Close. Just up ahead."

Voices echo through the walls, followed by pounding . . . music? It's hard to hear exactly, but there are definitely multiple people on the stage. Slinking quieter than cougars, Declan and I follow Pepper up a rickety metal staircase that takes us to the catwalk above the stage.

And it's only once we're up there that we understand what a monumentally *open the door on an airplane* level of stupid coming in here was.

"Okay, everybody, once more from the top!" A man sitting in one of those stereotypical director chairs is yelling into a megaphone. He's got on a bright red beret, a matching scarf, and a beard that is doing its absolute best to be a full goatee and failing spectacularly. On the stage across from him, over a dozen figures shift into position, and music blares from the speakers as the troupe launches into a (poorly) choreographed number. I take in the gaudy paper flowers, monstrous amounts of tulle on the costumes, and the backdrop showing a giant bubble next to some hastily painted corn. The troupe starts singing about how they're going to have the best time in a magic city, and oh my gods is this . . . ?

"*The Wizard of Oz?!*" Declan and I whisper-hiss in disbelief at the same time.

He cracks his first smile since his mom's phone call. "Jinx."

I'm glad he's feeling better, but this is no time to be laughing even if his laugh does make me want to do a happy cartwheel. Because the worst part isn't the fact that the costumes looked like they came straight from Party City or that these people are butchering an internationally beloved children's classic.

No, the worst thing about this situation is that every single person below us, from the director with his ugly beard to the actors prancing about onstage to the frazzled techies wrestling with extension cords in the back, has glowing golden eyes, marking them as people possessed by an adze.

Meaning our stupid butts just willingly walked into a building swarming with vampires.

"Declan, there's too many," I whisper. "We've got to retreat." I can't recognize anyone from this high up. I don't think I've seen any of these adze before, and that means I can't count on their loyalty to my aunt to protect me from them.

"And leave their hosts in danger?" says Declan. "No way."

"But we're outnumbered!"

"We were outnumbered at the zoo, and we got out of that okay! What makes you so sure I can't handle myself? Might I remind you which one of us has actually passed the Initiation Test?"

I've never wanted to hit someone with my shoe more than I do at this moment. I should leave Declan to the flying monkeys, but instead I say, "Yes, you. I heard you the first hundred times! But need I remind you that when the Nwoma says 'For life, always' that includes our own lives, too? If you get yourself killed trying to save others, all you've done is cause a different tragedy!"

Declan and I stare each other down, equally intense stubbornness in our eyes.

"A good warrior never backs down from a challenge," he spits.

"And a better one knows the difference between a challenge and a suicide mission," I shoot back. Wow, I can't believe I, Serwa "Stab First, Questions Later" Boateng, am the one arguing *against* going into battle. I must've spent too much time with Mateo, and now I'm going soft. "I get that you're upset, but throwing yourself into danger when you don't have to isn't the way to deal with it."

The last part gets to Declan. He breaks the stare by turning his head away. "Fine. We'll retreat, and Pepper will report this to the Okomfo when we get outside."

A whole bunch of Slayers converging on this location wouldn't be the greatest development for me, but I'll burn that bridge when I get to it or however that saying goes. Below us, the director yells "Cut!" and announces that they're taking a quick break. One of the techies runs onstage and starts handing the actors bags of chips and little drink boxes that my heightened senses immediately scent as blood. Ugh, that is equal parts genius and disgusting.

I start tiptoeing down the catwalk back toward the exit, and Declan moves to follow. And now I'm convinced that some god or creature or *something* out there has cursed me—probably Amokye, the guardian of Asamando. She *really* doesn't like me—because Declan's backpack catches on a hook on his way out. There's a ripping sound, and then we're both staring in sitcom-like horror as half the contents of his bag, including the last nyame dua, tumbles through the air.

Right onto the stage full of vampires.

13

How to Negotiate with the Wizard of Oz

"Leave no Slayer behind."

—From the *Nwoma*

THE NYAME DUA DROPS directly onto the head of the actor playing Glinda the Good Witch, knocking her tiara askew.

"Ow! Hayley, did you forget to secure the lights again?!" she shrieks. She reaches to grab the pot, then recoils as the protective magic in it burns her fingers. "What the—this is divine wisdom!"

The adze's unnaturally gold eyes rove the ceiling until they land on me and Declan clinging to the catwalk for dear life. "Intruders! Slayers in the rafters!"

Dozens of golden eyes turn our way. With a screech, Glinda launches herself into the air as she shifts into her true form. Compound bug eyes rip through her face, and a shiny hardened shell wraps around her skin as her fingers thin and lengthen into talons and she shoots up to eight feet. Miraculously, her giant pink dress somehow stays on even as a large pair of iridescent wings burst from her back. These send the firefly monster zooming toward Declan and me.

I scramble backward, but I can only move so far without falling off the catwalk. Declan's shoes still have the antigravity Adinkra drawn on them, which is why he's able to leap straight from the bridge and meet Glinda in midair. He wraps his arms around her neck as she zips around the air in a howling rage.

I finally make it to the stairs, where I find two more adze—one dressed as the Tin Man, the other behind him a munchkin—climbing up. The Tin Man's silver-painted nostrils flare wide when he sees me.

"Hang on . . . that scent," he says. "You're a—"

My foot collides with the Tin Man's face before he can finish that sentence, and he tumbles down the stairs. The adze might outnumber me, but I have the high ground (I've always wanted to say that!), and I'm not giving it up without a fight. I draw the akrafena Declan lent me and swing for the munchkin, who ducks beneath it.

"Why are you attacking us?" he cries, genuine hurt in his voice. "Aren't you on our side?"

"I don't side with people who can't even sing on beat!" I yell back.

The munchkin's hurt turns to indignation. "You insolent little— We've been practicing that number for weeks!"

"You've been sucking at that number for weeks, more like!"

The munchkin lets out a yell and barrels toward me, trying to pin me against a railing. But I jump up and use his head as a springboard to launch past him for the bottom of the stairs. There the Tin Man is back on his feet and definitely not happy about the faceful of foot he just tasted. His human mask slips in his anger, and rows upon rows of needlelike fangs glint in his mouth as he snarls my way.

"I'm going to enjoy taking a bite out of you, little brat!" he howls.

These two are scary, even with piles of stage makeup on, but I can tell from the way they move that they weren't trained for battle.

Unfortunately for them, I was.

I turn the small space into an advantage, moving not to get out of their attack range but to weave them into each other's. And sure enough, at one point the Tin Man's flying fist smacks the munchkin straight in the gut. The little guy yowls and retaliates with a very painful-looking kick right between the Tin Man's legs. Several blows later, they've both knocked each other out, and I'm leaping over their unconscious bodies on my way to find Declan so we can get the heck out of here.

Luckily for me, the lobby is completely deserted. All the vampires must still be onstage. At the main doors to the auditorium, where the audience normally enters, I slow. Even with the adrenaline pumping through my veins, all my training tells me that running in there would be a horrible idea. But Declan is still inside.

I can't leave him. Not after everything we've been through.

Now would be a great time for a silence spell to muffle my steps. But since I can't draw one of those, I nudge open the auditorium doors as quietly as I can and slip inside.

Judging from the unconscious munchkins, downed flying monkeys, and assorted Oz-related extras lying in dazed heaps around the room, Declan put up a good fight. But there were simply too many opponents for even a Slayer as good as him to defeat, and he's now on the stage wrapped up in a length of extension cord, Pepper unconscious beside him. The remaining adze—all six of them—are so focused on Declan that no one notices me creep to the stage inch by careful, silent inch to crouch beside the cart that still has a few chip bags and blood boxes on it.

"Let me take a bite out of him, boss. Just a quick nibble. I haven't eaten in days!" exclaims Glinda. She's switched back to human mode but doesn't bother to hide the slobber dripping from her fangs onto her poofy dress at the thought of sucking Declan's blood.

"Hey, if anyone feeds off him, it should be me!" the Cowardly Lion protests. "I'm the one who tied him up!"

"Only after I subdued him!" yells the Wicked Witch of the West. "I carried this whole fight, the same way I've been carrying the act-one finale!"

To his credit, Declan doesn't even flinch as the insect monsters discuss feasting on him like he's a freezer pop. I scan the area, but I can't see anything I can use to save him, not without divine wisdom at my disposal. There are too many adze left for me to engage in direct combat, and if I use my black magic, Declan will know what I truly am.

If I can't fight them off, and it's too risky to try distracting them and untying Declan by myself, then . . . then . . . then the best thing I can do is run and get help.

Even if that means leaving Declan all alone.

Shouts of protest go up among the troupe about who is the best fighter/spatial actor/vocalist, but the director silences them all with wave of his hand.

"No one is feasting off the boy." He levels a predatory look at Declan. "Not when he'd be so much more useful to us as a comrade than a meal."

At that, Declan stirs in his bindings. "I will never work with you," he spits weakly. Every word seems to cause him great pain.

The director laughs. "Let's see how long you think like that, Slayer."

He snaps his fingers, and a glowing pinprick of light floats out from backstage to hover above the director's cupped palms. A firefly. "You've been without a host for so long, old friend, but don't worry," he says to the bug. "Soon you'll be able to talk and run and laugh as freely as the rest of us."

Now Declan's mask of calm cracks; pure terror takes its place. These adze don't want to eat him—they want to turn him into one of their kind. Their host-less friend will enter his head, and when it does, Declan's mind and body will fall under the vampire's control. And he'll be conscious yet powerless the entire time.

As a child, I asked my parents hundreds of questions about how to prepare for any scenario a Slayer might encounter. How do you stay warm if you're tracking an adze across the tundra and it's dozens of degrees below zero? What's the best way to stop blood flow if you're injured mid-battle and your mmoatia isn't close enough to help? They answered all my questions no matter how absurd or macabre, and I loved them for never sugarcoating the harsh realities of our line of work.

The only time they ever hesitated was when I asked what I should do if I was ever possessed by an adze.

"That'll never happen," Dad promised.

"All the mental training and protective wards Slayers have make it very difficult for an adze to get in our heads," Mom added.

"But difficult isn't the same as impossible," I'd pressed. Even back then, when most kids were worrying about losing their baby teeth and learning to tie their shoes, I'd been laser-focused on my own survival. "What if the mental training and the wards all fail? What then?"

My parents both grew silent, and the implication of their non-answer was the first moment I truly understood that a Slayer's duty is to the death.

When an adze accesses its host's mind, the vampire sees every thought and memory, every feeling and emotion, that person has ever had. If an adze possessed a Slayer, they'd gain full knowledge of the Abomofuo's inner workings, exposing the thousands of people in our network and putting the millions of people we protect in danger. Passing the Initiation Test and getting your abode santann tattoo is a silent promise to die before ever letting yourself become the monster you fought against.

My hesitation vanishes as one crystal-clear thought burns in my mind:

If these vampires want Declan, they're going to have to get through me first.

Before I can think myself out of it, I snag one of the blood boxes from the cart and slip it into my jacket pocket. Then I run toward the stage, sword outstretched, and yell at the top of my lungs, "HEY, BUG BRAINS!"

"What are you doing? Get out of here!" screams Declan, but I ignore him as I take a running leap onto the stage. The adze shift into attack poses, fangs bared and golden eyes burning, but I slip past them to barrel into Declan. We go down in a huff, and before he can yell again, I jab my index finger into the pressure point on his neck to knock him out. The second I'm sure he's not getting up for a while, I crouch protectively in front of his and Pepper's slumped bodies.

The director's eyes fly from Declan to me, confusion

furrowing his brow. "I've never seen a rescue operation start with someone knocking the hostage unconscious."

"Let us leave now, or things are going to get ugly," I warn, channeling all my fear and adrenaline into sounding like something more than a terrified twelve-year-old.

The vampires just laugh as they circle the three of us. "Ugly how, little girl? Maybe they don't teach you kids how to count on *Sesame Street* anymore, but look around. You're outnumbered!"

"I can't remember the last time we got two new hosts at once," the Scarecrow chimes in with cackling glee.

The director's eyes narrow as he surveys me. "Something is off about you. Is that black magic I sense?"

Looks like the cat is out of the bag. Instead of replying, I let my human mask slip for the first time since I left the hotel so many hours ago. My fangs elongate and my eyes go crimson red, leading to several shocked gasps from the adze.

This is why I had to knock out Declan; this is the truth I couldn't let him see. Because while I'm sure these adze won't negotiate with a Slayer, they just might listen to an obayifo.

The director lets out a delighted cry at my transformation. "I knew I smelled something different about you! Welcome to our show, little sister!"

My fingers tighten around the blood box, but I don't pull it out. I . . . I can't. I swore I'd never drink blood, no matter how weak I got surviving on only human food.

But what matters more: my promise to myself, or saving Declan's life?

"I'm not your sister," I snap. "What are you even doing here?"

"You know our kind thrives in environments of immense

distress, and what place engenders more misery and woe than the community theater?" asks the director. "The high emotions, the backstabbing, the ever-shifting alliances—and that's only the props department! This place is a black magic paradise. The inherent turmoil in the performing arts make actors amazing hosts for us adze."

"A solid sixty-seven percent of Hollywood are actually vampires," chimes in a munchkin, and all the adze nod in agreement.

The director's golden eyes slide from me to Declan and back again. "I didn't realize you had claimed the Slayer for yourself. How about a deal? We'll let you feed off him as long as you let our friend have his mind afterward."

I'm literally shaking with rage at this point. I make a silent promise to myself right then that even if I am an obayifo, I will never be someone who discards another person's life so easily. My knuckles tighten around the blood box as the vampires inch closer.

Do it, Serwa. Stop keeping yourself from all that you can be.

"Or, counter-deal," I say, wincing as the voice clamors inside me. "You let us both go, no one gets bitten, and no one gets possessed."

The director's friendly smirk turns condescending. "Be careful how you talk to your elders, girl. I offered you a bite of the boy out of politeness, but we will force our way past you if we must."

They're less than a foot away now. Six against one.

I can't win this fight. Not the normal way.

I take a deep breath and one last look at Declan to make sure he's still unconscious. "I'd love to see you try, you wannabe Sondheim."

Oh, that insult does it. With a growl, the director lunges toward me.

Now, Serwa!

Just before the man's fingers wrap around my throat, I pull out the blood box and bite into it like it's an apple. This is where having fangs comes in handy, because the waxed cardboard punctures easily. I force back every hint of my humanity and give in to my most primal urges as I drink another person's blood for the very first time. Beneath my nausea, my adrenaline, my fear, there is nothing but hunger. And right now, the blood . . .

It tastes . . . it tastes . . . *good*. Almost like fruit juice. And the effect is immediate. The thick pounding that's been muffling my head for weeks clears, and the world becomes sharper, more focused as the theater swims into perfect clarity around me. When the box is completely empty, I toss it to the side, wiping the blood from my chin.

And then I let my black magic free.

Just like the day of the blackout, my obayifo power explodes outward in a wall strong enough that the adze stumble back, though they recover quickly.

"Ha, you call that black magic?" the director taunts.

Auntie Effi's voice rings in my ears. *Black magic is a moving current, not a stagnant pool.*

And maybe it's the blood I ingested, or the fact that it's more than just my life on the line right now, but her words hit a target they missed back at the hotel. The power is a current, but I am a rock against the surf. It can push all it wants, but I will not break. My magic bites at me, but I bite back, redirecting it farther and farther outward until a purple haze engulfs first the stage, then the entire building. It seeps into every inch of the

Lincoln Theatre until I can sense each nail, board, and screw of the structure as easily as I can feel my own breath.

"No. I call *this* black magic."

The adze yell in alarm as the ground pitches and rolls beneath our feet. Chunks of plaster fall from the ceiling. "Let me and my friends go *now*, or I'll bring this building down on all our heads," I warn.

"You wouldn't dare!" screams the director.

An ear-splitting crack fills the air as a fissure opens in the stage between us to prove that, yes, I actually *do* dare.

Because I'm angry.

And I'm scared.

And I'm tired.

And, most of all, I am *done* with other people telling me what I am and am not capable of. My black magic is ecstatic at being let free again, and it whispers to me that this building is nothing more than a collection of cracks waiting for just the right push. I could be that push; I could bring every board to its breaking point, just like I've been brought to my own breaking point time after time.

After all, adze might be impervious to a direct black magic attack, but no creature alive is impervious to a cave-in.

My braids whip around my face as the building sags, emitting a sound like a great beast's dying wail. Wires pop from the ceiling, and someone lets out a scream as a spotlight crashes to the stage, the lens shattering into a million pieces around us. I can feel the adze's own black magic scrambling to take control, but their power is nothing against mine. They can't stop me from pushing, pushing, *pushing*—

"Okay! You win!" screams the director as the ground pitches beneath our feet again. "Please, just go!"

I point to the fallen nyame dua, lying half-forgotten near Dorothy's basket. "Give me my pot."

The director fetches it for me, whimpering as the divine wisdom burns his hands. It burns mine, too, but I shove the nyame dua into Declan's backpack without letting my discomfort show. Just as quickly as I let my magic out, I pull it all back in.

Now, beneath the wave of pure, destructive power, I sense an undercurrent inside me that feels like wind and starlight and endless open sky. Something born of the place where my divine wisdom and my black magic meet. It's the same magic that answered my desperate call during the blackout in Rocky Gorge and spirited me deep into the forest when I needed to get away.

I wrap my hands around Declan and Pepper, then intentionally push into that undefinable magic for the very first time.

And just like that, we're gone.

14

How to Learn from Your Elders

"Never forget that it is because they who came before us did what they did that we now can do what we do."

—From the *Nwoma*

DON'T BELIEVE WHAT YOU see in the movies: Teleportation stinks. To be fair, this is only the second time I've actually done it, but that doesn't make it any less disorienting when Declan, Pepper, and I slam down onto the concrete near the African American Civil War Memorial several blocks away from the Lincoln Theatre. And not a second too soon, because Pepper starts to come to just then.

"Serwa? How are we back at the memorial? What happened?!" she demands.

"You and Declan were surrounded by the adze, and I ran to help you, but I misjudged my attack and accidentally knocked him unconscious." I babble while out of breath, because you try teleporting two people and a mmoatia across a neighborhood without passing out. All my atoms feel like they've been pulled apart and rearranged in the wrong order. At least my wheezing helps sell the lie. "I was able to distract them long enough to drag you both here, but they might follow soon."

Pepper narrows her tiny eyes at me, and honestly, I don't blame her. Me dragging someone Declan's size several city blocks without getting caught is pretty hard to believe. It's taking all my self-control to keep my human mask in place again after letting my obayifo side out so completely. But before she can poke all the holes in my story, Declan lets out a moan.

"S-Serwa?"

"Deckie-poo!" Pepper squeals (even though he technically called out for me, not that it matters or anything). I help him sit up against the memorial as Pepper begins healing the bruises on his face and the cuts on his arms. There's nothing life-threatening that I can see, but he's in no shape to be going anywhere for the rest of the night.

"Declan, where do you live?" I ask. "We've got to get somewhere safe where the adze can't reach us." I'd bet all my good crossbows we only have a few minutes max before the vampires come looking for us, and I don't think I'll be able to scare them off with only a threat again. And there's no way I can do any more teleportation now that Declan and Pepper are awake.

Declan mumbles something, but he's too out of it to be intelligible. I whirl on Pepper. "We need to get him home! Can you unlock his phone and call an Uber?"

"Why can't you call one?"

"I don't have a phone!"

The mmoatia scoffs at the idea of a kid in the twenty-first century without access to the internet at all hours of the day, but then Declan lets out another groan. Pepper's lip quivers, and I can practically see her mentally calculating the risk of letting me into their family home versus leaving her Slayer partner exposed out here. "He uses Face ID," she finally admits.

After some Face ID shenanigans and the world's most

awkward Uber ride (the driver takes one look at us and decides he actually doesn't want to know why two kids covered in plaster and bruises are hightailing it out of U Street in the middle of the night with a wriggling backpack), we reach Georgetown and pull up to one of the nicest homes I've ever seen. I've only ever interacted with the Amankwahs at Slayer events, never at their house. I knew they were loaded, but not like *this*.

Pepper punches in the code to the three-car garage and directs me where to half walk, half drag Declan to his bedroom. Once there, I dump him on the bed, clothes and all, with a silent apology to whoever has to do his laundry when this is all over. (Believe me, adze gunk is, like, impossible to get out of your clothes.)

"I'll take it from here," says Pepper. "Wait downstairs—there are snacks in the pantry and juice in the fridge if you're hungry." As annoying as her whole cutesy Tinker Bell act might be, I have to respect the fact that she's a supernatural being with more healing experience than I've got. I just nod, and I'm backing out of the room when the mmoatia adds, "And, Serwa . . . thank you. For saving my boy."

My eyes go blurry as I nod again. I make it all the way to the foyer before my legs give out, and I slide to the floor with my back against a wall. I curl up knees to my chest and head on my arms as the full weight of what I just did crashes over me.

Because, yes, I might've saved our lives, but I had to drink blood to do it. And honestly?

The full, ugly, horrifying truth?

It felt *good*. Using my black magic to save Declan felt right in a way nothing else has in a long time.

You did nothing wrong.

But I broke my promise to myself. I swore that even though

I was helping my aunt to free Nana Bekoe, I wouldn't hurt anyone to do it. Then again, I wasn't the one who harvested the blood for the boxes, so it's not like I hunted someone down to drink their blood. And if I hadn't done anything, there's no way Declan and I could've gotten out of the theater. What's worse, doing a bad thing for a good reason or doing a good thing for a bad one?

The familiar brain fog I get when my thoughts get too complicated returns. There's a tugging in my stomach, pulling me down toward . . . something. All right, Serwa. Stop focusing on what you don't know and start focusing on what you do. What I know right now is that based on the severity of his injuries, Declan's going to be out of commission for at least the next hour. And with Pepper fussing over him until he's back on his feet, that gives me plenty of time to search the house for any clues about the password to the secret exhibit in the museum.

I start in a wide, oak-paneled room on the ground floor that I assume is Dr. Amankwah's study. A giant CEO-type mahogany desk takes up most of the room, and tall bookcases line the walls. A quick scan reveals mostly medical and financial books, absolutely nothing useful for, I don't know, an extremely grouchy girl trying to sniff out the confidential dealings of a top-secret international monster-hunting organization. How rude. I wrap my hand in my sleeve before touching anything, taking care not to leave any fingerprints or anything out of place.

The last bookcase—the biggest one—is dedicated entirely to Declan. There are pictures of him ranging in age from a plump-cheeked baby in an Adinkra cloth onesie at his outdooring, the traditional Ghanaian ceremony to welcome children to the community, to a lanky kid posing with Dr. Amankwah in matching aloha shirts in front of Cinderella Castle at Disney World. A pang hits my chest at seeing these pieces of Declan's childhood so painstakingly preserved. Unlike my parents, who bopped from town to town hunting vampires as the Okomfo directed, Dr. Amankwah was stationed to watch over only DC, which means Declan has grown up in the same place his whole life. I used to think I preferred my family's way of life, but now, the thought of putting down roots in one place sounds . . . nice.

The second shelf is all trophies. Little League MVP, First Place in the Science Fair, Most Decorated Spelling Bee Champion in Sandy Elementary History . . . I roll my eyes at the last one. Of *course* Declan Amankwah would win an award for getting the most awards. I bet if there were an award for Most Likely to Be Crushed by a Falling Shelf Full of Their Own Awards, he'd find a way to win that one, too.

This room is a cute time capsule, but there's nothing that points to the secret exhibit. I could try breaking into his computer like I did the one at Rocky Gorge Middle School on Back-to-School Night, but he probably has wards on it to protect from magic interference like all Slayers are taught to do to their devices. All right, on to the kitchen. This room is way more chaotic than the study, with an open box of Cheerios, an over-turned glass, and a pill counter on the table. A wall calendar is stuck on the top half of the fridge, and the dates are filled with neat, color-coded writing.

SUNDAY: DAA PHYSICAL THERAPY 10:00 (ELKWOOD FACILITY)

MONDAY: DAD MEETING W/ GCPS BOARD (DON'T FORGET TO BRING SB REPORT!)

THURSDAY: BULK RECYCLING PICKUP @ 9:00

Declan must have annotated this calendar since I highly doubt Dr. Amankwah calls himself Dad. The schedule is packed, and it doesn't even have Slayer duties listed on it. Geez, when does Declan sleep?

Tomorrow's gala has been highlighted, but aside from that, there's no other information about the museum. I start rummaging through the drawers and cabinets looking for anything that might be useful. Come on, if I were a thirteen-year-old Slayer boy and I needed a secret password to a magic museum exhibit, where would I—

"Declan?" calls a voice from below.

I freeze. The call comes again, and it's too soft to be Dr. Amankwah. I start tiptoeing away, but then there's a *thump* followed by a small crash. My urge to make sure no one's hurt wins out over my instinct to run and hide, and I follow the sounds down the basement stairs.

Sprawled at the foot of them is an elderly Black man who is leaning heavily against the banister with his metal cane on the floor a few feet away. I rush down to help him up, and his eyes widen with surprise when he looks at me. "Akosua? Awurama Boateng's young apprentice, right?" he asks breathlessly.

I open my mouth and close it, not sure how to reply. This man . . . he thinks I'm my mom. He must be Declan's grandfather, the daa who was mentioned on the calendar. There's no sign of the night nurse; I guess she had to leave even earlier than she'd told Declan. Dr. Amankwah and my dad grew up as young Slayers in the Compound together, so it's definitely possible that the older Mr. Amankwah would've met my mom when she was younger.

"No, I'm not her," I reply weakly as I help the man into the puffy recliner at the edge of the room and fetch his cane. "I'm a . . . I'm a friend of Declan's. What happened down here, Uncle?"

"Oh yes, right, of course. Elsie forgot to give me my medication before she left. I tried to go get it myself, but I had a small tumble. It's these old joints—they're not what they used to be after my stroke," he says. "I'm sorry to bother you."

"It's not a bother! Here, one second." I run back upstairs, grab the pill counter and a glass of water, and run back down.

After he's taken the medication, Mr. Amankwah thanks me profusely. "It's good to see you again, Akosua. Are you still seeing that Boateng boy?"

"Um, yeah. I am." I read somewhere that when someone has memory issues, you're not supposed to fight their version of reality. Or maybe it's the opposite? I'm not sure. All I know is right now, it feels kinder to let this man think I'm my mother than to disrupt his thoughts. "It's—it's going well."

Mr. Amankwah smiles. "I'm always telling Richard he needs to be like Edmund and find a nice girl like you to settle down with! But he just says I don't know what I'm talking about and 'it's not easy to get married these days,' as if your generation doesn't have all these apps full of people left and right! I keep telling Declan, 'Put me on that Tinder. I'll have six wives by the end of the week, a looker like me will.'"

I laugh, sitting cross-legged at Mr. Amankwah's feet. "I'm sure you would, Uncle," I reply, and he physically puffs up at the compliment.

I don't have time to waste, but I can't bring myself to walk away. I never knew my grandparents, so something like this—listening to an elder's stories and hearing their wisdom about a world I am too young to have experienced—feels precious. Even more than the trophies and the awards, this living, breathing connection to an ancestor is what I envy most about Declan's life.

"Uncle, what were Dr. Amankwah and my da—I mean, what were Richard and Edmund like when they were younger?" I ask, hungry for something no food or blood can give me.

Declan's grandfather rubs his chin softly. "My Richard was always so boisterous. You'd think he was born with wings sprouting from his feet from the way he barreled into every room. Edmund was quieter. He was always friendly, but there was something . . . sad about the boy. Honestly, I'm glad you came along. He's smiled more since he met you than I can remember him doing all the years before."

My chest constricts as the image of my father at my age forms in my mind. I've seen pictures, of course, but Mr. Amankwah's words shed new light on the images.

My father used to be sad until my mother came along. Maybe falling in love with an obayifo didn't ruin his life as much as everyone says it did.

Mr. Amankwah continues. "Yes, Richard needs a nice girl like you, especially after all that business with Stacy. . . . I told him to leave that girl alone, but he wouldn't listen, and then look what happened. And the way it affected poor Declan! The boy pretends it doesn't bother him, but it does. Do you know I needed to get into his laptop the other day, and the password was her birthday? He uses it for everything." Declan's grandfather shakes his head. "It's a shame. The whole thing is such a shame."

Daa's words click something together in my mind. Stacy has to be Declan's mom. If Declan really uses her birthday as a password for everything, then maybe . . . "And just when is Stacy's—?" I begin to ask, but I'm cut off by heavy thudding on the stairs as Declan bursts into the basement, panting.

"Daa, I'm so sorry I'm late, but I can't find your medicine.

Did someone move—" He pauses when he sees me sitting with his grandfather, the pill counter on the small table beside the old man.

"There you are, Kodwo," Mr. Amankwah says, referring to Declan by his Akan day name. "If you'd made me wait any longer, I would've been skin and bones by the time you arrived! Luckily, Akosua was here to help me out. Good girl, this one."

A small line appears between Declan's brows. "Yeah . . . good thing Akosua was here . . ."

"It was nothing," I mumble.

There are deep bags under Declan's eyes, and even after Pepper's mmoatia healing, he still looks like a bus ran over him, then backed up to run over him again, then rolled right over him a third time out of pure spite. But he doesn't let his grandfather see how tired he is. Instead, he lets the old man talk his ear off as Declan leads him into the basement bedroom and helps him get ready for bed. I wait awkwardly on the couch, feeling more like an intruder in this moment than I did when I was literally sifting through the Amankwahs' belongings.

Sometime later, Declan reappears from his grandfather's bedroom with an empty tray in his hands. I jump up to take it from him, but he shakes his head. "You've already done enough. I've got it from here."

"Seriously, it was nothing."

The awkward silence that comes after seeing something private the other person wasn't quite ready for you to see stretches between us. I'm about to crack a joke to end it when Declan asks, "You wanna go outside?"

15

How to Use a Trampoline

*"Even in a lifestyle as hectic as ours, never
neglect the need for moments of rest and reflection."*

—From the *Nwoma*

THE CLOUDS HAVE ROLLED in, turning an already
dark night two shades away from pitch-black. Declan
and I sit on the top of the stairs leading from his back
porch to his wide, almost football-field-sized yard. My
gut tells me if I don't say anything, Declan might fill the
silence. Sure enough, he does.

"When I was little, I thought my daa was the strongest man in the world. No one and nothing could get
in his way if he put his mind to something." The words
are aimed at me, but Declan's eyes are planted on the
wood beneath his feet. "Then, about a year ago, he had
a stroke. He's recovered really well, especially for someone his age, but he's still not all the way back. It's . . .
hard to see him like this."

"I'm so sorry," I reply. I've spent my whole life griev-
ing my father's mother, who died before I was born.
Witnessing the slow decline of a beloved elder is a pain
I can't even imagine.

Declan sighs. "Honestly, I should be thanking you.

It would've been really bad for his blood pressure if he hadn't taken those pills before bed . . . And when he was talking to you, it was the most energetic I've seen him in a long, long time." Declan finally lifts his head, and a shiver that has nothing to do with the air temperature crackles down my spine. "So thank you, Serwa, for saving me twice tonight."

There's no arrogance in Declan's voice, no condescension. Just pure gratitude and another emotion I can't recognize. My mouth is all dry and my pulse is racing. . . . What is going on? Oh gods, I'm pretty sure these are the first stages of a heart attack. I'm too young for one of those!

A breeze cuts across the lawn, raising goose bumps across my skin. "You cold?" asks Declan.

"What? No, I'm fine, really!" I protest, but that doesn't stop him from slipping off his varsity jacket and wrapping it around my shoulders. I stick my arms inside the sleeves, which are so long I have to roll them up to see my hands. But the jacket is soft and warm and it smells nice—that same grass and apples and boy smell from our duel earlier today.

"Thank you," I mutter, and Declan just nods, and oh my gods, I might've grown up pretty sheltered, but even I know that every cheesy teen movie has the *Person A lends Person B their jacket* moment before one of them either confesses their love or they're both murdered horribly. B-but Declan's just being friendly. *Obviously.* He doesn't like . . . I mean, he could never . . .

Nope, nope, noooooo, not going there. Not even gonna think about it. Bad, brain, bad!

My eyes scan the lawn again to give my mind *anything* to think about besides how stupidly soft Declan's jacket is. They land on a dark shape near the back. "You have a trampoline?" I say excitedly. "I've never been on one!"

I wait for Declan to say something snarky about my limited life experience, but he just goes, "Well, there's a first time for everything."

And that's how Declan and I find ourselves racing across the lawn in the middle of the night to try the trampoline. I struggle at first, but after a few face-plants I find my balance, and soon we're bouncing and shrieking with delight like a couple of sugar-high toddlers in a Chuck E. Cheese. Part of me wonders if Declan should be goofing around like this so soon after recovering from his injuries, but he looks the happiest he's been all night, laughing and whooping as we rise and fall and rise again, no cares or worries besides seeing who can bounce the highest.

Minutes or maybe hours later—time passes differently on a trampoline, I swear—we collapse in a giggling heap side by side on the stretchy canvas base. Declan clutches his stomach, literally gasping for air. "Wow, I forgot how much fun this thing is. I haven't used it in years."

"I don't believe that," I reply between my own hiccuping laughs. "If I had one of these bad boys, my parents would need a bulldozer to separate me from it. This is amazing."

Declan's smile falters. "Yeah, well, it's hard to fit in regular trampoline sessions when your life is as hectic as mine."

My thoughts fly back to the overstuffed, color-coded planner on the fridge. Literally every second of that calendar was filled in. "Why do you keep your schedule so packed? Balancing school and Slayer duties would be a full-time job on its own, but soccer, academic clubs, picking up extra tasks like this nyame dua mission, and taking care of your grandpa? Declan, you're doing too much."

"You wouldn't understand, rookie."

I'm surprised by how much that comment stings. How is

it that I can be bouncing on a trampoline while wearing this boy's jacket one second, and the next, four little words from him have me blinking back tears? "And exactly what is it that I don't understand?" I bite back.

"Drop it."

"No, I won't drop it. I'm sick of people acting like the world is sooooo complicated that stupid ol' Serwa wouldn't know anything about it! Why can't I understand? Because I haven't taken the Initiation Test?"

"That's not—"

"Because I can't speak Twi as well as you do? Because I don't go to a rich school surrounded by rich friends who are obsessed with me? Because—"

"Because you have two parents who actually want you!"

Declan freezes, his mouth hanging open in the universal expression of someone who just said something they didn't mean to. I stare at him as he jerks away, covering his face with both his hands. After a long, long moment, he starts speaking again.

"My mom was already married to my stepdad when I was born," Declan finally says, and the air between us grows heavy with the implication of his words. "I lived with them the first few years of my life, and we were . . . we were . . . I know most people remember their early childhood fondly, but mine really was good. Both me and my stepdad didn't have any reason to think anything was weird, and my mom . . . well, she was a really good actress. They both treated me like their true son, because back then, I was."

The last time I'd seen Declan's mother was during his Initiation Test. I'd noticed she wasn't sitting with Dr. Amankwah, but I didn't think that was particularly weird—lots of people have separated parents. But I can already tell this story goes far deeper than something a few quick greetings would ever reveal.

"But my grandma—sorry, my stepdad's mother—started getting suspicious," Declan continues. "Lots of little things my mom said weren't adding up, and as I got older, I looked less and less like my stepdad. My stepdad's family confronted my dad and mom about it, because they had dated not long before she got married, but they denied everything. And you can deny what you've been up to and who you've been hanging out with all you want, but you can't deny the results of a paternity test. The way my mom tells it, there was a fifty-fifty chance I was either my dad's or my stepdad's kid, and, well, the coin landed on the wrong side."

Declan lets out a laugh with absolutely no joy in it.

"Honestly, once the results came back, my dad did a one-eighty. My parents agreed early on that I'd live with him full-time and spend some weekends and holidays at my mom's. At the time, I didn't really get why I had to move in with him. I was like six, and all I knew was that there was something wrong with me and that was why the people I thought were my dad and my grandma couldn't stand to be in the same room with me anymore. And there are lots of people willing to raise a kid who's not biologically theirs, but my stepdad's not one of them. For a while, it looked like he and my mom might even get divorced over the whole thing, but they went to marriage counseling, and I guess they worked it out, because they're still together. And now here we all are, one big, messed-up family."

"That is . . . Wow," I say, because what else is there to say?

Declan nods, his eyes and thoughts somewhere far away. "*Wow* is one way to put it. And don't get me wrong, I love my dad, but I can't forget how he only stepped up after the paternity test made him. So that's why, when he asked if I wanted to take the Initiation Test when I was only eleven, I said yes even though I didn't feel ready. That's why I can't complain about all the stuff he needs me to do now. Even though he won't say it out loud, I was never part of his grand life plan. So if I can be stronger, be smarter, be *better* than everyone else, I can prove he made the right choice by . . . by keeping me around. And my mom made the wrong choice letting me go."

The silence returns; neither of us rushes to fill it. There is no consolation to offer someone whose own family made it clear they don't think he should exist. Tears burn at the back of my eyes, both of outrage for what Declan had to go through—what he's *still* going through—and of shame at myself for all those years of petty rivalry, not even considering what ugly things might force someone to push past all their limits the way Declan has.

Every word I could say jams up in my throat. None of them really matter, so instead, I grab Declan's hand. A jolt of surprise pulses through him, but he wraps his fingers around mine. We stay like that for a while, long enough for the clouds to part so Osrane and all her moonlight can shine down on us.

When I feel like I can speak again, I whisper, "I know it's not the same at all, but I get what it's like to . . . to feel you have to prove yourself every second of every day. That was how I always felt with my parents, like if I didn't fill the massive shoes their legacies had left behind, I was embarrassment to the entire family. And I don't know what the answer is, but I know it's not pushing yourself until you break."

"It doesn't help that I'm one of the only immigrant kids in my whole neighborhood, either," Declan mutters. "I feel like if I fall behind, it just proves what too many of my neighbors secretly think—that my family and I don't really belong here."

I scoff. "Right, because when you overwork yourself into an early death, at your funeral people will comfort themselves saying, 'At least he showed those snooty boys at Cunningham Prep what's what!'"

He sighs. "The logical part of my brain knows you're right, but it's hard to make the rest of my brain believe it."

"All your brains can fight me in a Walmart parking lot, because they're not winning this argument."

Declan lets out a loud laugh that shakes the entire trampoline, and now I'm smiling, too. "You're really something, Serwa Boateng. You know that?"

"Oh, so you *do* know my name! And here I was wondering if I should check my birth certificate to make sure *rookie* wasn't listed there."

"Oh, it's definitely there, probably on the line right beneath *smart-aleck* and *lover of trampolines*." Declan sits up, and without really thinking about it, I sit up, too, like my body chose to mimic his before my brain could send it the memo to move. "But seriously, you know I'm just kidding with all the rookie stuff, right?"

I shrink inside the jacket. "It's pretty hard to tell someone is joking around when you only see them a couple times a year, and every time you do, they go out of their way to show you up."

"Show you up? Serwa, I have never tried to show you up!" he exclaims.

"But what about the rookie thing?"

"I thought it was funny how it flustered you, but I never meant it as an insult, really. I'm sorry I dragged it on so long if it really bothers you."

I . . . I . . . Huh. "So, the Easter egg hunt?"

"Everyone was trying to win that!"

"A-and the tournament at that one outdooring we went to? You weren't targeting me then, either?"

Declan shakes his head. Meanwhile, my own head can't process this information. My (apparently one-sided?) rivalry with Declan has been one of the constants of my life. And now he's telling me that after years of me scheming and stewing and secretly praying for his downfall, there was never any animosity on his end at all? It feels like someone just told me water isn't wet and now I have to rearrange my entire understanding of how everything works.

If we're not rivals, then . . . what exactly are we?

My face must look as shocked as I feel, because Declan goes, "So you really thought all these years that everything I did and said to you was part of some messed-up master plan to make you look bad?"

". . . Something like that."

"Serwa, I mean this in the nicest way possible, but not everything around you is actually about you."

I sigh. "Yeah, I'm definitely starting to realize that. My friend Gavin, he was the first person to show me how sometimes I'm so focused on what I think is happening that I miss what is actually happening." I lean back on my elbows, still floored over the whole *Declan Amankwah Has Never Secretly Hated My Guts* revelation. "He, our other friends Eunju and Mateo, and my cousin Roxy spent a whole month teaching me how to interact with other people like a normal human being. Eunju once called me 'battle smart, people stupid,' and every day proves how right she is."

I meant it as a joke, but Declan is giving me that searching look again from the soccer field. "Why do you do that?"

"Do what?"

"Put yourself down like that? You're not people stupid, or any kind of stupid. You're, like, really cool. And smart. And funny. And I'm not just saying that because you saved my life a billion times tonight."

All the air feels trapped in my lungs. This moment feels so breakable, like a single wrong breath will end it all, yet it also feels static and alive. Declan's looked at me before, but not—not like this.

Not like he sees everything about me, and that the person he finds there is someone worth believing in.

"You might just be a rookie now, Serwa, but I'd take you over a hundred full Slayers any day. And if you saw in you what I see in you, you would, too."

And that's when it happens.

That stomach-dropping, free-falling, tumbling-through-the-air-with-no-possible-hope-of-not-getting-smashed-to-bits-when-you-hit-the-ground feeling you've seen in every movie and read about in every book. Auntie Effi warned me this might happen, but it's only now, now on this trampoline with this boy and his smugness and his bravery and his insecurity that the truth of what I feel—what I've probably *always* felt—barrels into me with the speed of an out-of-control-bullet train with its brakes cut:

I like Declan Amankwah.

16

How to Complicate a Situation with an Unwanted Crush

"Never forget what we fight for and why."

—From the *Nwoma*

I LIKE DECLAN AMANKWAH.

I like Declan Amankwah?!

But how could this happen! *Why* did this happen?!

Wait, that's a stupid question. This happened because he's funnier and smarter and nicer than I ever knew. It happened because even when we were little, whenever he walked into a room, I couldn't focus on anything or anyone else. It happened because we're lying next to each other on a trampoline in his backyard after he poured his heart out to me while literally covered in moonlight.

This whole situation is the kind of revolting cliché my mom and I would've made fun of in those period dramas my dad is obsessed with, except it doesn't feel so cliché when it's happening to you, and oh my gods, in those stupid shows, this is the moment where the main character and the love interest kiss.

"You okay?" asks Declan, and I let out a high-pitched

laugh that would probably make a hyena want to scratch its own ears off.

"Me? I'm fine! I'm amazing! Never better!" I lie like every single one of my brain cells isn't screaming because I have a *crush* and it's on *Declan Amankwah.* Hanging out with him felt so natural just a minute ago, but now I'm too aware of my hair and my face and my everything, really. I need to put on a natural expression. What even *is* a good expression to wear when you're alone with your crush and they . . . might . . . kiss . . . you? And, even more shocking, you *want* them to?

It's in moments like this that I'm really glad my skin is as dark as it is, because I'm pretty sure if I was light-skinned, my face would be redder than a tomato.

"You sure you're okay?" asks Declan. "You look like you're going to throw up."

I feel like throwing up because behind these new feelings is something far more familiar, yet equally overwhelming—the hunger. It's just like my aunt said: An obayifo's bloodlust is stronger around the object of their affection. I thought I'd be good on blood for at least the next few days after the incident at the Lincoln Theatre, but it's like the realization of my crush has flung the floodgates of all my other uncontrollable urges wide open. I have to force myself to breathe as each new stomach pang racks through me stronger than the last.

I want to sit out here with Declan all night. I want to hold his hand. I want to bite down on one of those blood-filled arteries I can hear pulsing beneath his skin like a ticking time bomb.

My fangs push up against my gums, and now I suddenly understand why Auntie Effi said there isn't much difference between a first kiss and a first bite.

"I need water!" I exclaim, and I hightail it off the trampoline before Declan can ask any more questions or do anything stupidly cute to make me bite his head off. Once I get to the kitchen, I lean my forehead against the wall in shock. All the movies make being a vampire seem like this mysterious, super-hot thing that gives you cool powers and eternally ruffled hair. (I'm looking at you, Edward.) But so far my experience has been weird thoughts and even weirder feelings. It's like every-thing my mom warned me would happen with puberty but worse because it's *vampire* puberty.

I wish my friends were here. They'd know how to navigate this crush, and even if they didn't, Mateo and Roxy would com-fort me, and Gavin would try to make me laugh, and Eunju would probably crack some quip like *Of course the first person you ever liked would be someone who has sworn his life to putting stakes through the heart of people like you*, forcing me to quip back until we're so busy sniping at each other I forget to be sad.

And . . . I wish my parents were here. Not that I'd tell them about this crush—GODS NO! Do you know how much my dad would start crying because *my little girl is growing up so fast*??? Ick. It's just that my parents have been there through all my major firsts—first steps, first broken bone, first time disarming an enemy combatant. I'd never given much thought to what my first crush might be like, but I guess I'd subconsciously assumed that they'd be there for it, too. (And that they'd be oblivious of all details pertaining to said crush and remain completely in the background. Like all good parents should.)

The hour grows ever later, Serwa. Do not let childish dalliances distract you from your true purpose.

I take a deep breath. Everything feels like it's spinning out of control, but one thing isn't—my mission. If anything, tonight's events have made it clearer to me why we need the Midnight

Drum. The source of all my problems is the stigma against obayifo. If Nana Bekoe wants to end that, then I'm on her side, even if her tactics might be extreme.

When I look over at the fridge, an idea hits me. Daa mentioned that Declan uses his mother's birthday as a password for all his devices. If he's this particular about writing out his schedule, then his mom's birthday has got to be there, too.

A quick search of the rest of the year—November and December—reveals nothing. Luckily, this isn't one of those tear-away calendars, so the earlier months are still behind the current page. I sneak a quick look over my shoulder; the trampoline is too far from the house for Declan to see what I'm doing, but I still have to hurry. Heart in my throat, I gingerly remove the calendar from the fridge and start flipping through the earlier months. January, February, March—Nyame help me, where is it? I don't have time for this!—April, May, June, July . . .

There! The date July 28 is circled in red and has two simple words beneath the number: *Mom b-day*.

I see Declan's face crumbling at Ben's Chili Bowl when his mom called to cancel their kayaking trip. I hear the waver in his voice when he described his parents' complicated history. It's obvious that his love and pain are so closely tied that he can hardly separate the two.

July 28 is the code phrase to get into the Abomofuo's secret exhibit.

The last obstacle keeping my aunt from the Midnight Drum is gone.

"What are you doing?"

I almost jump several feet in the air when Pepper flits into the kitchen with her hair in rollers and her face covered in green goop. "Calendar fell off while I was grabbing some water," I lie. I quickly flip back to October, replace the planner, and open the fridge to get a bottle. The whole time, I can feel Pepper's eyes boring into my back like tiny lasers.

"Declan told you about his mom, didn't he?" she says.

The skin on the back of my neck prickles. "H-how can you tell?"

"The psychic bond between a Slayer and their mmoatia, remember? We've only been working together two years, but I can read his emotions better than he can." Pepper perches on a banana in the fruit bowl like it's a tiny throne, and while her pose is nonchalant, her tone is anything but. "I feel turmoil inside him whenever he talks about his mom."

"I can imagine. The whole thing sounds . . ." Messy? Unfair? Painful? "Hard."

"Mm-hmm. And do you know, in all the time I've known him, you're the only new person he's told the whole story to? He hasn't shared it with his friends at school, or his teammates, or his fellow Slayer initiates. Just you."

My heart does a funny slip-and-slide thing in my chest. Declan let me in on something that even the friends who see him every day don't know. He trusts me that much.

Pepper peers out the window in the direction of the trampoline, and her face softens into a smile that makes her look as sweet as the fairies she resembles.

"Do you know I'm only three hundred years old? That must sound ancient to you, but in mmoatia time, I'm a teenager. All I ever wanted was to become a Slayer's partner, but the older mmoatia kept me on archive duty for centuries because of my youth.

"Then, two years ago, word came down that I'd finally been partnered with someone. Not just anyone, but the second youngest person to ever pass the Initiation Test! It felt like fate. The day Declan and I became a team, I swore to myself I'd prove wrong every person who thinks being young means you can't make a difference."

Pepper turns to me again, all softness gone. Her eyes are like daggers, and I'm the helpless prey caught beneath her gaze. "The life of a Slayer isn't easy. Few live to old age, and even fewer do it without suffering major trauma. I'm determined to make sure Declan makes it into that last group, and that means not letting anything near him that could even potentially become a threat. Everyone in his life is either an ally or an enemy, and it's my job to know which is which."

The mmoatia leans forward, and even though I tower over her, I feel like she's the one looking down at me.

"So tell me, Serwa Boateng: Which one are you?"

I open my mouth to answer, but nothing comes out. Which one *am* I?

Ally or enemy?

Slayer or obayifo?

"I . . ."

"Everything okay? I was starting to think you got lost inside the fridge," jokes Declan, choosing now to walk in on what is quickly starting to feel like a hostage negotiation. He looks between his partner and me. "Did I miss something?"

"Serwa and I were just having a girl talk," Pepper lies smoothly. She flits over to Declan and rubs at the bruise on his cheek he got when he smacked into one of the trampoline bars after I bet him he couldn't do a backflip on it with his eyes closed. (He pulled it off because *of course* he did. Ugh.) "You weren't jumping around on that trampoline, were you? Why did I waste all that time healing you if you were just going to crack your head open on that deathtrap?"

"I'm fine, really!" Declan waves her off. To me, he says, "Now that we're both rested, it's time to plant the third nyame dua, the one for Esum. If we leave now, we can get it done before sunrise."

Amid the running for our lives, extremely personal confessions, and life-ruining romantic realizations, I had completely forgotten about the last nyame dua. My immediate thought is *Heck yeah, let's do this!* because even the prospect of traipsing through the city in the dead of night and coming across another supernatural horror that either wants to eat us or sing at us badly sounds fun if I'm doing it with Declan.

But instead, I blurt out, "Can I use the bathroom?"

Declan blinks in surprise, but he directs me to the bathroom, which I promptly lock myself inside. I close my eyes and count to ten, telling myself that for these ten seconds, I can wallow in self-pity over not being the person Declan thinks I am. The kind of person he'd . . . you know, *like* like.

I'm not going to help him plant the third nyame dua. Honestly, after tonight, I'm probably never going to see Declan ever again.

At least not on the same side of the battlefield.

He's a Slayer. I'm an obayifo. Now that I've got the code phrase, it's time I remembered why I'm really here.

When I open my eyes again, I'm back in mission mode. I grab a marker from my pack and write out a quick note on a scrap of paper I had at the bottom of my bag:

Aunt just messaged me on my iPad freaking out. Gotta go home now. Sorry I didn't make it to the end! Stay safe!

I leave the note on the counter by the bathroom sink, then get to work on the window. The bug screen comes off easily, and minutes later, I'm hauling myself through it. My body is moving on autopilot, like if I can keep my muscles occupied, my brain won't have time to stop and think about how betrayed Declan is going to feel when he finds me gone. The moon is back behind the clouds, making the world dull and dark.

As soon as my feet hit the lawn, I'm running harder than I've ever run before. It's not until Declan's house is just a blur in the distance that I stop, pull out the burner phone, and call my aunt to let her know I'm ready to come home.

17

How to Plan a Heist

"Things that seem too simple on the surface rarely are."

—From the *Nwoma*

"**AND YOU'RE ABSOLUTELY SURE** that's the pass-code? July twenty-eighth?"

I nod. "I'm sure."

Back at the Luciole's penthouse, I've just finished updating my aunt and her coven on the events of the night. I've only been gone for six hours, yet I feel like a completely different Serwa than the one who left this hotel thinking she was going to outwit her worst enemy. Oh, what a sweet summer child she was.

All the coven members react excitedly to the news, and why shouldn't they? It's everything they've been waiting for. I slink down in my seat as the conversation switches to logistics for tomorrow's heist—who will go where, who's responsible for what signal and at what time. Normally, pre-battle scheming is my favorite part of a mission, but I just sort of half listen with my head buried in Declan's jacket, Biri burbling anxiously at my feet. I can't believe I ran from Declan's house in such a panic that I forgot to give the jacket back to him. The right thing to do would be to anonymously mail it to his house, but it's my only proof that tonight actually happened.

That for a little while, he and I were on the same side.

When I arrived at the hotel wearing Declan's jacket, Auntie Effi lifted an eyebrow but didn't say anything. Even as she helped Zuri and Fern finalize the plan to infiltrate the hotel, she kept looking over at me with that face adults use when they're clearly concerned for you but trying to pretend that they're not. This goes one for a few hours until the plan is finally set and the coven disperses to prepare themselves before our big day tomorrow.

Now that it's just me and her, Auntie Effi leans against the whiteboard they were using to plot out positions, crosses her arms over her chest, and asks, "What's the matter with you?"

I pull my legs up so I'm curled into a ball on the armchair. "Nothing," I reply, too busy wondering if Declan ever planted the third nyame dua, and if so, where? I should've been there when he saw Esum, the Night, the last of Nyame's celestial children. But instead, I'm here.

"Hands in your pockets? Jacket collar over your ears? You're like the poster child for pre-adolescent petulance. What's going on, Serwa?"

"I said it's nothing, Auntie."

Auntie Effi crosses the room to stand in front of me, her hands on her hips. "Did something happen to you tonight?" Her voice is dangerously low, promising that if anyone had laid even a finger on me, she'd hunt the perpetrator to the end of this world and the next to make them pay.

"No."

"Then why are you sulking like a sasabonsam forced to take a bath?"

"It's just . . ." I fumble for the right words to express the hurricane of thoughts swirling in my head. "Do you think Declan will get in trouble for accidentally helping us steal the drum?"

I hate the way my aunt's eyebrows shoot up. I hate the sad, knowing smile on her lips even more. "And you tried so hard to deny that you had romantic feelings for the Amankwah boy."

Is my aunt technically right? Yes.

Is it a universally acknowledged fact that you get to go *I told you so* whenever someone close to you admits to a crush you saw long before they did? Absolutely.

But that doesn't make it feel any better to have the situation rubbed in my face, especially when she adds, "Another reason why you should've listened to your auntie. Tell me what hap—"

"Why should I?!" I explode. The surge of black magic that accompanies my outburst slams the coffee table between us against a wall, breaking off one of its legs. It feels good not to have to hold back how upset I am. I can't hurt her when we're made of the same destructive power. "Sorry that I don't want to have a big kumbaya heart-to-heart with someone I've only known existed for, like, a month! Stop trying to act like my mom, because you're not!"

For the first time since I met her, Auntie Effi's face crumples, and she looks like the abandoned little girl I saw in the memories she projected for me back at the tot lot. She lifts a hand like she might reach for me, then drops it back to her side.

"Trust me," she says, "one thing I don't need to be reminded of is how I'm not my sister and never will be."

I had kind of hoped she'd explode back at me, because fighting feels better than wallowing. But apparently, I hit on something that goes far deeper than this conversation. Her sadness cuts through my defensive fury.

"I'm sorry," I say. "That wasn't fair." What should I do? Go over and hug her? Will that make it worse?

People make it sound like being related to someone means you should automatically know how to treat them like family. But being part of a family is like trying to build a puzzle when you've never seen the image on the box—all you have are a bunch of random pieces that you have to make fit even when they don't want to.

"You were right," I say after a long, awkward silence. "I do like Declan. And I want to help free Nana Bekoe, but I hate having to hurt him to do it."

I don't realize there are tears rolling down my cheeks until my aunt is wiping them off. She wraps her arms around me tentatively, and I sink into a hug that is both as needed as it is hesitant. "I feel like no matter how hard I try, I hurt people, and I don't even have to suck their blood to do it," I say, hoarse and tired. "I know caring so much about someone who hates us makes me a bad obayifo, but I don't know how to stop."

"Serwa, look at me," my aunt commands, and I lift my head. "You are not a bad obayifo. Of course you're upset—you had to manipulate someone important to you. You should never apologize for caring about people. It's when you lose your compassion for others that you really become a monster."

"Even if that person's a Slayer?" I ask, eyes blurry with tears.

Auntie Effi stiffens. I can practically see her recalling all the pain and heartbreak the Abomofuo have put her through since she was a child. Yet she swallows down the trauma and simply says, "If someone hurting us was enough to make us stop caring for them, the world would be a far less complicated place. But that doesn't mean your compassion is inherently wrong."

I nod, knowing how hard it must be for my aunt to admit

159

that her enemies can be more than that to someone else. It makes the tornado of emotions inside me calm down a little bit. After the night I've had, this moment feels so calm and fragile that saying anything else is almost guaranteed to ruin it. But there's one more question I need to ask, one I've had since the night I learned the truth about my mom and Auntie Effi's past.

"Auntie, what happened to your father?" I whisper.

I've noticed that sometimes you can learn more about a person from what they don't say than what they do. In the past few weeks, my aunt has talked extensively about Nana Bekoe and my mom, but she's only ever mentioned her father—my grandfather—once. My gut tells me that whatever happened to him was probably awful even by obayifo standards, and the distressed look on my aunt's face confirms that fear.

"Why do you ask?"

"That night at the tot lot, you mentioned he taught you and Mom to speak Ga, so he was around at some point. What happened to him?" *Was he another victim of our family's black magic?* is what I want to add, but I can't bring myself to say the words. I need confirmation that our family being obayifo didn't have disastrous consequences for at least one important person in our lives.

My aunt lets out a long, bone-weary sigh. "I don't remember too much, honestly," she admits. "I was six and Akosua was nine when it all happened. Our father wasn't anyone particularly powerful or special—just a postman. I honestly can't tell you what he saw in my mother. But he was friendly and kind."

"What happened to him?" I ask again.

"He learned his wife and his two small daughters were obayifo," she says dully. "And once he had that information, he couldn't handle it."

My stomach fills with twisting dread. "Did he try to kill you and Mom?"

"No! No, never. But he couldn't handle being involved with something he'd been taught was monstrous and evil. Out of shame, he tried to hurt himself. Akosua found him and managed to save him before he did irreversible damage, and to make sure it didn't happen again, she erased his memories of the three of us." My aunt gives a small shrug. "My father is now in a nursing home back in Ghana. And he has no recollection that your mother and I even exist."

There are moments in life no words can fully capture. This is one of them. I had thought my grandfather being murdered was the worst-case scenario, but I was wrong. So wrong.

Tears fill my eyes as I imagine my mother—as a child even younger than me—finding her father on the edge of death's door and having to erase all his memories of her to save him from himself. I . . . I don't know what I would have done in her place. As mad as I still am at him, I'd rather have my dad hate me forever than forget me completely.

"That's horrible," I say.

Auntie Effi sniffs loudly. "Do you know what surprised me most when I came to this country? The way witches are glorified. People here dress up as us for Halloween. They fill their TV shows and social media profiles with our aesthetics. It's like they've forgotten that, for most of human history, witches were something to mutilate, not emulate. Women who were seen as outcasts—too queer, too brown, too unwell . . . Any one of us on the margins was a target. To me, a pointy hat and a broomstick are not a cute costume; they are a reminder that, for centuries, people were brutalized under the mere assumption they *might* be what we actually are."

My aunt stands up. "That's why I fight for this coven and the haven we have created for ourselves. We deserve safety and joy and to experience all the good things in life regardless of our powers. And I won't stop until no other obayifo is ever faced with a choice like the one my sister had to make all those years ago. And like the one you made tonight. Do you understand?"

It feels almost insulting to compare what I'm going through with Declan to what my aunt and mom went through with their father; losing a crush is nowhere near losing a parent. But it's weirdly comforting to know I'm not the first obayifo who's had to choose her own safety over a person she cared about. It's a reminder that as personal as my problems feel, they are a symptom of an issue far bigger than me.

"Not really," I admit as I slide my hand into my aunt's and let her pull me to me feet. "But I'm starting to."

18

How to Execute a Heist

"When the time comes, trust your team and trust your plan."

—From the *Nwoma*

IT GOES WITHOUT SAYING that my parents covered one or two, shall we say, less-than-lawful subjects as part of my Slayer training. How to hotwire a car, how to assemble a makeshift catapult, how to launder considerable sums of money through organizations fronting as local mattress outlets—you know, the basic life skills every kid should know. Included within this legally dubious education was how to steal.

Wanna know the number one most important rule for swiping an object straight out from under somebody's nose?

The easiest way to steal something from someone is to convince them to give it to you.

7:19 a.m. The Morning After My Patrol with Declan: The first staff members of the Smithsonian National Museum of African Art begin arriving on the premises.

Most of them are barely conscious since it's way earlier than when anything with a pulse should be awake, and they all mutter bleary-eyed hellos to one another between sips of coffee. Among the throng is Zuri, who clocks in to work the same way she's done for the last five months straight, as if today is just any other day.

9:06 a.m.: Zuri emails her boss that everything is still on track for the gala tonight. Sends a few choice texts confirming the same to Auntie Effi. She turns down a muffin from a coworker. Mentions apologetically that she already ate, but next time for sure, Lorraine! Doesn't mention that the meal that made her feel so stuffed was a one-liter coconut-pineapple-AB+ blood smoothie (with extra protein powder.)

10:01 a.m.: A group of tourists get in a loud argument with a security guard outside the museum. They've just gotten off a thirteen-hour plane ride from Luxembourg and now simply cannot understand why the site they were most excited to visit is closed.

The Middle Man security guard, a square-faced grandfather named Lawrence, is trying to explain to them that the museum is closed in preparation for a private event that night, but they're not having it. He mentally drafts his resignation letter, because he's way too old to be dealing with this mess, while the tourists shove brochures in his face and bellow about how if they say that the museum is open every day from 10 a.m. to 5:30 p.m., then the place needs to open at 10 a.m., goshdarnit!

10:39 a.m.: Exactly 361 feet away from the African Art Museum, a harried receptionist at the Smithsonian Castle signs for a large package of what she believes to be toilet paper for the restrooms but is actually more than two dozen bonsam packed into a cardboard box. She has the box sent to the second-floor custodial closet. Once there, the obayifo who smuggled in the bonsam lets them free, and the creatures fly into a vent and begin working their way through the building's central heating/cooling system.

10:50 a.m.: The disgruntled Luxembourgish family, who settled on visiting the Castle after Lawrence so rudely refused to let them into a closed building, hear a sound like a thousand cats running across a hardwood floor. Seconds later, the building descends into chaos. The lights begin to flicker, the temperature cycles between freezing cold and boiling hot, and the sprinklers start shooting moldy water everywhere, dousing the family and causing them to declare they are never returning to America EVER AGAIN!!!

10:55 a.m.: Lawrence is back at his post, weighing retirement activities against a new job search, when the abode santann charm he wears on a gold chain around his neck starts burning against his chest. He does a quick check of the building, but there's no sign of a black magic flare-up . . . at least not yet.

11:07 a.m.: The flare-up reveals itself when the security guard at the Smithsonian Castle (nice guy; they play mahjong once or twice a month; Lawrence always loses) calls Lawrence to tell him that the building is going absolutely haywire, and no one has any idea why. Lawrence laughs along. The second the call ends, he tries to send a text to his Slayer liaison, but the cell reception in the building is suddenly abysmal, which is 100 percent due to Zuri messing with the building's router and phone lines during her bathroom break. No one will be getting any calls or messages in or out until a tech can come and fix them.

11:15 a.m.: The black magic shows no signs of abating. Now Lawrence is really starting to panic. The Abomofuo have been secretly working on the opening of the Ghanaian Visionary

Artists Collection for months. Reporters from all over the country will be in attendance to cover one of the largest-ever initiatives to return stolen artwork to Africa and to highlight new talent from the continent, not to mention the school-children and other civilians attending. Guests are set to start arriving in a little over seven hours; he can't let all those people walk straight into a black magic hotspot! But as a Middle Man, Lawrence lacks the combat training to do anything about the black magic assault—that's the Slayers' job. He tries again to send a message to Dr. Amankwah asking what he should do. No luck. His dreams of resigning start to slip away as it becomes clear the Okomfo are going to fire him long before he quits.

11:30 a.m.: Things are looking hopeless. The black magic is getting worse. Lawrence has a tension migraine from all the chaos and confusion.

Which means it's finally showtime for Auntie Effi and me.

YOU'D THINK ZURI HAS had years of experience dealing with museum-related crises from the confident way she strides up to the security desk. "Lawrence, do you have any idea what's going on with the Wi-Fi? The board is going to murder me if I don't update them on the gala preparations by noon," she says. Behind her, Auntie Effi and I stand in the blandest tan delivery jumpsuits you can possibly imagine, caps slung low over our faces. Thanks to Zuri's work on the inside, we knew exactly which company the museum would use for today's pickup. An adze-possessed employee "lent" us the uniforms and van, and Zuri canceled the real appointment. The next part of the plan is totally dependent on Zuri's performance, but it doesn't make standing here in the open any less nerve-racking.

Poor Lawrence shakes his head, wiping his sweaty forehead with a handkerchief. "I think something similar is happening next door. I heard their system went down right before ours did."

Zuri's eyes go wide with fake surprise. "What does this mean for tonight?"

"I—I guess, since we haven't heard otherwise from the higher-ups, we should just carry on as we discussed earlier . . . ?"

"No way. There's too much at stake to leave it to chance. We need to move the transfer up—now, before the black magic hits us, too."

Middle Men aren't trained in battle like Slayers are, but they're just as loyal to the Abomofuo's secrets. That loyalty shows in the sharp way Lawrence asks, "How do you know about black magic?"

Zuri glances over both shoulders, pretending to be extra paranoid even though the museum is empty. Instead of saying anything, she pulls a gold charm identical to Lawrence's out of her purse. The security guard gapes at it as he touches his own abode santann necklace.

"Prayɛ, sɛ woyi baako a na ebu," Lawrence begins in Twi.

"Wokabomu a emmu." Zuri finishes the proverb.

When you remove one broomstick, it breaks, but when you put the pieces together, they do not break. It's an old proverb to remind the people that in unity, there is strength. The Middle Men adopted it as their motto. I don't know where Zuri got the charm—and I'm honestly too scared to ask—but like the code phrase that'll let us into the exhibit hall, this is a key part of the plan to get us to the Midnight Drum.

"I didn't realize they'd stationed another Middle Man here!" Lawrence says excitedly.

"I'm backup in case something like this happened," says Zuri. "But we've got to hurry. We need to clear the exhibit, and once the items are in a safe location, Dr. Amankwah can decide where they go next."

Lawrence's smile falls. "I still don't know . . ."

Oh gods, we've lost him. Not now, not when we're finally, *finally* so close to the drum.

"But he gave us the passcode!" I blurt out. Zuri gives me a sharp look because we'd agreed this morning that she'd do all the talking, but it's obvious we need to pick things up if we want to pull this off.

"It's true, he did," Auntie Effi chimes in. I can feel the black magic starting to pool in her palm. She'll knock Lawrence out if she has to, but we're all hoping it won't come to that. "He knew that there needed to be multiple fail-safes in place in the event of an emergency."

Lawrence looks at the three of us in what have to be the longest five seconds of our lives. I nervously lick my lips, then take another risk by adding, "I know it's against protocol to move without orders, but the items can't remain on the premises if the black magic attack happening next door reaches all the way here. There's too much at stake."

My heart clogs my throat as Lawrence stares directly at me. Beside me, Auntie Effi's hand clenches into a fist. If he doesn't cooperate, she is about to attack in three, two—

"All right. Let's get moving," says the security guard. I send up a silent thank-you to Nyame that things didn't have to get ugly as my aunt relaxes beside me.

Minutes later, all four of us are on the bottom floor of

the museum. We're in front of the statue of Funtunfunefu-Denkyemfunefu near the still-blocked-off entrance to the exhibit being unveiled tonight. The two-headed crocodile somehow seems larger than the last time I was here, and it suddenly occurs to me that if I'm wrong about the code phrase, a single bite of one of its jaws could snap me clean in half.

Lawrence says to it, "There's been a change of plan. Because of a black magic flare-up next door, we need to start moving the items out of this hall and onto the truck ASAP."

"No password, no entry! That's what our dad and grandpa told us!" yells Righty. "We're a good guard!"

"Though *good* is a subjective measurement based entirely on one's personal moral code," adds Lefty.

Now's my turn. I step right up to the statue, pretending not to be freaked out by all four of its reptilian eyes swiveling my way. Sweat pours down my back. Either I'm right, and my aunt will finally be able to accomplish what she has worked toward for the last twenty years, or I'm wrong and . . .

Well, I've come to the bridge. Time to burn it down.

"The code is July twenty-eighth," I say.

I immediately brace myself for the worst, but then Righty makes a strange sound . . . I think it's trying to imitate the blare of trumpet, but it comes out more like metal grinding against metal. "That's it! Yay! We don't have to eat you now!"

"They probably would've given us indigestion anyway."

Zuri, Lawrence, Auntie Effi, and I all shield our eyes as golden light shines from the wall, and the Adinkra-covered door Declan walked out of yesterday reappears among the concrete and stone. My eyes burn, and I can't tell if it's from relief that I'm not crocodile food or disgust at my betrayal of Declan. I take a step forward, hand hovering over the doorknob, and pause.

The abode santann carved into the knob peers back at me with a hollow sort of knowing. It feels like it's looking not at me but through me, to a corner of my soul it has already cast judgment on.

I need to calm all the way down. They call this Adinkra the All-Seeing Eye, but the Abomofuo aren't omnipotent. They can't see everything, everywhere, all at once, or else they would've caught my aunt and her coven a long time ago.

Swallowing down my fears, I open the door.

19

How to Realize Something Is Very Wrong

"A fool hopes a plan won't fail. A wise person plans for it."

—From the *Nwoma*

GROWING UP AROUND MAGIC means I have seen my fair share of rooms bigger on the inside than on the outside, but comparing those rooms to the Abomofuo's secret hall feels like pitting a dollhouse up against a mansion.

Behind the door is the single largest room I've ever seen, easily ten stories higher than the museum itself. The magic in here is so thick I can practically taste it; the door must have been some kind of portal, and now we're on the other side of the veil. Wooden shelves over a dozen feet high extend to the left and right as far as the eye can see, broken up every now and then by tall, masked mannequins in multicolored ruffled garments. They're so lifelike, I jump as we pass the first one.

"Masquerade outfits," Zuri explains, rubbing at her temples. Being around so much divine wisdom can't be easy for her or Auntie Effi. My mixed heritage is the only reason I feel just a dull ache and not a pounding migraine from being in here. "Often worn at events like the Fancy Dress Festival back in Winneba."

I approach one of the mannequins, only to flinch back when the laughing mask that forms its face turns my way. "They're enchanted!"

"To deter thieves," says Zuri. "Come, we don't have much time. The items marked for today's retrieval are this way."

Glass orbs engraved with nsoromma, the star Adinkra, float around the room, bathing us and all the objects in an eerie silver glow. Warm water laps at our ankles, not unlike the star-flecked river in Asamando that marks the border between the realm of the living and the realm of the dead. Gods are often tied to bodies of water, so it makes sense that the Abomofuo chose to hide so many of their most important objects in a place with this much magical power.

We're lucky that Zuri has the list of items the Abomofuo want to move, because without it, we'd be beyond lost trying to navigate this place. It seems like any object that a Slayer has ever owned is hiding down here. We pass whole armories' worth of akrafena, stacks of golden stools emanating soft glows, and rows upon rows of Adinkra cloths, each one representing a Slayer who lost their life in the line of duty. Above the rush of water there's a quiet murmur in the air, as if the owners of each item are reaching across the centuries to tell us who they were and why they are worth remembering. I swear, the masquerade mannequins turn their heads to watch as we pass. This whole thing is starting to feel very Belle trespassing in the Beast's castle.

The section holding the items for transfer is marked off by a floating velvet rope, and it becomes obvious just how hard our task is going to be. Even though this narrows down the area we have to search, there's still easily hundreds of objects to sort through. How are we supposed to find the Midnight Drum among all this?

And something feels . . . off. Like someone-shifted-all-the-furniture-in-your-house-two-inches-to-the-left-but-you-can't-prove-it off. We haven't seen or heard anyone else since we entered the exhibit, but I still can't shake the feeling of someone standing right behind me.

"All right, this will go faster if we split up and start emptying different shelves at the same time," says Zuri while Lawrence uneasily wipes sweat off his forehead. She gestures to me. "You go down to the end there while we start loading the section over here."

That's our agreed-upon code for me to look for the Midnight Drum while Zuri and Auntie Effi keep Lawrence distracted. But when I turn to walk away, Zuri grabs me by the arm and says very quietly, "I was wrong about what I said to you yesterday. What you pulled off with the Amankwah boy proves you really are one of us. You always have been."

Her approval makes my throat go tight. I simply nod, and when she lets me go, I make my way through the aisles, feeling like a lost kid in the world's largest, most dangerous toy store. I pass a whole family of mechanical gazelles enchanted to hop over a hedge in an endless loop, a spear made of pure gold that hovers inches above its shelf, and golden Akan paperweights hiding secret compartments for tiny knives and poison, but not a single drum. Now I'm starting to worry. What if we risked everything only to be wrong, and the Midnight Drum was never in the museum at all?

But my freak-out is premature, because that's when I see it. Between a pot labeled ALL THE WISDOM IN THE WORLD and a pumpkin-sized bronze carving of a warthog with large gold nuggets for eyes sits an ordinary-looking djembe drum. Its jet-black wooden body is about the size of a human torso, and there's a creamy white goatskin stretched over the top. My breath catches in my throat.

I'm looking at the Midnight Drum.

For the first time in my life, I'm looking at my grandmother.

I approach the instrument with trembling hands. I've wanted this for so long—not the drum, which I only learned about a couple of months ago, but the chance to know more about my family, more about where I come from.

I know Nana Bekoe is not perfect. But we're family. That has to mean something.

. . . Right?

"Auntie Effi!" I call out, in my excitement forgetting that I shouldn't be using her real name in public. "I found it!"

But the moment I pick up the drum, I can tell something is wrong. Everything else in the room is giving off varying amounts of magic energy, from the tiniest coin to the largest statues. The Midnight Drum was created from both divine wisdom and black magic, so it should radiate both.

But the object in my hands right now . . . I can't sense either divine wisdom *or* black magic in it.

It isn't giving off anything.

"This is a fake," I say aloud, seconds before a high-pitched scream rips through the air. Auntie Effi! Zuri!

I whirl around, ready to run to their aid, only to see none other than Declan Amankwah standing right behind me. Before I can even yell, he has his arm wrapped around my neck in the same chokehold I've put so many other people in over the years.

"I meant it when I said you were good, rookie," says Declan as I kick and scream in his grasp. "Too bad for you, I'm still better."

With that, he jabs his finger into the side of my neck.

And the world goes dark.

20

How to Embarrass Yourself in Front of a Boy, Part Two

"Know when you are beaten. There is often more to learn in defeat than in success."

—From the *Nwoma*

IF I HAD TO list the absolute worst things to wake up to after being knocked unconscious, a conversation about baby pajamas would definitely be in the top five, right after an arsonist clown juggling chainsaws in my face, but before my math teacher springing a pop quiz on my birthday.

"Which do you like more? The polka-dotted ones bring out his eyes, but the striped ones come with matching booties."

"Either would be a good choice, Nana Nsiah."

"But I don't want just a 'good' gift—I need the best. My grandson deserves nothing but the best!"

Ughhh, my head feels like someone wearing soccer cleats tap-danced across my brain. Even cracking my eyes open takes serious effort. I'm sitting on the floor of the exhibit hall in one of the few places not covered in water. Lawrence and Zuri are nowhere to be seen, but beside me, Auntie Effi is stirring awake.

"Serwa? Are you all right?" she groans. A thin trail of blood trickles down from a nasty cut on her forehead.

"I'm fine," I assure her, even though all my instincts say that probably won't remain true for long. Matching rope bindings are wrapped around both our wrists. "What happened?"

"What happened is that you have been caught attempting to pilfer valuable Abomofuo property," says the oldest of three figures in the room with us, the man who was cooing over baby clothes. Nana Nsiah. Nana Nsiah . . . Why does that name sound so—

Wait, Nsiah as in *Okomfohene* Nsiah? The leader of the entire Abomofuo?! I didn't recognize him because I've only ever seen him at formal summonings, when he wears this really cool lion mask, but now I remember his voice from the day my parents received their mission to go after my aunt. He's the kind of old that could either be sixty or ninety, but it's clear from his energy that he's as alert as someone half his age. The man next to him is taller, with a shaved head, glasses, and a thick beard. He gives off major Nick Fury vibes—if Nick Fury dressed like Colonel Sanders.

Dr. Richard Amankwah. Which means the third figure, the shortest of the trio, can be none other than—

"Declan," I groan. He flinches, then turns his head away. I'm not sure why I said it aloud, but his rejection snaps away the rest of my haze, and the last few minutes before I passed out come rushing back.

My aunt's intel was correct—there was a Midnight Drum hidden inside the African Art Museum.

But it wasn't the real Midnight Drum. The whole thing was a trap, and we walked right into it.

When I jump up from the ground, I don't have a plan—any rational person would realize there's no way I can get past three members of the Abomofuo on my own. But I left rational behind with the giant two-headed crocodile. However, when I rush forward, two of the masquerade statues from earlier appear behind me to grab me by the shoulders and haul me back.

"Apologies for the multiple levels of protections, but it's for your safety as much as our own," says Okomfohene Nsiah.

Several words come to mind, all of them the kind that would get me grounded into the next century if my parents heard me say them. I try to call on my black magic, but it fizzles and sparks sadly. Closer inspection reveals several nyame dua Adinkra drawn on our bindings. Neither Auntie Effi nor I can use black magic as long as we have these on.

I glance over to my aunt, who—judging by her grimace—just came to the same realization I did. Me being captured is one thing, but I can't believe they got her, too. She's one of, if not the, most powerful obayifo in the world. She should've been able to take them down easily.

Unless she got distracted trying to protect me.

Despite her wounds, my aunt finds the energy to snarl, "Ah, Nana Nsiah. It seems Owuo has found you too ugly to descend his ladder again, leaving you to terrorize the land of the living for another year."

"It's quite a shame. I heard the god of death throws marvelous parties down in Asamando." The head priest smiles. "I'd say it's good to see you again, Boahinmaa, but a man of the gods shouldn't let lies pass his lips."

I have no idea how my aunt is staying so calm. My body can't decide whether it wants to pee or throw up from fear, and there is a not-zero chance both might happen at the same time. But Auntie Effi is nothing but cool detachment, even without her magic.

"What's going on?" I cry. "You've made a mistake, let me go!"

It's Declan who steps forward and hisses, "So you can try to steal the Midnight Drum again, witch?"

There's so much venom in that last word that I flinch. Less than twenty-four hours ago, Declan was spilling his heart out to me on the trampoline. Now he's looking at me as if we never had those moments, or any of the others that brought us together last night. As if I've only ever been, and ever will be, his enemy.

I'd been warned this would happen—I'd known this would happen. But knowing a blow is coming never makes it hurt any less.

"I—I don't know what you're talking about."

"Don't play stupid, Serwa. Everyone here knows you're an obayifo," says Dr. Amankwah. The world falls away beneath my feet. It feels like the walls are closing in on me and there's not enough air, nowhere to run even if I weren't bound.

"So, you caught us. Bravo," spits my aunt. "How did you do it? Spies? A double agent within my forces?"

The head priest's smile goes wider. "Why, young Serwa herself led us to you."

That cracks my aunt's facade, and she looks at me with an expression of pure shock.

"I didn't!" I cry, because I need her to know I haven't betrayed her like every other member of our family has. "I didn't tell them anything, I swear!"

"It's true, she didn't reveal anything to us directly," Dr. Amankwah confirms. "But we didn't need her to divulge your plans when she led us straight to your hideout."

They found the hotel. But how? I definitely didn't tell them the address, and any of the women and creatures hiding there would die before giving up the location. I'd double-checked that

I wasn't followed the two times I've gone back to the Luciole since seeing Declan at the museum yesterday morning. But how did they find the hotel, then? Did they use a tracker? I'm pretty sure I would've noticed if Declan had drawn any Adinkra on me.

Unless . . .

"The jacket," I say hoarsely, and Declan's silence is all the confirmation I need. "There was a tracking spell on the jacket you gave me."

Dr. Amankwah nods. "And when you wore it last night, it led us right to that den of witches and vampires. Our forces are seizing control of the building as we speak, and we've taken the other obayifo who was here with you into our custody as well."

Auntie Effi lets out a small, choked sound, and for an instant, genuine anguish fills her face. The majority of the obayifo hiding in the Luciole aren't like her and me—they haven't trained their whole lives to defend themselves in case of an assault. It's all too easy to imagine the Slayers overrunning the hotel's lobby, snatching up poor Biri and all the other baby bonsam, capturing Fern, and further traumatizing all the obayifo like Zuri who have already been through so much.

My aunt lost her home and I lost the place that kept me safe when the entire world fell apart, all because I was stupid enough to trust a boy who never once trusted me.

"How long have you known?" I ask Declan. I don't know Dr. Amankwah or Okomfohene Nsiah, not really. But I know Declan. Focusing on him is the only thing keeping me from freaking all the way out.

"Since you were spotted near the site of the black magic flare-up at the museum's fountain yesterday morning," he replies coolly.

If Declan realized I was an obayifo yesterday morning, then that means I spent an entire evening trying to hide a secret we both already knew. "B-but if you knew I was an obayifo, why didn't you turn me in right away?" I ask, hating how high-pitched and hysterical my voice sounds. "Why did you let me go with you to set up the nyame dua?"

Why did you pretend to be my friend? Why did you make me like you?

"Isn't it obvious?" says Dr. Amankwah. "Your parents reported you missing weeks ago, yet you seemed well taken care of when you were sighted at the museum. We figured that if we tracked you long enough, you'd lead us right to whichever black magic creatures you were aligned with. And you did so beautifully. Thanks to you, Boahinmaa and her associates are finally in Abomofuo custody. They won't be able to terrorize the public any longer."

I wish I could go back in time to the Serwa of last night and scream in her face about how *stupid* she is with her silly little crush and her silly little hopes. She of all people—*I* of all people—should've known better than to think I could outmaneuver the Abomofuo. The whole time I thought I was laying a trap for them when I had never actually left the Slayers' web.

If everything last night was fake . . . Declan pretending not to know why I was in DC . . . telling me all that stuff about his family . . . Oh gods, was the whole bit about his grandfather just a part of his sick plan? "I can't believe you used your own grandfather just to get me to trust you."

"Daa had nothing to do with this!" Declan explodes.

Dr. Amankwah frowns. "Nya abotare, Declan," he says, ordering his son to calm himself in Twi. "It's in an obayifo's nature to sow distress."

How dare he speak about my nature. He doesn't know *anything* about me.

"So you set up the entire gala and new exhibit just to lure us out of hiding?" my aunt asks incredulously.

Okomfohene Nsiah shakes his head. "The gala and the exhibit have been in the works for months. Though when we got word in August that you had been sighted in the DMV area, we did start seeding hints that the Midnight Drum would be involved, in case that might lure you out of hiding. Declan only became involved after Serwa was spotted at the museum yesterday. However, we did take certain . . . precautions with the hope that if Serwa was in the area, she would eventually make her whereabouts known."

Certain precautions? My mind goes back to when I ran into Mateo yesterday morning. It had felt like almost too much of a coincidence that the GCC's mural had been selected out of dozens of entries to be featured at the gala.

"You rigged the art contest to bring my friends to the museum just to try to lure me out of hiding?" I ask in disbelief. I know the Abomofuo always have backup plans on top of backup plans, but this feels way too *1984* even for them.

Instead of replying, Okomfohene Nsiah bends down and trawls his hand through the water like he's drawing an Adinkra. A sphere of the liquid rises into the air and flattens into a kind of dripping screen. Light swirls within it until it reveals Mr. Riley, Eunju, Gavin, Mateo, and Roxy sitting in the art room at Rocky Gorge Middle School. A rush of longing and regret washes over me as I stare at the GCC's old meeting spot.

My chair's still in the same spot. Even though it's been weeks, no one's moved it.

"I just got a text that the bus should be here in thirty

minutes. Does everyone have all their belongings gathered?" asks Mr. Riley. "The school will be locked when the bus drops us off after the gala, so anything you don't bring with you, you won't be able to get till Monday."

My friends all nod. Everyone's dressed to the nines for the event. I wish I could reach through the screen and warn them they're being used as bait.

"What are the odds we'll run into Serwa?" asks Eunju. She's trying to play it off like she doesn't care about the answer, but there's no mistaking the hope in her voice. She's missed me—and the worst part is, without her memories intact, she has no idea why.

"If Mateo saw her at the museum yesterday, I bet she'll be there tonight," Gavin chimes in, while Mateo nods vigorously next to him. "Maybe she'll let us know why she and her family dipped so quickly?"

"Or maybe she'll just blow us off again," mutters Roxy. I've never heard my cousin sound so bitter, not even when she was describing how her former best friend, Ashley, became her biggest bully, or the struggles her family had after her dad's deportation. Did me leaving upset her that much?

A line appears between Mr. Riley's eyebrows. I didn't have time to erase his memory before I left, so, unlike the four kids, he remembers everything about me up until the blackout. But he has his own supernatural secrets to protect, and from the way he carefully picks his next words, I can tell he didn't expose the truth to my friends when they came back not knowing anything about magic.

"I know we're all disappointed that we didn't have a chance to say good-bye to Serwa before she left Rocky Gorge," Mr. Riley says slowly. "But I'm sure she and her family had their reasons.

It's not fair to her or ourselves to go around in circles asking what-ifs or why when she's not here to explain herself. All we can do is cherish the time we had together and know that sometimes, when our friends make painful choices, it usually has more to do with what they're going through than any desire to hurt us."

My throat closes up with emotion to see Mr. Riley defending me even after all this time. Without realizing it, I lift a hand toward the water screen, like if I just reach out far enough, I can step through and tell them everything. But at that moment, Roxy lifts her head and stares straight at me. Her eyes lock with mine, and even though I know it's just a coincidence—we can see them, but they can't see us—I jerk back like I accidentally touched a live wire. The image disappears and the water falls back to the ground, dragging me back to my quickly unraveling reality.

"Leave my friends alone. They have nothing to do with this!" I yell as the full weight of what the Okomfohene just showed me hits me. Mr. Riley and the GCC are on their way to the museum right now. They're walking straight into the heart of the Abomofuo's web, and they have nobody to protect them when they get here.

"No harm is going to come to your friends," the head priest promises. "I showed them to you as a reminder that your recent actions have affected far more people than just yourself. They are on our radar now solely because you put them there."

I swallow thickly because there's nothing I can say to that. If the Abomofuo's plan was to rattle me, then it worked; I've never felt more thoroughly defeated.

Auntie Effi glances at me, and despair gives way to rage on her face. Even though she can't use her black magic, she's still a terrifying sight with her eyes glowing red and fangs fully extended. "You think yourselves heroes, but what kind of heroes manipulate a little girl? What kind of heroes destroy the home of dozens of helpless women and creatures?"

"I don't think anyone who drinks the blood of innocents deserves to be called helpless," sneers Dr. Amankwah. He's lucky we're bound, because without these ropes, I'm pretty sure my aunt would be wringing his neck right now. "You can gnash your fangs all you want, but the nyame dua wards Declan planted last night make this whole building too strong for even your magic to break through. You are powerless within these walls."

My aunt practically trembles with rage, but there's no denying the ugly truth in front of us: We've lost. There's no trick that'll get us out of this scenario, no loophole, no spell crafty enough to deliver us from inside the enemy stronghold.

It's over.

"So what happens now?" I ask, fighting to keep my voice even. They've already won—they don't get to have my tears, too.

"After the gala, a team of Slayers led by Dr. Amankwah will return to escort Boahinmaa to the Compound. There, she will stand trial to answer for her crimes against our people," says Okomfohene Nsiah. "Her fate is in the gods' hands now."

My stomach turns at the thought of what the gods' idea of justice might be. In the stories, they can turn cruel or forgiving at the drop of a hat. There's no telling where they'll fall when it comes to my aunt.

"And as for you, young lady," he says, turning to me. "I think it's about time you went back to your parents."

21

How to Hold a Grudge

*"Deal with the wounds of the past before they become
the scars of the future."*

—From the *Nwoma*

TEN MINUTES LATER, WHEN my parents quite literally burst through the secret exhibit's door, the world stops.

They look haunted, as if the few weeks we were apart were actually twenty years for them. Gods, I'm the world's worst daughter for making them this scared. I shrink back like I used to do when I was a kid and I knew I was about to get in trouble. "H-hi, Mom. Hi, Dad. I can expl—oof!"

My parents crash into me like a two-person tsunami, and the feeling of their arms around me is so familiar, so right, that for a second I just let myself lean into it. I'm no longer being held in a creepy magic exhibit hall by a boy I thought liked me and the world's most vengeful grandpa. I'm four years old again, my parents are consoling me after a nightmare, everything is easy, and I'm safe.

I'm safe.

"Serwa, are you all right? How do you feel? Are you

hurt?" Even my mom's voice sounds older, and her clothes are all mismatched and wrinkled like she threw on whatever was closest to her when she got the call that I'd been found. Tears flow down Dad's cheeks as he runs his hands over my face and checks the rest of me for injuries. Boulder and Avalanche, my parents' partner mmoatia, climb out of Mom's bag to greet me. Boulder in particular shows more emotion than I've ever seen on him.

"Serwa, don't you ever scare me like that again!" thunders the small, gnome-like creature. "Let me take a look at you. Are you bleeding anywhere?"

"I'm fine! I promise! Auntie Effi took really good care of me!" I say in a rush.

That's when my mom finally notices Auntie Effi sitting on the ground beside me. My aunt gives her a wary nod. "Good to see you again, sister."

I saw the full power of my mother's vampire side in the memories my aunt showed me all those weeks ago. I watched Mom pull grown men apart with her bare hands and display a viciousness more like an animal's than a person's.

That's why—even given my tendency to exaggerate—you should know I am being 100 percent completely and utterly serious when I say I have *never* seen my mother look as enraged as she does right now.

"You stole my child," she hisses, and the pure fury in her voice makes me throw myself between them before any more blood can be shed today.

"She didn't steal me—she saved me!" I cry. "Auntie Effi found me wandering in the woods after the blackout and took care of me! She didn't do anything wrong!"

Out of the corner of my eye, I see Dr. Amankwah shake his

head and put a hand on Declan's shoulder. "Only a truly evil creature would poison a child against their own parents."

Mom's chest rises and falls rapidly. There's something different about her beyond the anger and the fatigue, something I can't quite put my finger on. Fists shaking at her sides, she looks past me to my aunt. "And what do you have to say for yourself?"

With her hair disheveled and her makeup ruined, Auntie Effi's beautiful armor is gone, revealing the little girl who sat on the streets of Ghana begging for someone to love her. She breaks the stare first, lowering her gaze to her reflection in the water near us.

"Only that I wish I really was the monster you believe me to be," she whispers.

How many times can a heart break before there are too many pieces to put back together? I look at my aunt, my mother, my father, me—this twisted little family that no one can save from itself.

Maybe it's time we stopped trying.

Dad wraps his arms around my shoulders so tight it would take a jackhammer to separate us. Then he turns to Okomfohene Nsiah. "Undo these bindings. Serwa isn't a threat to anyone."

Even though he means well, my heart sinks a tiny bit. Which is it—am I his harmless little girl, or a vampire so strong I couldn't be trusted with the truth of my own powers?

"We'll undo them before you leave," says the Okomfohene. "But while she's not wearing any form of magic seal, Serwa will be required to remain under Abomofuo surveillance at all times."

Hold on, constant surveillance?! I never agreed to that!

"What happened? How did you find them?" presses Mom.

Dr. Amankwah steps forward and quickly explains the plot to use me to get to Boahinmaa and the Luciole. Trust me—the only thing more embarrassing than learning your former crush never actually liked you is hearing his *father* break down how much your former crush never actually liked you. Cruel and unusual? Meet punishment.

However, my parents look just as shocked as I did when I first heard the story. They didn't know about Declan's trap, either. Now, that's a surprise. The Abomofuo knew my location for at least twenty-four hours and didn't alert my parents.

"And why were we not informed of Serwa's whereabouts before now?" Mom asks the Amankwahs. Only someone who knows her as well as I do can hear the rage simmering beneath her cool tone.

Dr. Amankwah says, "It was decided that, given your emotional closeness to the situation and how much was at stake, it would be best to keep you unaware of the mission until we had everything under control. But I assure you, Serwa was never in any true dan—"

Declan's father lets out a strangled yelp as my dad grabs him by the front of his shirt and slams him against one of the shelves. Several glass figurines fall from their perches and shatter at their feet.

"You used our child as a pawn and *didn't tell us*?" roars Dad. My mom might be the creature of black magic, but right now, my father is the one out for blood. He's usually so friendly that I sometimes forget he is one of the most powerful Slayers in the history of the Abomofuo. If he ever decided to turn against the organization that raised him, things would get ugly fast.

Okomfohene Nsiah must realize this as well because he

orders sharply, "Kwabena, let him go. Awurama would be ashamed to see you acting in such a brutish manner."

Mentioning my dead grandma is a low blow, but it works. Dad lets go of Dr. Amankwah with a growl and Boulder climbs onto his shoulder to offer his partner some comfort. Declan's dad just readjusts his tie as if he hadn't been seconds away from having his head cracked against a shelf. Okomfohene Nsiah steps between them, his patience clearly growing thin, while Auntie Effi looks like she wishes she had a Slurpee and a tub of popcorn as she watches all this unfold. My mom just steps closer to me, one protective hand on my shoulder, another resting on her stomach.

"Kwabena, Akosua, when you received your abode santann, you both swore that you would work in the best interests of our society, no matter the cost," says the head priest. Mom and Dad both instinctively touch the spot on their chests where the All-Seeing Eye that represents the Abomofuo is seared into their skin. "It is unfortunate that the mission to rescue Serwa had to unfold the way it did, but it is over now. She's safe. The means do not matter when they lead to the desired end."

It's weird watching your elders interacting with their elders. When you're little, you can't even imagine there was a time when your parents weren't your parents, but seeing them get chastised is a reminder that every adult is still a kid to someone. My parents lower their heads. I can tell they don't agree with the priest, but they don't contradict him, either. Declan looks at me with pity. I turn my head away.

Okomfohene Nsiah clears his throat, and just like that, the prim grandpa is back. "I hate to cut a family reunion short, but we still have a gala to prep for. Boahinmaa will remain in here until the time comes for her to be escorted to the Compound.

Kwabena, you and your family should go get ready. Tonight's event is black-tie optional, and I'd hate to see you show up in"—he eyes my dad's beat-up Crocs with a grimace—"that."

Dad pulls a face. "Actually, Nana Nsiah, while we appreciate your kind invitation, I think my wife, daughter, and I won't be able to attend tonight. We have a lot to recover from as a family."

"Nonsense. I can't think of a better reason to be out celebrating than the return of a prodigal daughter!" He turns an intense gaze on my father when he says, "Besides, there have been . . . rumors among some of our members about conflicting loyalties among our ranks. We wouldn't want to add fuel to the fire by having the family at the center of these falsehoods absent, now would we?"

I silently yell at Dad to stand up to the priest, because how dare this man question his loyalty? My father has given everything to the Abomofuo. His own mother even gave her life for their cause. How is all that sacrifice not enough to earn their trust?

But instead of fighting, Dad's shoulders sag. He's clearly considering the implications of our family missing such an important event and not liking the possible consequences. "Of course, Nana Nsiah," he says reluctantly. "We'll be there."

"Splendid! I'll see you all at eight sharp," says the Okomfohene with a smile that no one else in the room returns. "Make sure you try the mini quiches when you arrive. They're to die for."

22

How to Get Ready for a Party (That You Were Threatened into Attending)

*"It is oftentimes those closest to us
who can cause the most harm."*

—From the *Nwoma*

I DON'T THINK THERE'S anyone on earth who would make worse guests at a party tonight than my parents and I, but what the Okomfo want, the Okomfo get.

My parents take me back to the hotel in DC where they've stayed while searching for me, and there we get ready for the gala in complete silence. You'd think there was a tennis match going on in my head from the way my emotions keep pinging back and forth. One second, I'm so grateful we're all together again I could burst out singing like a Disney princess. The next, I'm angry at them for abandoning Auntie Effi, then I'm disgusted at them for rolling over for the Okomfohene without a fight. And *then*, one of them will smile at me or gently touch my cheek, and the gratitude will return and the full, messy cycle will start all over again.

"Perhaps this gala will be good for us," ventures Dad as we stand awkwardly in the small sitting room waiting for Mom to finish her makeup. "A chance to de-stress after everything that's happened."

"Uh-huh," I say, arms crossed over my chest. I hate playing the cliché surly preteen daughter, but I don't have anything to say that isn't about the massive elephant in the room my parents have made an Olympic sport out of ignoring. From his vantage point on the hotel bed next to Avalanche, Boulder gives a disapproving tut. Even after all our bonding in Rocky Gorge, the reunion between the mmoatia and me was strained. When push comes to shove, Boulder is loyal to my father over me, which means there's no point trying to make him understand why I did what I did the day of the blackout.

Honestly, I'm still trying to understand it myself.

Dad flips the hotel remote back and forth between his hands as the sound of rushing water marks that Mom is *still* not done. Then he leans toward me with a conspiratorial grin. "You know what we're probably going to see tonight?"

It's impossible to stop the smile that comes to my mouth at his familiar tone. "Big Hats?"

"Big Hats!"

You know how some families play I Spy or the license plate game when they're on long car rides? My dad and I play the Big Hat game. The name says it all: When one of us sees some truly humongous headwear—I'm talking like a cowboy hat big enough to drink a gallon of milk from or the largest beret the world has ever seen—they yell "Big Hat!" and the other has to stop whatever they're doing and sing the Big Hat song my dad made up when I was a toddler.

It was as silly back then as it is now, but it was always my special thing with Dad—Mom never played because she couldn't appreciate the fundamental hilarity in a top hat tall enough to brush the ceiling. It wasn't until years later I realized it was my father's subtle way of making me excited about being on the road all the time for Slayer business. The game taught me to look for joy in all the different places and people I got to see, even though it meant we couldn't have a stable home in one place.

Dad grins and immediately jumps into the Big Hat song, using the remote as an impromptu microphone. It's a moment so familiar that on instinct I open my mouth to sing along.

But then I stop myself. There's no way a silly preschool song is enough to make me forget everything that's happened.

"You lied to me," I say softly, cutting Dad off mid-note. "I had no one else to believe, and you lied to me."

My father lowers the microphone and rubs at his face. "We did," he says simply. I can't tell if I feel better or worse that he doesn't even attempt to deny it. "But we weren't going to for forever. Your mother and I agreed that once you were eighteen, we'd tell you the truth—about your black magic, about Nana Bekoe, about everything."

"That doesn't give you any right to put a seal on me and never say anything!" I shoot back.

Dad stares at me for what feels like an eternity before he softly says, "The day you were born, you came out of the womb screaming."

I scoff. "Most babies are born screaming."

"Your cries weren't just newborn wailing. You were shrieking and thrashing like . . . like your body was fighting a war against itself just to stay intact. And you were glowing, these bright flashes of alternating gold and purple light, the divine wisdom and black magic inside you battling each other for dominance."

My dad's shoulders start to shake, his voice growing heavier as if just by telling me this story, he's reliving the horror all over again. "Your mother and I didn't know what to do. The midwives and the mmoatia had never seen anything like it, and the Abomofuo had no record of a child being born with both divine wisdom and black magic. Our options were to try to seal one of your powers right then and there or wait to see if your magic would stabilize on its own. The choice didn't feel fair, but you were so little and perfect, and you were in so much *pain*, and I just—I couldn't . . . We were so excited to bring you into the world, and to think that all you'd do was suffer . . ."

Dad stops to take a shaking breath. Sometimes I forget that in the grand scale of age, my parents aren't really that old. They'd had me in their early twenties, only a few years after my grandma Awurama had died. To go through something like that without any guidance from your own parents or family . . . I can't imagine it, and I hope I never have to.

After a few minutes, Dad finds the strength to speak again. "I'm not going to pretend like I've been a perfect father. None of this would've happened if I'd just believed you when you tried to tell us about the adze in Rocky Gorge. But, Serwa, I swear to you with all that I am that everything, *everything*, your mom and I have done has been to keep you safe. And from the bottom of my heart, I'm sorry we thought that lying to you was the only way to do it."

The expression on Dad's face—equal parts pain and remorse—rips my heart in two.

And I'm a worse person than I thought, because even though I know he means every single word, I still can't forgive him.

"Having good reason to hurt someone doesn't make it okay," I reply.

My father bends over like I punched him straight in the

heart. And because everyone in my family has horrible timing, Mom exits the bathroom just then.

"Was that the infernal Big Hat song I heard earlier?" she asks. She's stunning in her traditional kente-print blouse and skirt, which only makes me feel like even more of an impostor in my matching dress. Mom looks at me and her face twists into the universal parent expression for *You must be out of your mind if you think you're going out looking like that.* "Serwa, what are you doing with your hair?"

Turning from Dad's pained posture, I tug at my braids in their usual style. "Ponytail."

"This is a formal event. You can't just . . . Come here, let me fix it."

Mom drags me into the bathroom, undoes my ponytail, and begins expertly weaving my braids into an elaborate updo. While she mutters to herself about "looking like someone actually raised you," I compare our faces in the mirror. For the first time I can see why people think we look alike, to the point where Declan's daa mistook me for her. Those are my fingers I see in her gentle movements weaving my hair into place. Those are her eyes and her mouth making up my annoyed expression.

This is such an ordinary moment after everything we've been through; there are probably millions of moms all over the world grumbling about their daughters' hair at this very second and just as many daughters irritated about it.

An ordinary mother-daughter moment for two people who are anything but.

"Auntie Effi is going to lose the trial," I blurt out. I'm not ready to bring up what Dad just shared with me because it was hard enough watching one parent relive that trauma. However,

I can't stand playing happy family when a member of ours is being held against her will.

Mom's voice is even, though her hands slow down. "The Okomfo will decide her fate and mete out justice as they see fit."

"But look at how Okomfohene Nsiah talked to her tonight! Do you really trust him to give her a fair trial?"

"It's not our place to question whether the Okomfo's tactics are fair or not."

"How can you let them treat your own sister like that?"

Mom turns me around so she can look me in the eyes. I'm expecting anger in hers, but all I see is a bone-deep exhaustion. "There's more to family than just blood, Serwa," she says. "Boahinmaa chose her path, and I chose mine. It's a shame they diverged, but each of us is responsible for the choices we make. My sister's path led her here, and now it's time for her to face the consequences."

My whole life, my mom has been my favorite person in the world. Forget the gods—she was my real hero.

Now I'm not even sure if the person in front of me is someone I like.

"She misses you. All she wants is to save your mom and be a family again," I say, my voice cracking. This is so unfair, and my parents helped make it this way.

At the mention of her mother, Mom's gaze hardens. "Effi—I mean, Boahinmaa can want our mother back all she wants. That doesn't mean it can or should happen. Nana Bekoe chose her thirst for revenge over nurturing her remaining children. I haven't spent years undoing the damage she did to me to welcome her return with open arms."

I don't think my mom is as unaffected by Nana Bekoe as she likes to pretend she is; her whole body tensed at the mere mention of my grandmother. But pointing that out isn't going to get us anywhere, and it certainly isn't going to free Auntie Effi.

"If the Okomfo do anything to her, I will never forgive you. *Ever*," I say.

I rarely make ultimatums like this, which is how my mom knows I mean every word. A part of me wishes she would yell or scream back, because surely an argument would feel better than this heartbreak.

But instead, my mom just sighs, hand on her belly, and kisses me on the forehead. "If you hating me is the price I have to pay to never again go through what I did when you were missing, then fine."

"Uber's here!" Dad calls, breaking up our mother-daughter stare-down.

Mom pulls back, and the inches between us feel like miles that neither of us knows how to cross. "Come on. We don't want to be late."

23

How to Put the Pieces Together

"A true Slayer does not stop a hunt until
every path has been taken and
every stone has been unturned."

—From the *Nwoma*

FOR A GROUP OF people who spend the majority of
their time hiding in the shadows battling monsters of
unspeakable horror, Slayers sure know how to throw a
party. The museum has been transformed into an event
space for the night, and the only thing louder than
the chatter of the crowds who've come to celebrate
the sneak preview of the Ghanaian Visionary Artists
Collections is the DJ blasting Afrobeats all throughout
the building.

If you've never been to a Ghanaian hall party, you
need to add that to your bucket list, because there's
nothing like it. The food, the dancing, the outfits—I'm
just saying it's like twice as much energy as Coachella
without the having to sleep next to strangers in the
mud part. The art all around us only adds to the festive
atmosphere. A celebration of Ghanaian culture, with
tiny deviled eggs and mini quiches for all. Yippee!

I feel like I'd be enjoying the party more if I wasn't being held hostage in plain sight. The moment we arrive, Okomfohene Nsiah sticks to my family like glue, and I have to stand awkwardly at my parents' side as they make small talk with the other gala attendees. It does seem that the Okomfohene was being truthful when he said no one else knew about the mission to capture me. I don't think any of these people even knew I was missing. They ask me how my studies are going, and I give the polite, practiced answers I'm supposed to. Something tells me it wouldn't be a good idea to admit I've been too busy training with witches these last few weeks to crack open a textbook.

"Aren't the decorations just wonderful?" huffs an old uncle with jowls longer than a basset hound's.

Yep, my absolute favorite element is the woman currently being held in a secret magic room like this is one of those freaky gothic novels with the wife in the attic! So cool!

"Yeah, it's okay."

Dad knocks me with his elbow, a silent warning to stop making my displeasure so obvious. My parents don't want to be here, either, but they know how to act like they do. I guess this is how our community solves it problems. Maybe if you keep acting like nothing is wrong, everything will just magically fix itself. My parents keep checking on me every thirty seconds, but I don't know why they even bother; Declan's magnified nyame dua spell covers the whole building with protective divine wisdom. I couldn't cause a black magic scene right now even if I wanted to.

The whole time we're circulating through the building, I keep my eyes peeled for Mr. Riley and the rest of the GCC. Every now and then I think I see Eunju's braid or Mateo's glasses, but then the person will turn and it'll just be a stranger. The paranoia feels like a living, breathing thing currently clawing up my insides. Is it just a coincidence I haven't run into them yet? Or are the Okomfo playing more mind games with me by keeping us apart when I know they're in this building somewhere?

My friends' presence here does exactly what the priests hoped it would. There's no way I'm going to risk making a scene if it could put the GCC in any kind of danger.

After about an hour of everyone getting to mill about the new art pieces and mingle with one another, it's time for the sit-down dinner in the exhibition gallery. I slow when my parents and I approach our table, because the only seat left is next to none other than Declan Amankwah. His eyes practically bug out of his head when he sees me. My scowl deepens. I know I rarely wear dresses—nothing against them, they're just not very easy to fight in—but his staring just adds insult to injury at this point.

Declan clears his throat as I throw myself into my chair with enough force to make the utensils rattle.

"You look . . . different," he says. If I didn't know better, I'd say Declan is almost impressed by the sight of me in traditional formal wear. Yeah, right. Not falling for that again.

"Sorry, I left my witch's hat and broom at home," I snap under my breath. My nostrils flare from how hard I'm breathing to keep myself from going ballistic at him.

He winces. "Look, about what hap—"

"Nothing happened. You did your job. You're the better Slayer, and everything that happened last night was an intricately planned lie. Now leave me alone."

I don't want to talk to Declan Amankwah. I don't want to hear an apology that's probably just another lie. All I want to do is drink my nasty sparkling water, eat my overpriced fancy dinner, and sulk my last night of freedom away before I'm locked in the Compound until I'm old and gray or, like, forty.

But I guess Declan can't take a hint because he continues. "My house wasn't part of the plan. . . . The trampoline wasn't part of the plan. Neither was Daa. I know you don't believe me, but it's true. You were never supposed to meet him last night."

That's right. If the adze at the theater hadn't attacked him, I never would've had to drag Declan back to his home for his own safety, which would've meant no conversation with his daa or heart-to-heart between us on the trampoline. That part of the night being real makes everything hurt even worse.

"But if your plan was to lead me to the fake Midnight Drum all along, how would I have ever found out the password to the secret room if your daa hadn't leaked it?" I ask him.

Now it's Declan's turn to look embarrassed. "The third nyame dua is planted right here at the museum. After we'd activated it, I would've offered to show you the exhibit myself—"

"And your dad and Okomfohene Nsiah would've been there waiting to ambush us," I finished. The levels to the plan are kind of blowing my mind right now. If I had stayed, I would've walked right into their trap. And by leaving when I did, but taking Declan's jacket with me, I brought my aunt and the hotel into the trap. No matter what action I took last night, I was destined to lose.

Why did I ever think for even a second I had what it takes to go toe-to-toe with these people?

I can feel Declan looking at me, but I keep my eyes planted on the dais, where his father is giving a speech.

"On behalf of everyone at the Mid-Atlantic Ghanaian Preservation Society, let me welcome you all to tonight's gala. This community is the whole reason we do what we do, and there'd be no community without any of you. I'd like to give a special shout-out to the local students joining us tonight!"

While everyone applauds, I search the room for the Rocky Gorge table, but I don't see Mr. Riley or my friends anywhere. Strange . . .

Mr. Amankwah continues. "You know how hard it is to tear today's kids away from those phones of theirs long enough to teach them about art?"

Laughter ripples throughout the crowd, and I roll my eyes. Wow, how original; young people are obsessed with their phones. What next, a joke about airplane food?

From there, Dr. Amankwah launches into a long story about the importance of returning stolen artifacts to their communities and filling the space left behind with art that creates a new narrative about Africa and its peoples. Three minutes in, my brain shuts out his droning and turns to something that's still bothering me. This whole situation with my aunt and me versus the Slayers should be over and done. They won, we lost, the end.

But there's one open thread I can't let go of, and that's the location of the Midnight Drum.

If the drum in the exhibit was a decoy, then where's the real one?

I could tell the one in the museum was a fake the minute I touched it. And not in the way I know one plus one equals two, but like an understanding deep inside my bones that something was wrong. Is it because Nana Bekoe is my grandmother? No, the feeling went beyond that.

The Midnight Drum and I were both made with equal parts divine wisdom and black magic. We're both a walking paradox, two halves that shouldn't fit together but somehow do.

What if . . . what if . . . what if I don't *need* to look for the drum? What if I could home in on its specific magic resonance and follow *that* to its true location?

It's a risky move attempting to call the Midnight Drum when I'm literally sitting in a room full of Slayers, and it might not even be possible with Declan's wards still hovering over the building. But I have nothing to lose by trying. Not anymore.

While everyone else is still focused on Dr. Amankwah, I close my eyes and zero in on that tugging sensation inside me, the one that goes down, down, down past the world I know into another where magic lives in every nook and root. I follow the thread into a forest, deep and battle scarred, a forest too old to have a name, an entity too ancient for humans to wrap their minds around. The forest smiles at me, not with lips or teeth like a living creature might, but with rustling branches and twisting vines.

Hello again, Serwa, croons the voice that's been whispering to me for weeks now. *I've been waiting for you to return.*

And I smile back, because I know where the Midnight Drum is now.

To get it, I will once again have to find my way to the land of the dead.

24

How to Leave a Party in the Worst Way Possible

"Avoid causing bodily harm to others when not completely necessary."

—From the *Nwoma*

A FEW WEEKS AGO, my friends and I visited Asamando—the land of the dead—to retrieve a magic sword for the earth goddess Asaase Yaa. (There was a rock concert with some ghosts, and then the sword was eaten by Eunju's dog, and, look, it was a whole thing.) But at the very end, I heard this voice talking to me, and I had a vision of this destroyed forest in the underworld where the Slayers fought one of their worst battles against Nana Bekoe. At the time I thought it was just a hallucination from the stress of the whole journey (see again: ghost rock concert and weapon-eating dogs), but that was no hallucination.

That was the drum. It called to me then and has been calling to me ever since via the connection that the instrument and I share. It might have even been my grandmother herself, reaching out to me every moment I felt most alone to remind me that I wasn't.

If I want the Midnight Drum, I have to get back to Asamando.

The sound of thunderous applause snaps me out of my revelation. Dr. Amankwah has finally stopped delivering the world's longest speech, and now it's time to actually eat. My parents keep eyeing me over the food, but I don't engage—not because I'm sulking, but because I'm scheming.

I have to convey this information to Auntie Effi, but how? I doubt the password to the secret exhibit hall is the same as it was before, and without it, there's no way I can get past Funtunfunefu-Denkyemfunefu. But how can I possibly make it to Asamando without help? Last time it took assistance from a literal god to get there, and I don't think the Okomfo would like it if I interrupted their big party to set up a shrine to Asaase Yaa.

"What's that face for?" asks Declan several minutes into my silent plotting session.

"What face? I'm not making a face," I protest.

"Yes, you are. It's creepy. It's the face of someone about to give a bunch of kindergartners Red Bull just to see what happens."

"I'll have you know, Declan, that not everything— Hey, watch it!" I cry as someone walking past our table bonks right into me, knocking a bowl of soup all over my dress. I jump up and yell, "Ever heard of sorry?"

But the soup assaulter has already disappeared back into the crowd. Ugh, people these days! Dad tries to soak up the spill with a napkin, but I fight him off. "What, I can't even go to the restroom by myself anymore?"

I'm really pushing it with the backtalk today, but since I'm already about to be grounded until the end of time, I figure I can't really make the situation any worse. Even my ever-patient dad looks seconds away from snapping at me, but he wouldn't dare do it in public. "Just be quick. Go to the restroom, then come straight back."

"Go to the restroom, take a small detour to become an internationally wanted criminal, come back to the table. Got it."

I run to the restroom before I can face the consequences of my snark. While I'm not thrilled to be covered in tomato bisque, it is nice to get away from the party. Once I've washed off as much soup as I can, I exit the bathroom and pause. To the right, the hallway leads back to the gala, while the left goes deeper into the museum. All these people are up here laughing and chatting while somewhere beneath our feet, my aunt and the other obayifo are trapped.

"This is a bad idea, this is a bad idea, this is a bad idea," I mutter to myself as I plunge deeper into the museum. I probably have five, maybe ten, minutes max before my parents come looking for me, but that should be enough time to release my aunt and tell her what I've realized about the drum. After that . . . Well, that's future Serwa's problem. Current Serwa has enough to deal with already.

I make it down to the level right above where Funtunfunefu-Denkyemfunefu stands guard. But the rest of the staircase has been blocked off because of the gala, and the elevator to get down that far requires a keycard to operate at this time of night. I bite back a growl of frustration and wipe at the sweat dripping down my neck. I can't use black magic to make the elevator do my bidding, because the Okomfo have put protective wards all over the building. Could I try my divine wisdom again? I don't have anything to draw an Adinkra with, even if it did work this time. Maybe I could—

"You're not supposed to be here, witch."

I whirl around to see none other than Dr. Amankwah

standing behind me, power rolling off him in waves. Every time I met the man as a child, he'd always been friendly and smiling, but now there's nothing but pure hatred in his face. "I told Nana Nsiah we should've left you below with the rest of your kind, but he said you deserved a chance to prove you can ignore your destructive instincts. Clearly you can't. You monsters are all the same."

"I'm not—" I begin, tears burning at my eyes. I'm not evil? Not any different from the girl he watched grow up alongside his son, the girl who was just in his house yesterday learning all the painful secrets Declan holds close to his heart?

But none of that matters. I'm an obayifo, and to someone like Dr. Amankwah, that means I'm a monster. Nothing more.

"Come on. Since you clearly can't be trusted to behave properly among civilized society, we'll gather your parents and all three of you can go to the Compound at once."

"Get off me!" I scream as Declan's father grabs my arm and starts pulling me back toward the gala. I claw and yell, but the man's got arms like tree trunks. Even with my enhanced strength, I can't break his grip.

"Quit fighting, witch. You—oof!"

All of a sudden, Declan's father releases me and falls to the ground. I stumble backward, chest heaving, and stare in awe at Roxy standing above Dr. Amankwah's still body. Her mouth is open in a small O of surprise, the painting she just knocked Declan's father out with trembling in her hands. We both stare at each other in shock until a head full of midnight-black hair in a long braid pops out from behind Roxy with a long-suffering sigh.

"Well, so much for not making a scene," groans Eunju.

25

How to Catch Up with Your Friends in a Museum Bathroom

*"It is important to recognize when you've been wronged.
It is just as important to recognize when you have
wronged others."*

—From the *Nwoma*

UNDER ANY OTHER CIRCUMSTANCES, my normally happy-go-lucky cousin knocking a grown man unconscious with a painting of a dancing giraffe would make me laugh so hard I'd pee my pants. But given the twenty-four hours I've had, all I can do is stare as Roxy and Eunju double-check that Dr. Amankwah is actually just unconscious and we're not all about to be arrested for first-degree museum-murder.

"Wh-what are you—" I begin, only to be interrupted by two more figures racing around the corner to join us.

"Serwa!" cry Mateo and Gavin, and now my brain is basically a whirling beach ball that just keeps repeating *They're here. They're here. They're here.*

My friends are here.

Everyone is as they looked when the Okomfohene scryed on them: Mateo with his glasses, Gavin with his blue twists, Eunju with her braid, Roxy with her goth aesthetic. I'm the one who's changed beyond all recognition. But right now I don't even care because they're my friends and they're here and I'm not alone anymore.

Gavin nudges Dr. Amankwah with his foot. "Between Back-to-School Night and now this, we have *such* a bad track record with parties."

"You guys remember Back-to-School Night!" I cry, taking running steps toward them. Wait a minute . . . Hang on . . . I pull away, suddenly suspicious. "You guys remember magic? How?" That memory-erasing spell I cast on them was airtight; there's no way any of them should've been able to shake it off.

Gavin opens his mouth to speak, but Mateo shakes his head and glances over his shoulder. "Not here. T-t-too open. R-r-restroom."

We all pile into the women's restroom and push a trash can in front of the door so no one else can enter. I'm not sure what I was expecting for our big friend reunion, but it definitely wasn't Eunju grabbing me by the front of my dress and shaking me silly.

"Now that we're alone . . . WHAT IS WRONG WITH YOU?" she screams. "HOW COULD YOU JUST LEAVE US LIKE THAT? DO YOU KNOW HOW WORRIED WE WERE, YOU BIG STUPID JOCK? YOU COULD'VE GOTTEN YOURSELF KILLED! DO YOU EVEN KNOW WHAT WE WENT THROUGH? HOW—"

"Easy, Eunju!" says Gavin, pulling her off me. Whoa, I forgot that even without magic powers, the girl has, like, Hulk strength when she's mad. The whole room is spinning. "Keep shaking her like that, and she might start thinking we're upset or something."

Eunju takes a deep breath, eyes shimmering. Holy poop balls, is she about to cry? "I am upset!"

"Yeah, well, get in line," mutters Gavin.

"I think Serwa owes *all* of us an expl-pl-pl—owes us all answers," adds Mateo, and the hurt in his voice makes me flush with shame. Roxy doesn't say anything, just looks away from me with her arms crossed tightly over her chest. My cousin once burst into tears because I killed a spider instead of letting it go outside; if she of all people is mad at me, then I've really screwed up.

"Wh-where's Mr. Riley?" Yeah, I'm dancing around the metaphorical rhinoceros in the room, but you try facing down four people who should barely remember you exist without getting nervous!

"Back upstairs," replies Gavin. "I think he wants to marry this place. He's been going on for hours about how lucky we are to be surrounded by such a 'treasure trove of community-revealing artwork.' Whatever that means."

"We snuck off t-t-to look for you while he was b-busy fawning over a first issue of *Black P-Panther*," adds Mateo.

I nod. All right, no use putting this off any longer. "Okay, that's cool, but how come you guys . . . How come you remember me after, you know . . ."

"After you lured us into the forest in the middle of a citywide blackout, wiped our memories without our consent, then left us in the wilderness to have our entrails eaten by rabid raccoons?" Gavin asks dryly.

"There weren't any raccoons," I mutter.

Roxy finally pipes up. "You forget you weren't the only person in this group born with magic."

My eyes grow wide as the realization hits me. Both Mr. Riley and Roxy are Keepers, people descended from magical ancestors stolen from Ghana during the transatlantic slave trade. When those ancestors arrived in America, their divine wisdom and black magic evolved to better help them survive in this new land. According to Mr. Riley, there are Keepers all over the country with powers that fall outside the usual divine wisdom/black magic binary. Riley's divine wisdom has specialized into healing powers, while Roxy's ancestor was an obayifo, which gives her a connection to the dead. Her powers remained dormant until I came to town and dragged her to Asamando, where the ghosts loved her so much they basically tried to crown her their new queen.

So, while Roxy may not be a full blood-drinking obayifo like me, I guess she's impervious to direct black magic attacks. That was something I didn't even consider when I wiped everyone's memories because I was too busy panicking over my own powers bursting to life.

"I was so confused when I woke up in the forest and no one else remembered who you were or all the things we had done together," says Roxy, confirming my suspicions. "I tried to find Boulder, but your parents brought him with them to DC. It took me weeks, but I finally figured out the right combination of Adinkra to undo the spell on everyone else."

Whoa, undoing a memory erasure on multiple people is . . . a huge deal. Especially when someone's had minimal training. If the Abomofuo had any idea how powerful my cousin is . . .

Roxy continues. "Your parents have been coming back to my place every couple of days to see if maybe you'd returned to Rocky Gorge. That was why I picked up your dad's phone when you called the other day. Do you know how hard it was pretending in front of Auntie and Uncle and Boulder that I knew nothing about the Abomofuo? And my poor mom, who has no idea what's going on!"

My cousin's glare is too hot to meet, so I turn to Mateo and ask, "If Roxy undid the memory wipe, then when you saw me here yesterday morning, you knew who I was?"

He nods. "I wanted t-to say something but couldn't. B-b-but I figured you'd be here t-t-tonight, even though you said you wouldn't, and we came up with a plan to t-t-ry to talk to you."

They all stare at me, clearly awaiting their long-deserved explanation. I look down at my too-tight borrowed dress shoes. So many words in the world, but when you need them most, they leave you.

"Sorry," I mumble.

Roxy's face twists with pure outrage.

"Sorry? Sorry?! You leave us in the woods without our memories, you disappear for weeks with nothing but a super-freaky phone call, and all you have to say for yourself is *sorry*?" she screams.

Eunju nods along. It's amazing to see how shared anger at me brought two ex-best friends closer than ever. Maybe Declan was right—I *should* be a therapist. "What is going on, Serwa?" she demands. "Why did you do that to us?"

"Did you have something to do with the blackout?" Gavin chimes in.

"What happened to your f-f-fangs?" Mateo asks quietly.

More lies bubble up in my throat. A part of me still thinks with the right one, I can weasel my way out of this. Things were already bad when I left my friends behind; I can't tell the truth and get them even more involved in this mess now that it's gotten worse.

But . . . they came to find me. Even though I hurt them, and even though they're rightfully angry as all get-out, when my friends thought I was in trouble, they came. If that's not deserving of the truth, then what is?

"There's something I need to tell you. Something I didn't know myself until the day before I left Rocky Gorge."

Careful, Serwa, mutters the voice I now know is coming from Asamando, but I ignore it. Heart pounding in my throat, I pull tight on every thread of magic within me.

And I drop my mask.

When I open my eyes again, they're crimson red. Eunju lets out a little squeak of terror, and Gavin flinches, while Mateo and Roxy stare at the fangs protruding over my lower lip. It feels like I'm standing in front of them naked. No, worse than naked—it feels like my chest's been ripped open, and now my heart is completely vulnerable in all its squishy, mushy glory. There's no going back from this reveal, not this time.

But I don't want to go back. And I can't move forward if I don't do this.

"I'm an obayifo." I force myself to look into each of my friends' eyes even though all my instincts scream at me to climb into a toilet and hide. "I always have been, but I didn't know it because my parents put a seal on me when I was a baby to suppress my black magic. But the seal is broken now and . . . and . . . here I am."

I then launch into a speed-run recap of everything that's happened between me leaving them at Sweetieville Amusement Park and us communing in a bathroom after knocking out a beloved member of the DC Metro Area Ghanaian community. When I finish, there is Complete. Silence.

Then Gavin goes, "OH MY GOD, YOU LIKE DECLAN AMANKWAH!"

My face goes hotter than Mount Vesuvius right before it barbecued Pompeii. "How is that the part of the story you're focusing on?!"

"Because it's the part that's freaking hilarious!"

"Wait, wait, was he at dinner?" asks Eunju. "Which one was Declan?"

"I think he was sitting at the t-t-table next to Serwa," answers Mateo.

"Oooh, he was cute!" says Eunju while Gavin nods along.

Roxy pulls a face. "Eh, I've seen cuter."

"Serwa Amankwah . . . Serwa Amankwah Boateng . . ." muses Gavin. "Hey, if you get a middle name that starts with *T* and then add his name to yours, your initials would be S-T-A-B. Stab."

"Why would she want her initials to spell *stab*?" asks Eunju.

"Who WOULDN'T want their initials to spell *stab*?"

"Serwa's m-middle name already starts with an *A*," mutters Mateo. Now I'm flushing for a different reason. He remembered my middle name's Acheampomaa? I think I only told them that once. I didn't realize Mateo paid such close attention to me. "She d-d-doesn't—she doesn't need Declan for that."

"Can we please focus, people?" I butt in. Not that this hasn't been incredibly awkward for everybody involved, but I've been away from the table for way too long. My parents are gonna start looking for me soon, if they haven't already. "Forget my initials. How do you feel about the . . . the vampire thing?"

My friends look at one another and then Mateo asks gently, "How d-do *you* feel about it?"

How do *I* feel?

For weeks, I've been so focused on what being an obayifo meant for my mom and Auntie Effi and their screwed-up history that I never really thought about what it means to me. I haven't loved constantly running for my life, and I don't think I'm ever going to enjoy needing blood to survive.

But between all the fear and anxiety, breaking the seal on my black magic has led to some incredible moments, too. I got to know my aunt and become part of a community of powerful, magical women, like Zuri.

"I feel like . . . like . . . this is a big change, but I'd rather stay like this than go back to how I was before," I say, and despite all the pain being an obayifo has caused me, I mean it. "It really isn't all bad! Like, I basically have night vision and super strength now! And my fangs are so sharp, I'll never have to buy scissors again!"

My fingers move to touch the spot behind my right ear where the seal once was. For so many years I used to rub that spot when I was nervous or overwhelmed. I thought it was just a tic, but now I know it was because deep down, I sensed a part of me was missing. Me regaining my black magic was inevitable—while I wish it had happened in a less catastrophic way, my true self was always going to come out no matter how hard the world tried to shove her down.

"And for the first time ever, I feel . . . complete. Like I'm the person I'm supposed to be. Or on the path to becoming her, at least."

There's nothing scarier than putting your heart in other people's hands not knowing if they're going to protect it or rip it to shreds. I didn't realize how much I was bracing for the worst until Gavin says, "We're not mad at you for being a vampire, Serwa."

"You're not?"

"Of course not," chimes in Eunju. "How can we be upset about something we didn't know?"

"We're m-m-mad at you because you abandoned us!" says Mateo.

"You used magic on us without our permission to take something you had no right to steal!" Roxy adds,

"I didn't know what else to do!" I say. "And I didn't think you'd want to be around me anymore—"

"That's right, you *didn't* think!" Roxy's voice cracks with emotion. "How were we supposed to prove you could trust us when you had already decided for us that we didn't?"

Frustration bubbles up inside me. Why can't I make them understand that all I wanted to do was protect them? Why can't they—

. . .

Oh gods.

I sound exactly like my parents justifying why they had to seal up my black magic in the first place.

The realization rocks through me like a lightning strike. I've spent so many weeks mad at my parents for making decisions about my life without my consent, and here I am defending why it was okay for me to do the same thing to my friends.

"You're right," I say, lowering my head in shame. "About all of it. I'm scared, but that wasn't an excuse. I know it's not enough, but I'm sorry. I'm so, so sorry."

When I lift my head again, my voice is barely above a whisper. "And I know I have no right to ask this, but all I want is one day when you can trust the new Serwa as much as you did the old one."

Sometimes, fighting with people you care about makes everything worse.

But every now and then, a fight is exactly what you need to break through the resentment to reach the understanding on the other side.

After a long beat of silence, Roxy finally nods. "Thank you."

With that, the tension leaks out of the room. Gavin breaks out in a grin. "Well, seeing as new Serwa hasn't tried to tamper with our minds yet, I say she's already at least a forty-six percent improvement over the old one."

Mateo nods vigorously. "You're our f-f-friend. No f-f-fangs can change that." He lets out a small gulp as his eyes flick to my mouth again. "Even if they are super sharp."

Eunju punches me in the shoulder with juuust a little bit more force than necessary. "But for real, if you ever try to erase my memories ever again, I'll sic Dubu on you." Eunju's dog once ate a sacred magic item, so that's a very real threat.

"We trust you. Just like you should've trusted us," says Roxy, though her smile is tight.

Okay, ouch, that stings, but I deserve it.

"But the real question is," Roxy continues, "do we need to worry about you going all"— her voice takes on what has to be the world's worst Dracula accent—" 'I vant to suck your blood!' on us?"

"No! I've never bitten anyone, and I don't plan to!" I'm still uncomfortably aware of every flutter of my friends' hearts, but my self-control is way better now than it was when I first broke my seal. I'll have to drink more blood eventually, but I'll rob a blood bank before I ever hurt anyone.

"Okay," says Mateo. "I g-g-guess we have t-t-to take your word for it." He rubs his neck nervously.

"One more thing," Gavin interjects. "What did you do with our wristbands?"

After our mission in Asamando, Asaase Yaa gifted each of my friends with a magic wristband that let them control one of the elements—air for Mateo, water for Gavin, fire for Eunju, and earth for Roxy. The wristbands have been with my belongings at the Luciole ever since the blackout, and said belongings are now in the custody of the Abomofuo after the raid on the hotel. I explain as much to the others.

"They have no right to keep those," says Roxy. "Those wristbands are ours." That was more than just a magic object to my cousin—it was a connection to her patron deity Asaase Yaa, and more importantly, her deported father, who raised her on the myths and legends of Ghana.

"I'll get them back for you, I promise," I say. "But there's something more important than the wristbands right now, and that's the Midnight Drum."

There's no way I'm getting out of this museum on my own. But with my friends here, retrieving the Midnight Drum suddenly doesn't feel so impossible anymore. They seem sympathetic when I explain Nana Bekoe's true history with the Abomofuo and how the organization aided the death of my aunt. We might be just a bunch of kids, but we see the injustice more easily than a lot of the adults around us seem to.

"You're sure it's in Asamando?" asks Gavin.

I nod. "Remember when we were down there, and I just completely zoned out? I think that was the drum calling to me even though I didn't realize it. I need to tell my aunt. Help me break her out of the museum, and I promise as soon as we have the drum, I'll get your wristbands back for you."

"But last time we could only access the underworld because of Asaase Yaa," chimes in Eunju. "How are you going to get there without her?"

That is a very excellent question that I very much do not have an answer for. We don't have the time or materials to construct another makeshift altar to the earth goddess, and even if we did, something tells me she'd ask for something outrageous—like for us to free all the pandas from the National Zoo or become vegan or something—in exchange for her help. But I'm also not the biggest fan of dying, which is the other way to get to the underworld (as long as you're okay with not coming back).

We're all stewing over my *getting into the underworld without having to unalive ourselves* problem when Mateo's eyes light up. To Roxy, he says, "You still have that vial Antoa g-g-gave you?"

Roxy nods, pulls a small bottle of yellow liquid from her pocket, and hands it to me. "Never leave home without it! Mostly because I almost put it through the laundry once," she admits sheepishly.

My cousin won the vial from Antoa Nyamaa, the Akan goddess of justice and retribution. The bottle contains pure, unfiltered divine wisdom that can create anything without needing Adinkra to power it, though Antoa warned us it'll only work once.

"This came straight from a goddess. If it won't open a portal to Asamando, nothing will," I say, turning the vial over in my hands and deciding not to think about how the golden liquid looks a lot like pee.

"Okay, you have a how, but what about a where?" asks Gavin.

"You said magic is strongest near water, right?" asks Eunju.

I nod, and all our eyes fall simultaneously to the toilet bowl. Technically it *could* . . . Nope, no way, absolutely not. The few standards I still have are telling me to draw the line at toilet travel.

Also, if I'm wrong and the vial isn't enough to get me all the way to Asamando, I really don't want to be fished out of the plumbing.

"There's the fountain here on the bottom floor?" suggests Roxy.

I shake my head, imagining the circular layers of the museum's floor above our heads and the secret magical layer below us. "Too out in the open. We'd get caught right away."

"The Enid A. Haupt G-G-Garden!" exclaims Mateo. At our blank looks, he sighs. "Didn't *anyone* read the b-b-brochure Mr. Riley gave us?"

We all shake our heads. He sighs again. "The famous garden b-b-between the museum and the castle?"

"Oh, I know what you're talking about!" I exclaim. "I was up there with Declan yesterday."

"You were up there with Declan!" sings Gavin. If I didn't need his help, I'd shove him straight into the toilet.

"There are a l-l-lot of fountains up there. Those should work," Mateo continues, and I'm grateful there's at least one person in this group who isn't determined to roast me over my stupid crush.

"To be clear, *just* you are going to Asamando this time, right?" asks Eunju.

I nod. "Free Auntie Effi. Get to the garden. Get to Asamando. Get the drum," I repeat. It's not much of a plan, but I've pulled off more with less. Plus, it keeps my friends out of trouble. As for my parents, well . . .

Maybe I understand their choices a little better now, but that doesn't change the fact that the Abomofuo aren't as perfect as they wanted me to believe. Freeing Nana Bekoe is the first step to righting so many of the group's wrongs.

"First, let's try to get my aunt out of her holding place. Everyone ready?"

Nods all around. We take a minute to readjust ourselves, and I change my eyes and retract the fangs so I'm once again totally-not-a-vampire Serwa. We got this. We can do this. We have a chance as long as we have a plan. . . .

A plan that immediately goes awry when a several-ton, two-headed crocodile bursts its head through the restroom door and screams, "YOU GUYS KILLED MY GRANDPA!"

26

How to Ride a Crocodile

"At times when stealth is not an option, making a scene often achieves the same results."

—From the *Nwoma*

ALL RIGHT, I'LL ADMIT it: I forgot all about Funtunfunefu-Denkyemfunefu. That's my bad. This one's on me.

"Grandpa?" mouth the others, but there's no time now to explain that Declan created this metal monstrosity, which is why it is understandably upset at the fact we attacked his technical grandfather, Declan's dad. The crocodile swipes a clawed foot through the bathroom door, taking out one of the sinks in its attempt to get at us. My friends and I press ourselves against the wall, as far as we can get from the flailing metal.

"Uh, any ideas, Serwa?" calls Eunju as Funtunfunefu-Denkyemfunefu strikes the mirror and glass goes flying everywhere.

"Give me a second!"

A crocodile snout replaces the arm, and Funtunfunefu-Denkyemfunefu gets one of its heads all the way through the door before it can't go any farther. Still, it's long enough for its teeth to snap and gnash in our direction.

"Grandpa was one of my two favorite people!" cries Righty. "He always told me stories of the world outside the museum! Now I have fifty percent fewer favorite people! That's less than half!"

"Your math's n-n-not—" Mateo begins, stepping forward, but I yank him back, because correcting the angry metal reptile doesn't seem like it'll help our predicament. Out of the corner of my eye, I see Eunju peel herself off the wall and slowly head toward the monster.

"Eunju, don't!" I cry, but she ignores me to walk directly into the creature's biting range, hands out like a zookeeper trying to calm an enraged beast.

"You've never left the museum?" she asks.

Righty nods, cracking the doorframe in the process. "All the other art was made outside and brought here, but we were made in here. We've never even walked all the way to the top floor," Righty moans. "We've never seen the sun! Never eaten a hot dog!"

"Never strolled full of melancholy down the Champs-Élysées at midnight with the moonlight washing over our scales," chimes in Lefty's voice from the hallway.

"How do they even know what that is?" mutters Roxy, and Mateo and Gavin and I just shrug.

When Eunju finally makes it to Righty, she starts rubbing the croc's snout. "Poor babies. That must be so lonely," she croons in the same voice she uses whenever she's petting her dog, Dubu. "You don't want to hurt us at all, do you? You're a big softie—er, softies, aren't you?"

And would you believe it, Righty actually nods, tears brimming in its eyes. Eunju moves to scratch its chin, and a *thump-thump-thump* fills the hall outside—it sounds like she's got

Funtunfunefu-Denkyemfunefu wagging its tail like some kind of giant golden retriever.

"Who's a good boy? Who's a good boy?"

"I am! I am!"

"Wait, me too!" cries Lefty, and there's some awkward shuffling and maneuvering until Lefty has poked its head into the bathroom for scratches, too. Eunju shoots me a quick glance over her shoulder. That's my cue.

"We want the same thing you do—to leave the museum," I say. "Why don't you come with us? We can show you the world!"

"Shining, shimmering, splendid!" Roxy adds behind me while Mateo and Gavin nod vigorously.

"But Dad might get sad if we leave our post," mumbles Lefty.

"Pleaaaaaaaase?" asks Eunju, and now she's got Lefty's tongue lolling out of its mouth from how hard she's rubbing its chin.

"Oh, why not," Lefty finally acquiesces. "The universe as we know it is on an inevitable, unstoppable crash course toward oblivion anyway. Might as well enjoy ourselves while we still can."

"Yippee, I've always wanted to be a delinquent!" cheers Righty. "Climb aboard, kids!"

Funtunfunefu-Denkyemfunefu backs up, allowing the five of us to run out of the bathroom and clamber onto it. I sit behind Righty's head while Eunju and Roxy take Lefty, with Mateo and Gavin in the rear.

"How'd you know that would work?" I yell to Eunju as the crocodile begins the ungainly task of turning itself around to reach the stairs. It's not easy to maneuver yourself when you're bigger than a semitruck.

"I know a dog when I see one. This thing's just a puppy with scales!" she yells back, patting Lefty's head for good measure.

For my sixth birthday, my parents took me to a petting zoo where I rode a pony for the first—and so far only—time in my life. Riding Funtunfunefu-Denkyemfunefu feels just like that, minus the saddle, or the reins, or the fur, or any of the other things about riding a pony. But aside from all that, it's basically the same!

"Can you get us into the Abomofuo's exhibit hall? I need to get my aunt!" I tell the crocodile. In response, it starts lumbering down the stairs, plowing through the rope barrier to the bottom floor.

Mateo lets out a groan at our bumpy ride, wrapping his arms around my waist and pressing his face into my back. Even after our time apart, the interaction feels so natural. "I think I'm gonna be sick."

"If you have to hurl, do it on the priceless art, not me!" I cry.

At the bottom floor, when we reach the spot where Funtunfunefu-Denkyemfunefu used to stand guard, both heads cry out in unison, "Pumpernickel!"

"That's the new password?" snickers Gavin.

"Maybe Serwa's future husband really likes bread," adds Eunju.

"I literally hate all of you!" I scream as the door to the exhibit reveals itself in all its creepy-eye-covered glory. But so does another problem: There is no way we are getting Lefty and Righty through this door. Either Auntie Effi has to somehow find her way up to us, or we have to abandon the safety of the crocodile and go in there and get her ourselves.

"Auntie Effi!" I yell down. No response.

I'm debating which action to take when a voice screams

from the central staircase, "Serwa! Stop this right this instant!"

A whole contingent of Slayers are running from the upper floors down to where we are,

Mom and Dad leading the pack. There's no time to fetch my aunt now; I have to trust that at least with the door open, we've given her enough aid to get out on her own.

"Sorry!" I cry to my parents before directing Funtunfunefu-Denkyemfunefu to dive straight through the oncoming onslaught. It does so, and the Slayers all dive out of the way as the crocodile barrels through them in a mad dash to the exit on the ground floor above us. Righty and Lefty may have a single working brain cell between the two of them, but they are also the work of an extremely powerful enchantment. As we go higher and higher toward freedom, the effect of this magic rolls over all the other art in the museum, bringing it to life in similar ways. Sensing that magic shenanigans are afoot, some of the artifacts and artwork start cheering for our escape.

"To freedom!" yells a seven-foot-tall serpent mask hanging on one of the walls.

"Send us a postcard from the outside!" yells a dancing woman from a painting. Several clay figurines even pick themselves up off their platforms to run under the Slayers' feet, tripping a few of them. The civilians who managed to get out of the main event hall yell and scream at the sight; the Abomofuo are going to have a field day mind-wiping them later. The whole thing is chaotic, magical, and somehow the most fun I've had in a long time.

That is, until people start shooting crossbow bolts at me.

"DUCK!" I yell as a bolt whizzes past my face to embed itself in a sculpture of a little boy carrying a basket on his head.

"Actually, I prefer geese," replies Righty. "The higher fat content gives it that delicious oomph."

"Everyone knows duck roasts better!" snaps Lefty.

"Can the two of you argue about this later?" I cry.

Another bolt flies past and hits one of the crocodile's legs. It regains its balance, but not before stumbling so hard Gavin slips off its back, accidentally pulling Mateo down with him.

"Gavin! Mateo!" cries Roxy.

"We gotta go back for them!" yells Eunju.

"No time—hang on tight!" yells Righty. The crocodile leaps from the banister onto a tapestry, then swings up to the second floor from the top like a scaly Tarzan. Forced to take the normal route, Gavin and Mateo run for their lives up the spiral staircase, the Slayers in hot pursuit. I might be their main target, but they're not letting my friends out of here without mind-wiping them first.

"I knew I should've tr-tr-tried harder in gym class!" screams Mateo.

"Less yelling, more running!" wheezes Gavin.

We finally make it to the last flight of stairs leading up to the ground level. "There's the exit!" I yell, but it's quickly clear there's no way Funtunfunefu-Denkyemfunefu is going to fit through the glass doors.

"Brace yourselves!" yells Lefty. Eunju, Roxy, and I all duck as Funtunfunefu-Denkyemfunefu crashes headfirst through the door, taking down a good chunk of the wall in the process. The ensuing cloud of dust sends us all into coughing fits, but we're outside!

"Thank you so much!" I yell as Roxy, Eunju, and I scramble off the crocodile.

"Good luck, little obayifo!" says Righty. "We'll send you a souvenir from Paris!"

"Only if the shipping rates aren't as horribly inflated as everything else in this dismal economy," adds Lefty.

With that, Funtunfunefu-Denkyemfunefu runs off toward the National Mall. The Slayers switch paths to follow it, because a giant walking, talking two-headed crocodile gallivanting around the monuments is a *way* bigger problem for them than a few stray kids. Not only that, several of the pieces in the museum are attempting to make a similar grand escape. Masks fly through the air toward the Capitol building, and there is one moving garment composed of Ankara print and tinkling bells trying to tuck itself into the basket of a Capital Bikeshare. My friends and I take advantage of the general confusion to slip into the garden.

Compared to the chaos near the museum's entrance, the Enid A. Haupt Garden is eerily calm. The largest source of water across the four acres is in the Moongate Garden, located between two nine-foot-tall pink granite gates. The square pool on the ground is bisected by two stone paths, separating the water into four distinct sections with a large bowl in the center. I turn to face my friends.

"I guess this is where we part ways," I say awkwardly.

"Yeah," says Eunju. "We need to find Mr. Riley before the man has an aneurysm."

"And somehow convince him that the entire museum looking like a scene from *Chicken Run* isn't our fault," adds Gavin.

Only now do I realize I was secretly hoping my friends would change their minds and decide to accompany me to Asamando just like old times. But I can't blame them for being cautious, especially seeing as how we barely got out of there last time. I've taken a step toward fixing things with them, but there's no guarantee things will be the way they were ever again.

With nothing else to say, I bring my attention to the vial and the fountain. I've never used pure divine wisdom before, so I have no idea how this is going to work. Using my knowledge of Akan spiritual traditions as a guide, I press my palm to the fountains and give a quick prayer to Antoa to thank her for her assistance and ask for her aid in entering Asamando one more time. Then I pour a few drops of the vial into one of the sections of the fountain.

To my surprise, all four sections start glowing faintly. I pour the rest of the vial in, and soon the whole pool is glowing golden. The five of us anxiously watch the golden light flicker and swirl until an image of swaying palm trees and a long, star-flecked river comes into view. Yes, that's Asamando! It worked!

I step in front of the fountain. On the count of three, I'll jump in.

One . . .

Two . . .

On three, the bowl at the center of the Moongate Garden cracks open. My friends and I huddle together in alarm as another bolt hits the bowl, shattering it completely. The quadrants flicker wildly between regular water and Asamando, the portals no longer stable now that the structure is crumbling.

Behind us, Declan stalks into the garden with his crossbow in hand. "This ends now, witch," he seethes.

I hate how even now a part of me does a weird little flutter when I see him. I'll definitely need to unpack that later.

Roxy puts herself between us, teeth bared. "Don't you talk to her like that!" she yells.

As much as I love my cousin for standing up for me, there's no way she or any of the others would walk away from a match with Declan unharmed. And if he captures them, they are going to be in a world of trouble when the Abomofuo realize Roxy has the ability to break through mind-wipes.

My first instinct is to push my friends through the portals, but I force it back. If I'm going to do better than my parents and the Okomfo, then I need to let people make their own choices.

"The portals," I say to them quickly. "You can jump through so they don't catch you and mind-wipe you again."

"But you said we didn't have to come this time!" Eunju protests.

"I know what I said!" I cry. "But it's either the portals or the Slayers—you pick!"

Declan fires another crossbow bolt into the fountain, which destabilizes the portals further. Gavin looks between Declan and the underworld, and he's the first to decide that the former is way scarier than the latter. He jumps into one of the quadrants, and as soon as he's gone, the water returns to normal. Eunju groans but she goes next, pinching her nose and jumping like she's taking a high dive. Mateo and Roxy both approach one of the portals together, but the water buzzes and froths until they back away. The implication is clear—only one person per portal.

Mateo pulls at the sleeve of his nice dress shirt, looking at me in concern. "There's t-two more portals and three of us," he says with a gulp.

I give him what I hope is an encouraging smile. "Good to know you can still count, smarty-pants," I say with an affectionate bump to his shoulder. "Don't worry about me. I can take care of myself."

That seems to be enough for both Roxy and Mateo. They each take the last two portals, not without concerned glances over their shoulders.

But then they're both gone, leaving just me and a boy who trusts me even less than I trust him.

"Don't move!" barks Declan, his crossbow pointed at me as

I slowly turn to face him. I don't need my heightened senses to see the way his hands shake around his weapon. Even after everything, he doesn't want to hurt me.

I turn my back to the fountain, where the last traces of Antoa's magic leave the water flickering weakly. I take a step toward him, and then another when he doesn't pull the trigger. "You don't have to do this, Declan."

"Stay back!" he warns.

I'm not sure where the other Slayers are, but right now, they don't matter. It's just us, and if there's a chance I can reach him, I have to try. He's aiming for my shoulder, not any of my vital regions; he only intends to slow me down, not kill me. But a wound from that thing is still going to hurt real bad no matter where it lands.

"I'm sorry I used you to get the password for the exhibit hall." I'm only a foot away from him now. Declan's close enough to shoot me straight in the heart. We both know that he won't. "But even though I lied about why I was there, everything I said on the trampoline . . . I meant every word. I wasn't lying about any of that, even if you were."

"I wasn't lying." His voice is so soft it's hard to hear him over the pounding of my own heart. "What I said about trying to be your friend when we were growing up . . . that was all true."

"We can still be friends." I'm inches away from him now, closer than we were on the trampoline. "Put down the bow. We don't have to fight just because they say that's what Slayers and obayifo are supposed to do."

Declan's breath hitches. He slowly starts to lower the weapon, and my heart swells. If I can reach him, then maybe, just maybe—

"Declan!" calls Dr. Amankwah from somewhere outside the

garden. The man must finally be back on his feet after Roxy knocked him out.

At the sound of his father's voice, something shutters in Declan's face. He lifts the bow again, his finger moving to the trigger.

The next few seconds feel like they happen in slow motion. Declan presses the trigger on the crossbow, but in the same instant some primal survival instinct in me takes over. I shove my elbow into his gut, and the shot goes wide. Declan and I both tumble to the ground, crossbow clattering to the stone beside us. I recover first, scrambling to my feet with a surge of terror and bloodlust rushing through my veins.

I take one look at the exposed skin at the side of Declan's neck and grab him by the shirt.

Then I bite.

27

How to Go Too Far

"Those who jump without looking do not get to complain about where they land."

—From the *Nwoma*

AUNTIE EFFI WAS RIGHT: Fresh blood *is* better.

Its effect on me is like what happened at the theater times 1000 percent. My black magic is an engine, and for the first time ever, it's firing on all cylinders. A purple haze consumes my senses as the power in me builds to a crescendo. There should be guilt—over biting Declan, over breaking my promise to my friends and myself—but right now, there is nothing but pure, undiluted power, and it's *mine*.

Without a second glance, I drop Declan to the ground and dive into the fountain. There, my own teleportation abilities latch on to the last remnants of Antoa's magic still swirling through the water. The two amplify one another, creating a wall of force that tosses me around like a doll trapped in a hurricane. The last thing I see is a vortex of light closing in on all sides.

And then I'm gone.

ASAMANDO IS EERILY QUIET when I land butt-over-heels in some kind of darkened room. I let out a groan as the rush of power that brought me to the underworld is quickly replaced by horror.

I just bit Declan Amankwah.

Oh my gods.

I have to stop myself from licking away the dribble of his blood running down my chin.

I feel weirdly . . . numb? That's a good sign, right? Because numb is better than freaking out about doing the one vampire thing I swore I would never, ever do. Besides, it was self-defense. Declan was going to hurt me; I hurt him first. It was him or me. I feel like my picker for what is right and wrong has gotten so wildly out of whack, all I have anymore is the bad choice versus the worse one.

Nyame help me, what if I killed him? Or turned him into a vampire? Wait, I need to calm down. Only an adze can turn other people into vampires, and there's no way I drank enough blood to kill him. He'll be fine . . . eventually.

Even if he won't be, too much has happened now to turn back. Declan and I are never going to be friends, or anything more, no matter what we said to each other at the fountain.

I have a bigger problem right now: I have no idea where I am or where the rest of the GCC went. A second inspection of my surroundings reveals kitschy floral wallpaper and woven hangings with slogans like BLESS THIS MESS! and DON'T GO BACON MY HEART. Am I in someone's farmhouse? But this is definitely Asamando—I can see the underworld's perpetual twilight through the open window, and feel the pull of the Midnight Drum stronger than ever.

But where are my friends?

I exit the room onto a wide wraparound porch. Yep, this is definitely a farmhouse. At least there's no sign of Amokye, the guardian of the underworld. Antoa's magic must be stronger than Amokye's because I can see the river glittering in the distance. I'm really glad I don't have to deal with the threshold guardian, but unlike last time, I don't have a clear way to return to the mortal world. Even if I find the others, will I be able to teleport all five of us home?

Well, one problem at a time.

My connection to the drum pulls me off the porch and deeper into the grounds. Here, the trees are cracked and gray; sap runs down their bark like tears. The earth is scorched to the point where nothing new can grow.

"Eunju?" I call out softly into the oppressive gloom. "Mateo? Gavin? Roxy?"

Nothing. No sign of my friends; no sign of the Midnight Drum.

So close, Serwa. Keep going.

The trees finally thin out into a wide field of tall, thick grass. Various wispy blue spirits stalk the land, harvesting the plants. I'm pretty sure there's a myth regarding spirits and a farm, but for the life of me I can't remember what it is. (Hey, *you* try memorizing every single legend and dozens of Adinkra without forgetting any. It's not easy!)

"Excuse me?" I call out to the closest spirit. "I'm looking for—"

"WAAAAAAAAAAAAAAAAAAH," the poor creature screams before immediately poofing away in a mini tornado. I sigh. Usually people at least let me introduce myself before they run off screaming.

The same thing happens with every other spirit I approach. The second they notice me, they disappear in a burst of wind.

Okay, something's really off about this place. Spirits in the underworld are hardly that unusual, but the energy of this farm is unlike anything I've ever felt before.

The pull of the Midnight Drum brings me to the very edge of the field, where grass meets forest again. There is a large barn-shaped structure with a thatched roof. Loud sounds of banging and drilling are coming from within.

I knock on the door, though I have no idea how whoever is inside is going to hear me through all that noise.

"H-hello?" I call out. "Excuse me, but I'm looking for directions."

A big crash, followed by a stream of cursing, fills the air. "You threw off my groove!" screams a deep voice. "Ugh, fine, come in, come in!"

I don't get a chance to follow the command, because Asamando does it for me. The ground pitches like a wave beneath my feet, sending me careening into the barn. Rows of storage shelves line the mud-brick walls. They're filled with large objects, each one about as tall as a person.

Wait . . . not *about*. Every single one *is* person-sized, though the exteriors are different.

Coffins. I am in a building filled with coffins.

Specifically, I'm in a building filled with efunu adaka, fantasy coffins. Many Ga people in Ghana believe that because a person's existence continues in the afterlife, their coffin should reflect something important about their personality for the journey. I see coffins carved to look like animals, such as lions and elephants; one that reminds me of an iPhone; and even a coffin in the shape of a giant doughnut.

At a worktable in the center of the barn stands a man muttering to himself as he runs a sander over a large hunk of wood.

With sinking dread, I realize *exactly* where I am and who is here with me.

In my haste to escape Declan and grab the Midnight Drum, I teleported myself straight onto Death's farm.

Owuo lifts his head and squints one glowing eye at me. Guess I'm dealing with the cyclops version today. He's shorter than I expected, stockier and squatter than two of his siblings, Tano and Bia. "You'd better have a good reason for interrupting me when I'm— Wait, Serwa Boateng? Is that you?"

Cool, the sadistic god of death knows who I am. Cool. Cool, cool, cool.

"I am so sorry to intrude upon your domain, Nana Owuo," I say hurriedly.

"Nonsense. I've been expecting you! Pardon the clutter. Come in, come in."

The god of death ushers me inside. A checkered tablecloth appears on the worktable beneath the unfinished coffin, and a pot of tea and a plate of cookies materializes on top of it. Owuo procures two chairs out of thin air and pushes me into one. "Please, help yourself! Teleporting across the fabric of reality always works up such an appetite!"

I swallow thickly as I nervously glance at the desserts. "Are those . . . Um, are there any . . . 'human by-products' in those?"

Owuo's face falls. "You feed a boy the flesh of his own sister *one time*, and suddenly you're the bad guy! Though I'm not sure why a vampire such as yourself would turn away such a delicacy." The god twirls the other chair around and sits in it with the back facing me like an adult trying to prove he's "hip" and "with it." "Anyway, what can I help you with today, my fine fanged friend?"

All right, I am officially freaked out. The Owuo in the stories

I was told growing up was a sadistic murderer who reveled in the pain and suffering of others. That's the kind of being I'd expect to be guarding the Midnight Drum, not Old MacDonald over here. The man in front of me is wearing a faded T-shirt, cloth shorts, a floral sun hat, and a thick leather apron that reads DEATH'S NO EXCUSE TO BE A BUMMER!

"Have you seen four kids about my age come by here?" I ask. Even though finding the drum is my main objective, I'm not doing that until I know my friends are safe.

"Seen them? Why, they're right over there!" Owuo waves a hand toward four unmarked coffins lined up in a row against a wall. A small window opens in each one, revealing the faces of Eunju, Mateo, Roxy, and Gavin frozen mid-scream.

I let out a strangled cry. "You— You—"

"Killed them?" Owuo shakes his head. "No, I have nothing to gain from their deaths—not now, at least. They're simply suspended for the time being as I thought it would be better for the two of us to speak in private."

A closer inspection shows that my friends' eyes are still moving even in their frozen state. Bile sloshes around my stomach, but I force myself to meet Owuo's gaze. The god hasn't killed them yet, but that doesn't mean he won't. If we're all going to get out of this alive, I need to play his little game.

"Do you happen to know where I can find the Midnight Drum?" I ask through gritted teeth. Even now, the drum is calling to me, pulling me forward, but I don't dare take my attention away from Owuo.

"Lucky for you, I happen to have exactly one drum, and it's midnight colored!"

"I see. Can I have it?"

"Absolutely not!" Owuo's smile grows wider. Having the

full force of it turned my way makes me feels like a mosquito trapped under a thousand-power microscope. "Do you know you're the third generation of your abusua to seek my aid, young Serwa?"

Abusua is the Twi word for *family*, specifically your maternal line. I blink in surprise. "You've met my mom and my grandmother?"

"Yes, Nana Bekoe came to me after your aunt, Abena, passed. Oh, what a state she was in! I have never seen such grief and rage so tightly woven together! She wanted power to rival that of the enemies who destroyed her child. And, being the source of all black magic, I of course gave it to her . . . for a price."

Owuo stands up, pulls a rag from his apron pocket, and starts wiping down his worktable without a care in the world. "So, imagine my surprise when, several decades later, one of her *other* children arrives, this time asking for a power that can stop the very same mother I aided before! I've had many people seek my assistance against their enemies, but never their own family. It was all so fascinating that I obliged, and that's how the Midnight Drum was born—with a pinch of divine wisdom, of course. And then, a few years ago, when the daughter bargained with me to hide it for her, I agreed."

If I have my timeline correct, Mom was a teenager when Nana Bekoe was finally defeated. It's easy to imagine a version of her, only a little older than me, trying to negotiate with a god who I'm starting to realize is several Froot Loops short of a full cereal bowl, if you know what I mean.

"And now here *you* are, trying to undo the actions of your *own* mother! Oh, what a twisted little cycle we've found ourselves in! I'd ask my oracle how many generations this familial backstabbing might go on for, but I ate my last soothsayer for putting too much smooth jazz on my workout playlist. A pity."

"That . . . is rather unfortunate?" I reply.

But that must have been the wrong answer, because suddenly Owuo is right in front of me, tilting up my chin with a hand so ice-cold it burns. I didn't even see him move. I try to pull free, but his grip is too strong.

"You're not like the other two, are you? Fascinating, so fascinating," he mutters. "You are a wonder, Serwa Boateng. A contradiction simply by existing. There are people who have been *granted* both divine wisdom and black magic, like your mother—and she requires a seal to be able to function at all—but to have been *born* with both? It's a miracle you didn't explode at birth!" The god starts giggling uncontrollably. "Can you imagine it? A nurse pulls a newborn out of the womb, and then KABLOOIE! Tiny baby chunks everywhere! Ha!"

Anyone legitimately laughing at the thought of a dead baby would be bad enough, but after I've seen how traumatic my birth was for my dad, Owuo's disregard fills me with rage.

"You're a monster," I spit.

"I am all I ever was," Death says simply and unapologetically. "I see so much potential—so much *power*—in you, but you're out of balance. You spent twelve years leaning too far into your divine wisdom, and now you've gone too far into the black magic. Until you're truly in sync with yourself, you'll only be a shadow of what you could be."

"I already know I have both powers!" I yell. "No one ever lets me freaking forget it!"

"Ah, you say you have both, but have you truly mastered each? If you needed your divine wisdom right now, could you harness it?"

I can't, and we both know it. For all Owuo's talk of my

strength, I have never felt more powerless. "Look, enough of the mind games. Name your price for the Midnight Drum so we can get this over with."

For the first time since we arrived, the smile drops from Owuo's face. "Owuo mpɛ sika," he says in a voice colder than the depths of a crypt at midnight. *Death does not want money.* It's an old proverb warning that all the wealth in the world won't save you from dying. "I may revel in violence and suffering, but there is nothing in this world I loathe more than someone who thinks they can buy their way out of the inevitable."

My heart is racing so fast I might pass out. No amount of training in the world could've ever prepared me for something like this, but I can't just say whatever I want with my friends' lives on the line. "I'm sorry, I didn't mean—"

"There is no payment you can offer me for the Midnight Drum. But I'm willing to trade you for it." The god of death snaps his fingers, and suddenly the four coffins holding my friends begin to shrink. He must have removed the suspended animation on them as well because they all start to scream at once.

"Serwa!"

"It's a trap! Don't listen to him!"

"Four friends and only one of you! Who are you going to save, Serwa?" cackles Owuo. "Last time you walked through my domain, it was with Asaase Yaa's blessing, but she won't help you now!"

I run to the nearest coffin—Mateo's—and start clawing at it, but then I whirl around when I hear Roxy calling my name. The coffins are shrinking too fast—there are probably only a few minutes left until my friends are pulverized inside, if they don't run out of air first. But by the time I pry one of them open, the other three will definitely be crushed.

Eunju, Gavin, Roxy, Mateo—I only have time to save one. But who do I choose? *How* can I choose?

"Serwa!" Tears blur my vision as my friends scream my name.

"Just let them go, please!" I beg Owuo. I don't care about the Midnight Drum anymore. I don't care about siding with the obayifo or the Slayers. All I want is my friends safe and sound. They don't deserve to die just because they made the mistake of believing in me. "I'll do whatever you want. Please, stop this!"

"What I want is for you to choose." There's no more friendliness in the god's voice, no more cheerful farmer. Just like he said, Owuo is all he ever was—inevitable, unflinching death. "More than your blood, more than your magic, your choices will determine what you truly are."

My friends' screams are getting louder, and the world is spinning. I need to do something, but my feet won't move. I can't—*I can't* . . .

My mind goes back to that very first black magic lesson with Auntie Effi in the hotel's fitness room, back when my powers were something I feared and hated. But they're a part of me now, and when I call on them, they flare up in response to my anger and outrage at being turned into a pawn in a cruel god's game. With the screams of my friends rising in my ears, I jump into the air.

And teleport directly into the face of Death.

"I said, let them go!"

I slice my hand through the air just like Auntie Effi taught me. My black magic follows the motion in a perfect arc, and Owuo's eyes widen in surprise as his head falls one way and his body falls the other.

28

How to Make a Deal with a God

"Some costs are too high."

—From the *Nwoma*

I STAND THERE SWAYING on my feet as Owuo's head bounces underneath the table.

Nyame help me, I think I just decapitated a god.

The efunu adaka holding my friends all sag before disappearing completely. Eunju and Roxy both fall to their knees, coughing and sputtering for air, while Gavin is hyperventilating with his head in his hands. Mateo is the one who recovers first—maybe he can hold his breath longer because of his connection to the wind? I make a mental note to test that theory when we're not all fighting for our lives—and he runs to meet me halfway. We throw our arms around each other, too relieved to remember to be embarrassed.

"S-Serwa! Are you all right?" he cries.

"Me? What about you?"

"I'm okay!"

"Never better," says Eunju weakly while Roxy throws a shaky thumbs-up.

"Oh, I think my splinters have splinters," moans Gavin.

I am so angry on their behalf. They weren't even supposed to come to Asamando this time. Why is it so difficult to keep the people I care about from being used as pawns against me?

Mateo's eyes go from me to Owuo . . . er, what's left of Owuo. "Serwa, d-d-did you kill the god of death?"

"I—I think so?"

As if in response, Owuo's head lets out this high-pitched hyena laugh. "Marvelous, oh, simply marvelous!"

Like a puppet being controlled by an invisible puppeteer, Owuo's body lifts itself off the ground and twitches and jerks its way across the room to retrieve it's still-laughing head. We all gag as the god squishes his head back onto his shoulders and gives it several solid twists like a lightbulb until he's facing front again.

"I like you, Serwa Boateng," Owuo says with a chuckle. "I like you a lot. I should disembowel you all and hang you from my ceiling by your entrails for that stunt, but I've met few creatures in my eternity of existence who would even think of laying a finger on me, much less someone who would actually do it!"

Owuo gathers his arms in front of him, and a dark object about the size of a grown man's torso appears between his hands. The Midnight Drum. Like the decoy back at the museum, it's goblet-shaped and made of the purest, deepest black wood with goatskin stretched across the top. But that's where the similarities end. Most djembe drums will have Adinkra or other artwork drawn on their body, but this one has nothing. It's like a drum-shaped black hole sucking in all the light from around it.

"I made a bargain with your mother that I would protect this drum," Owuo hums. "If you want it back, you'll have to make another even more powerful than hers."

I can't even imagine what my mother promised this horrible god to get him to protect the drum, or what I have to offer that she couldn't. "What did my mom bargain away to get you to hide the drum for her?"

"Ah, now that sounds like a mother-daughter conversation to me."

I sigh. Great; more awkward conversations with my parents. Just what I need. "What do you want now?"

"I have existed since before the dawn of time. I have known so many people, each one having passed through my awareness to make it to the afterlife. Billions come, but no one ever stays. Even your parents only came because they wanted something from me, and they left once they got it."

The memory of the day my parents left me in Rocky Gorge—their car getting smaller and smaller as I stood there with no idea when we'd see each other again—flashes across my mind. My shoulders sag. "Yeah. They do that."

"That is what I require, Serwa," says the god of death. "A companion. Promise that you'll bring me someone to share these immortal days with, and I will give you the drum."

Owuo wants . . . a friend. Someone who will stay down here with him in the gloom and the dark, not living but not dying either, forever.

I can't do that. I can't rip someone away from their chance at a happy afterlife.

But I didn't come this far to leave without the drum, either.

"How long do I have to fulfill this bargain?" I ask.

Owuo clicks his tongue, deep in thought. "These days, seven is the number of power, but people forget that in the past, it was nine. That was why your people used to sacrifice the ninth child.

So, you have nine turns of seven days to bring me a soul. If you don't, I'll take yours instead."

Nine turns of seven days must mean nine weeks. I have a little over two months to bring someone to Owuo or else I'll be the one trapped with him forever. I've heard enough folktales to know that bargains like this always end badly for the people who make them. But what choice do I have? This is one fight I truly cannot punch my way out of; I may have injured Owuo's physical body, but no one can truly defeat death. I can either agree, or I can leave.

I look over at my friends, who have already sacrificed so much to help me. "Do you think I should do it?" I ask them breathlessly.

They all look at one another. Mateo and Roxy shake their heads while Gavin and Eunju reluctantly nod. Two against two. They're as torn as I am.

I turn back to Owuo and reach out my hand. "Okay," I say before I can let my nerves talk me out of this. "You have a deal. The Midnight Drum in exchange for a companion."

The god of death wraps his hand around mine, and a jolt of ice-cold fire travels up my arm and through my body. When he pulls away, there's a tattoo of a black ladder on the inside of my right elbow. It's the Adinkra owuo atwedeɛ—death's ladder—one of the few Adinkra Slayers are forbidden to draw because of its destructive power. Instead of only four rungs, this version of the symbol has nine—one for each week I have to fulfill my promise to Owuo.

Owuo hands me the drum, and I flinch, waiting for booby traps or, like, a giant boulder to appear and squash me like a bug.

Nothing happens. The god hums again.

"Remember our bargain, Serwa," the god says as he picks up his sander to return to his gruesome, never-ending work of filling the land of the dead. "Because I certainly will. Now, up the ladder you go."

Owuo snaps his fingers one last time.

And just like that, my friends and I are back in the garden with the Midnight Drum in my arms . . .

And an extremely angry Declan Amankwah standing right in front of me.

29

How to Realize the Truth Too Late

"When the time comes to take a stand,
do so with both feet planted where they need to be."

—From the *Nwoma*

"YOU BIT ME!" SCREAMS Declan, his hand flying to the puncture wounds at the side of his neck.

Huh? I blink several times like someone waking up from a dream. It felt like we were in Asamando for hours, but Owuo returned us to the exact moment I left. The only difference is that my friends are standing dazed and confused beside me, the Midnight Drum is in my hands, and the bargain I made is inked into my skin.

Now, Serwa, quickly! Let me out now!

The sound of my grandmother's voice stirs a deep longing inside me. It's the same yearning that drew me to Declan's daa and that has always craved connection with those who came before me. The Midnight Drum vibrates with power and promise in my hands, but I don't move. Warring memories flash across my mind: playing the Big Hat game with Dad; Mom teaching me how to protect myself in a world she knew would never protect me; bonding with Auntie Effi over silly crush talk; my mother and aunt holding on to each other as terrified children in Ghana, trying to please Nana Bekoe when her heart only craved revenge.

Owuo's words from earlier echo through my mind. *More than your blood, more than your magic, your choices will determine what you truly are.*

Do I free my grandmother or not? What's the right thing to do when any choice I make will honor one part of my family and break another?

My split second of hesitation is long enough for Declan to snatch the Midnight Drum from me and clutch it to his chest.

"Okomfohene Nsiah was right about you," he snarls. My friends gather around me protectively even though he could take down all four of them with minimal effort. "It's just like the Nwoma says—there really is no good witch."

It feels like someone has taken a knife to my heart and twisted it. But before I can say anything, the pull of the drum recedes from my chest as it turns its attention from me to its new holder.

Declan. Now the Midnight Drum speaks with a younger voice—one I don't recognize but Declan clearly does. His mouth falls open and his eyes glaze over.

"Mom?"

Declan, baby, it's me. Help me, please!

Black magic seeps from the drum and surrounds Declan in a haze too strong for even the nyame dua wards to repel. Right then, as I watch my grandmother worm her way into Declan Amankwah's mind, I realize it doesn't matter whether I trust the Abomofuo or the obayifo. It doesn't matter what I am or am not. The only thing that matters is that Owuo himself—a being who enjoys nothing more than despair and discord—played a part in freeing Nana Bekoe. If the god of death himself put a finger on the scale to make this encounter happen, then Nana Bekoe absolutely should not, under any circumstances, be let out of the Midnight Drum.

Declan, baby, please. I'm sorry for everything! Help me. Let me out now!

"Declan, don't!" I scream. "It's not real!"

But I'm too slow to stop him from raising a hand and playing a single, clear note on the top of the drum. The moment he does, the Midnight Drum explodes.

30

How to Meet Your Grandmother

"To face a witch is to face fear itself."

—From the *Nwoma*

THE BLAST THROWS US all off our feet. A tear opens in the air above the shattered pieces of the drum, like someone cut a slice out of the sky with a pair of scissors.

One brown, withered hand pokes through the slice.

And then another.

And just like that, Nana Bekoe hauls back into the real world for the first time in almost twenty years.

I can't breathe. I can't move. My grandmother is shorter than she looked in the memories my aunt showed me. Stooped with age, Nana Bekoe is now only a few inches taller than me. A full patterned black-and-white kaftan hangs loosely over her shoulders, and her hair is giant cloud of gray curls. Honestly, she looks like the kind of little old lady you'd find at a senior center giving out candy to children and playing bingo on Sundays.

Except for her eyes. There is nothing nice or kind in her crimson eyes as they sweep over the garden and land on Declan. "Thank you for your assistance, young man. I couldn't have done it without you," she croons.

He takes a few shocked steps back. "You're not my mom," says Declan, his voice cracking.

Nana Bekoe ignores him and turns to me. One corner of her lip curls up over her fangs, but not in a smile. "And you must be my little halfling granddaughter. Come, let me take a look at you."

When I don't move, she twitches a finger.

Tendrils of black magic wrap around my waist and yank me forward until I'm floating upside down inches from her face.

"Serwa!" my friends cry.

That not-a-smile on Nana Bekoe's face grows wider. "You are the spitting image of Akosua. You poor wretch, having her for a mother."

I'm too terrified to speak, and the fact all the blood is currently rushing to my head certainly isn't helping. Nana Bekoe takes one look at the necklace I'm wearing—Grandma Awurama's—and kisses her teeth. "Now where have I seen this before? Wasn't this that horrid Slayer woman's trinket? What was her name . . . ? Ah yes, Awurama Boateng, wasn't it?"

"Please, don't," I beg, but it doesn't stop Nana Bekoe from yanking the pendant off my neck and crushing it in her fist.

"There, that's much better. It's bad enough you have the blood of the enemy—you don't need to wear their trophies, too."

Sometimes, on those lonely nights when my parents and I were on the road, moving from one town to another with no one knowing or caring about us in either place, I would fantasize about having grandparents. In those fantasies, my grandmother was someone loving and sweet. She'd like to bake, and she'd tell me stories, and she'd love me just as much as I loved her. I knew even then that those were just rose-tinged thoughts, and the reality would probably be less Disney-movie sappy.

But even in my worst nightmares, I never could've imagined someone like this.

Nana Bekoe looks around. "You're here, but where could that useless daughter of mine possibly—"

Her neck snaps back as an arrow pierces her forehead. A familiar voice behind me screams, *"Put her down!"*

Nana Bekoe's black magic falters, and she drops me to the ground. But she recovers immediately, simply yanking the arrow from her skull and tossing it aside. The discarded shaft hums with divine wisdom from the nkyimu Adinkra drawn on its flint. I've seen one of those take out whole teams of adze, but this one didn't even make my grandmother *flinch*. They told me Nana Bekoe was powerful, but this is beyond anything I've ever seen.

"There you are, Akosua. I was starting to think you'd forgotten all about me," she says as my parents burst into the garden with a host of Slayers in tow. Only a minute has passed since Dr. Amankwah called out to Declan, but the entire world has changed.

"Kids, get behind me!" my dad orders, and the six of us scramble to do as he says while he, my mom, and the rest of the Slayers plant themselves in a protective half circle in front of us.

"I don't want to hurt you, Mother," my mom says, shaking. The strongest Slayer in a generation, the person who taught me everything I know about battle, is *shaking*. Dad steps closer to her, his own sword raised, the look in his eyes just daring my grandmother to make a move.

"'You don't want to hurt me'?" Nana Bekoe parrots in a mocking tone. "What was turning your back on me after I brought you into his world, if not hurting me? What was leaving me to waste away for *twenty years* if not hurting me?" Fury spikes across my grandmother's face. "Really, Akosua, where are your manners? Is this any way to introduce a grandmother to her grandchild?"

Even though my grandmother is looking at me, she's still speaking to Mom. "An obayifo child who also has divine wisdom flowing through her veins. Of course it wasn't enough for you to banish your own mother. You also had to taint our bloodline with those who would see our kind dead. I had such high hopes for you, girl. I would have made you my heir had you not disappointed me time and time again. Abena never would have let me down like this."

My mom always used to tell me that the way you let people talk to you is the way you let them treat you. I've seen her call people out for acting snide or condescending because they made the mistake of assuming she wouldn't stand up for herself. But she says nothing as Nana Bekoe insults her in front of all of us. In the presence of her own mother, my mom becomes as powerless as a child hiding from a monster.

My grandmother stretches her neck like she's trying to get a crick out of it. "Enough idle chitchat. Akosua, get over here. We're leaving."

Instead of moving, my mom looks at me. Whatever she sees makes her square her shoulders, turn back to Nana Bekoe, and spit out, "*No.* I'm not going anywhere with you."

Suddenly, I wish I could run over to Mom and wrap my arms around her, because now I understand the full cost of her refusal. Nana Bekoe's eyes were already red, but they glow like embers with rage at my mother's defiance.

"You think you're grown?" she screams. "You think you're a big girl now, Akosua, and you can do whatever you want? How dare you say no to me!"

My grandmother raises her hand, and the black magic pooling in her palm has streaks of golden light, the same color as an adze, threaded through it. "You're not the only one who has changed during our time apart."

Nana Bekoe thrusts a hand forward, and a column of the mutated black magic shoots toward my mother. But Dad shoves her away at the last second, taking the full brunt of the attack straight to the chest.

"Daddy!" I scream as he slumps over. I try to run to him, but Mateo and Gavin hold me back. Mom scrambles to my dad's side.

"Kwabena? Kwabena!" My mother reaches for my father . . .

Only to duck out of the way when he slashes his sword at her face.

"Dad! What are you doing? Stop!" I scream. No! No, this can't be happening! My dad would never, *ever* attack my mom.

"Like my new trick?" my grandmother says with a cackle. "They said an obayifo's black magic couldn't control minds like an adze's can, but it's amazing what abilities you can develop after twenty years trapped in a magically volatile object. You were so concerned about getting me into the drum, you never stopped to think what being in there might do to me."

You can practically feel the terror that passes through the Slayers as the implication of Nana Bekoe's words sinks in. She was already a master of an obayifo's kind of black magic, but her time in the drum has given her an adze's ability to take over a person's mind.

My grandmother can turn anybody she wants into a vampire.

When Dad stands, his normally dark eyes are ringed with gold, and his top lip curls up to reveal fangs even sharper than my own. Nana Bekoe lifts her hands, and my dad mirrors the motion like a character in a video game taking commands from a controller.

With a yell, I rip myself from my friends and sprint over to my dad. I can fix this. Most people don't remember their true selves when they're under black magic mind control, but Roxy managed to reach Ashley when Ashley was being controlled by an adze.

He's not a monster. He's not a vampire. He's my *father*. If I can't get through to him, no one can.

"Dad, Daddy, it's me. It's Serwa," I say breathlessly.

"Serwa, get back here!" screams Mom, but now two other Slayers have planted themselves in front of her, waiting to see what happens.

"You've got to snap out of this!" I say to Dad. "Don't let her control you."

My father blinks at me but doesn't move.

I take a step closer. "It's me, Dad. It's me. R-remember the Big Hat game? Remember Mom and Boulder and your garden? Remember *me*?"

I take one last step forward, hand raised to reach him.

And freeze when my father lifts his sword and aims it directly at my heart.

"D-Dad?"

I feel like I'm watching everything that happens next from somewhere outside my body. My dad swings his sword as Mom pushes past the Slayers to jump between us. She lets out a howl of pain that echoes through my body, and a bright bloom of blood spills from the newly opened gash in her arm. Nana Bekoe is laughing as her own child bleeds before her, and behind us, Okomfohene Nsiah is screaming for everyone to retreat. This isn't happening this isn't real because my father would never raise a weapon at me he would never hurt my mom he wouldn't hurt me he loves us *this isn't happening*—

"Portal's ready!" yells a voice from somewhere behind me. While my family was embroiled in our violent reunion, several of the Abomofuo opened a new portal inside the fountain. Through the dim light I can just make out the orange-painted walls of the Compound.

"Everyone, retreat, now!" booms Okomfohene Nsiah, repeating the command again in Twi. "Obiara san n'akyi!"

"Come on, Serwa, let's go!" cries Roxy. She and the others yank at me, but I twist and thrash in their hands.

"Get off me!" I scream, but I'm not screaming, because this isn't happening. "Dad! Daddy!"

An arm wraps around my waist, hauling me effortlessly off my feet. Even with her injuries, my mom's obayifo strength is fearsome, and I can't stop her from dragging me toward the portal.

"Let me go!" I sob. "We can't leave him!" But my mother ignores me even as her blood drenches my shirt. I'm so overwhelmed, the scent of the blood doesn't even do anything to me. "Dad! Dad!"

The last thing I see before the portal closes around us is my father's blank, emotionless face and my grandmother's triumphant grin.

And then the world goes dark.

31

How to Go into Hiding

"Regroup. Rethink. Refocus. That is all one can do when one has lost beyond all measure."

—From the *Nwoma*

"LOOK UP."

I follow the mmoatia's command and turn my eyes toward the too-bright fluorescent light hanging above my head. I'm in one of the Compound's many healing rooms, which would be indistinguishable from your average pediatrician's office if the posters didn't say things like HOW TO RECOVER AFTER A SASABONSAM ATTACK and HAVE YOU BEEN VACCINATED AGAINST MAGIC LICE BITES? The mmoatia checking on me isn't Boulder. He's currently under surveillance to see how his psychic bond to my father will be affected by what happened in the garden a few hours ago.

"Do you feel any dizziness?" asks the forest spirit, whose face is taken up almost entirely by a bushy white mustache.

"No."

"Shortness of breath?"

"No."

"Any pain, anywhere?"

"No."

I can tell the healer doesn't believe me, but I'm not lying. I don't feel any pain.

I don't feel anything.

With a reminder to come back if I notice any new injuries, I'm discharged. My mom is waiting for me outside, her own arm wound already healed up.

"Your friends are still being treated, but there weren't any major injuries," she says, her voice as hollow as I feel right now.

I nod. "Cool."

We stand there for several tense, silent seconds. "Serwa, I . . ." Mom begins before trailing off. I don't know what she wants to say to me right now, and honestly, I'm not sure she knows, either. What words are left when your world has been torn apart by the very family you've tried so hard to save?

The silence feels like it'll continue forever until a woman in a crisp white pantsuit walks up to us. "Please come with me," she says, a hint of a British accent lilting her words. She must be one of the priests' personal assistants. "The Okomfohene would like to speak to you both."

We follow the woman into a conference room with a long rectangular table that has a large magic-forged holographic globe of the world hovering over the center of it. Hundreds of glowing dots pepper every continent, even Antarctica. Okomfohene Nsiah leans toward the map with his fingers tightly gripping the edge of the table. The head priest has his lion mask back on, the one he wears during formal Abomofuo proceedings. Declan, his father, and Pepper are seated around him. The older Amankwah gives my mother and me a disgusted glance, while the younger one won't even look my way. The bite mark on Declan's neck is healed at least. That's one good thing, I guess.

And, to my surprise, Auntie Effi is sitting there, too, though she's in chains and flanked by two Slayer guards. Yeah, no getting her out of this one.

"Is it true? Is Mother free?" she asks Mom and me, and our silence is all the confirmation she needs. Her face brightens with hope. "Did she—did she ask about me?"

"No," Mom says dully.

My aunt's face falls, but she gathers herself quickly, folding her shackled hands in her lap. "She'll come back for me," she says haughtily.

No one responds.

I can't see Okomfohene Nsiah's face, but I can sense his frown at my aunt. After a beat, he finally speaks. "Our forces only arrived in the garden the moment after the Midnight Drum was destroyed, and Nana Bekoe's black magic shut down all the cameras in the building. Can you explain to me exactly what led to her release?"

I open my mouth to speak, but the priest puts up a silencing hand. "I wasn't talking to you," he says coldly. I shrink back as he turns to Declan. "Young Slayer Amankwah, explain. How did Nana Bekoe escape the drum?"

Declan lifts his head, dark circles lining his eyes. It's weird—for so long I thought he had everything together, but now I only see a scared kid who is in way over his head.

Just like me.

Declan glances at me, and his apologetic look tells me what he's going to say before he does. "After Serwa bit me, she and her friends disappeared into a portal. They reappeared moments later with the Midnight Drum. I—I tried to intervene, but I wasn't fast enough to stop her from freeing her grand-mother."

There are spells a Slayer can cast to determine whether someone is lying, but they're not going to use one on Declan. Why would they? He's the golden child, everything a Slayer should be. If I told the truth, it would be his word against mine. No one here would ever believe that, at the last second, I chose not to free Nana Bekoe while Declan's insecurities made him vulnerable to her manipulation. It doesn't even matter that my friends would back me up, because the Okomfohene would just assume they're lying to protect me.

The truth only matters until it's told by someone people don't want to believe.

Dr. Amankwah shoots my mom and me a look of pure hatred. "Don't you ever come near my son again, witch," he warns me.

Mom and I don't respond, though she puts a protective hand on my shoulder. Normally, my black magic would flare at the direct threat, but the Compound is so thoroughly warded with divine wisdom that I can't call on it in here. This deep in the Abomofuo's fortress, I can't use either of my powers to protect myself.

Auntie Effi sneers. "Something tells me that son of yours isn't as innocent in this as he wants you to believe."

"How dare you talk about my—"

"Enough," the Okomfohene interjects before another fight can break out. "There will be time for punishment later. Right now, the most important thing is figuring out where Nana Bekoe went, what she wants, and how she plans to get it."

"The last two are easy," says my aunt, casually inspecting her nails like there aren't cuffs around her wrists. "What she wants is the complete destruction of the Abomofuo, and how she plans to get it is swiftly and violently. Which is no less than what you deserve given the amount of torment you've caused my people over the centuries."

The sharp warning in Auntie Effi's—no, here she is Boahinmaa—voice is clear. Even if she knew what Nana Bekoe was up to, she would not share that information with the Abomofuo willingly.

A shiver runs down my spine as I remember the corner of Asamando my grandmother destroyed the last time she was free. How much more damage can she do now with her new, heightened abilities? How many more people will she turn into vampires against their will, ripping them from their lives and loved ones to build her army?

Okomfohene Nsiah nods. "Noted. I have sent word across the global mmoatia network that we are under a code red. All Slayers in nonessential roles are to return to the Compound immediately. The damage at the museum has been dealt with, as have all the civilian witnesses."

Dealt with definitely means *mind-wiped*. I wonder if they got Mr. Riley, too, and if they did, if his Keeper powers allowed him to resist mind-wipes like Roxy's do. I don't know which would be worse, him forgetting us or him being racked with guilt that several students vanished on his watch.

The head priest looks at me. "As for your classmates, seeing as they broke through a memory alteration once before, we will keep them here for their own safety as we plan our next steps."

"But what about their families?" I ask, shocked. "They're going to notice they're gone!"

"We have the resources to handle that with minimal disruption to all parties involved."

"We've done it often enough," adds Dr. Amankwah.

I get that everyone is in crisis mode right now, but these are four people's lives, and four families, he's talking about. And the worst part is, I don't doubt the Abomofuo have the power to pluck Eunju, Roxy, Mateo, and Gavin out of their lives without anyone noticing they're gone.

This is all my fault. None of this would've happened if they hadn't made the mistake of being my friends.

"We're assembling a team now to confront Nana Bekoe before she can amass too much power," continues Okomfohene Nsiah. "Akosua, I am sure you understand that given both your emotional connection to this situation and your current condition, you will be sitting out this mission."

My mom places a hand on her stomach. "I understand."

Hang on, what does he mean by *current condition*? My mom looks fine to me. . . .

Oh my gods. "Are you pregnant?!" I screech, thinking back to how she did the same belly touch back when we were getting ready for the gala and how something has seemed different about her ever since we reunited.

Mom gives a small nod tinged with sorrow. "I wanted to tell you after we picked you up in Rocky Gorge, but then you disappeared, and there hasn't been any opportunity to share the news since we got you back. I'm only a few months along."

Boahinmaa lifts her eyebrows. "And here I am without a baby shower gift! Let me know if you'd like help setting up the nursery. I'm sure we have time to hang up the mobile before Mother razes this place to the ground."

Ignoring her sister, Mom stares at me earnestly, clearly bracing herself for my reaction. I don't blame her, seeing as the last time she surprised me with life-changing information, I almost destroyed an IHOP parking lot.

I feel like Nyame himself could jump up from under the table and hit me in the face with a pie and I'd be less shocked. My mom's pregnant. I'm going to have a little sibling. And right now, my dad is off somewhere under the mind control of his evil mother-in-law.

"How could you have another kid after everything you've put me through?" I snap, remembering Dad's retelling of my birth. Will this new baby be forced to wear a seal, too? But obayifo are always women, cis or trans. If my new sibling isn't a girl, will everyone like them more than they like me because they don't have black magic?

Did my parents need to have another baby to prove they can make a kid who doesn't ruin everything, since they clearly failed with me?

I groan and put my face in my hands. "This family is so screwed up!"

"I know it doesn't seem like it now, but this baby is a *good* thing," Mom tries to argue.

I just cross my arms over my chest and turn away, but not before seeing the anguish on Mom's face at my rejection.

The Okomfohene clears his throat. "Serwa, Declan, please leave the room. It's time for us to discuss confidential matters regarding the mission."

"But what about my dad?" I argue. "He hasn't done anything wrong! How are you going to save him?"

"When an adze possesses a host, they gain access to all the latter's memories," explains the Okomfohene. "Every thought they've ever had, every piece of information they know. If Nana Bekoe's powers now function in a similar manner, that means she now knows everything your father knows."

"Edmund and I were both raised in the Compound," says

Dr. Amankwah solemnly. "He comes from one of the founding Slayer lines. He knows our locations, our secret workings, and our weaknesses, which means Nana Bekoe knows them, too. The magnitude of this threat cannot be understated. Even during the last war, the forces of dark magic didn't have one of our own under their command."

"So what's going to happen to him?" I look around the room. No one will meet my eye. "Someone answer me! What's going to happen?"

"If we can reach Kwabena, our forces will, of course, attempt to extract him from Nana Bekoe's control," the Okomfohene says slowly, and it feels like all the air in the room is sinking into my lungs. "However, as you saw in the garden, she is highly resistant to our divine wisdom. We will do everything in our power to save him, but if that can't be accomplished, then we will have no choice but to . . . neutralize the threat."

"What do you mean by neutralize the—"

The full meaning of the head priest's words hits me like a speeding truck. Beside me, Mom lets out a sharp, shuddering grasp. Despite her devil-may-care facade, Boahinmaa's focus shifts to her sister with an almost protective sort of pity.

Okomfohene Nsiah can dress it up as politely as he wants, but the truth is obvious to everyone in the room—if they can't rescue my dad from Nana Bekoe, they'll have to kill him to protect the organization.

Just like I've done my whole life when the world got too scary or too big, I reach for my mom. She wraps her fingers around my own, and to my surprise, her hand isn't that much bigger than mine anymore. No matter what has happened between us up to now, we need each other to absorb our world falling to pieces.

Mom might be the best Slayer in the world, but at the moment, she's powerless to protect the people she cares about most. If our family is going to survive this ordeal, I need to be strong enough for both of us.

No—the *three* of us. My mother, me, and my new baby sibling. They might be a bad idea, but they're mine to protect now, too.

"Do you understand?" asks Okomfohene Nsiah.

Beneath my sleeve, Owuo's mark throbs gently. I force myself to look up at the man who might have to order my father's death. "I understand."

AFTER THAT, DECLAN AND I are kicked out of the room so the adults can talk. Two Slayers are ordered to take us to our respective locations in opposite directions of a sleek linoleum hallway. The abode santann is painted on the wall in regular intervals, the eyes seeming to follow our every move.

Declan pauses before he goes, "Serwa, wait." He shuffles nervously from foot to foot. "You still owe me an answer."

What in the world is he talking about? Wait. I forgot that silly promise I made before our duel on the soccer field. Declan wants to cash that in now of all times?

My lips curl up in a sneer. "Sorry, your dad says I can't be near you. And there's nothing more important than keeping Daddy happy, is there?"

He flinches like I slapped him in the face; I low-key wish I could. A small part of me feels bad for how tortured he looks—I know all too well how a single moment of weakness can lead to unimaginable chaos. I'm honestly not that mad at him for giving in to the Midnight Drum's call when I almost did, too.

But lying about it in front of the Okomfohene and placing the blame on me because he knows his word matters more than mine to these people? That's something I'm not sure I can ever forgive. Especially when his foolish actions mean I might lose my dad.

"Serwa, I'm—" Declan begins, but I turn my back on him and follow my guard down the hall.

My escort stops in front of a plain door and tells me I'm supposed to wait inside the room until my mother finishes speaking to the Okomfo. Just like Dr. Amankwah, he doesn't hide his disgust at an obayifo sullying the Compound's sacred halls. I wonder if he knows that I'm not wearing a seal. Not that it matters—the wards render my black magic useless in here.

The door opens into a surprisingly modern-looking lounge where I see Roxy, Mateo, Gavin, and Eunju all flopped on beanbag chairs with several sodas and pizza boxes around them. They take one look at my face and run over.

"Hey, it's going to be okay," says Eunju, her tone unusually gentle. "Everything is going to be okay."

I don't realize I'm crying until Mateo hands me a wad of napkins. "S-sorry they're kind of crumpled," he mutters, and this small gesture of kindness breaks the dam completely. With my friends wrapped around me, I fall apart, hiccuping apologies through my snot and tears.

"None of this is your fault, Serwa," says Roxy after I've calmed down enough to explain what's happening. "None of it."

I nod and sniff. Mateo awkwardly pats my back. "No offense, Serwa, but your g-g-g-randma is kind of the worst."

For the first time in hours, I let out a laugh. "She's not my grandma. She's just a lady that gave birth to my mom." The only grandma I care about now is dead, and nothing can change that. I touch the empty place on my chest where her pendant used to hang. "Enough about me. What about you guys? How are you holding up?"

"Aside from the fact we're being held hostage by the Ghanaian Illuminati? Never been better," jokes Gavin, earning him a punch in the shoulder from Eunju.

"They t-t-told us we can't leave until the security threat has been d-dealt with," says Mateo. "And they'll make it so our families d-d-d—our families don't worry."

"My mom is going to be all alone," whispers Roxy, her eyes glassy. It's impossible to miss the wave of terror coming from her—from all of them—beneath all the jokes.

"I'm going to fix this," I promise them. "I am going to stop Nana Bekoe, rescue my dad, and get you all back to your families. I swear on everything that I'll make this right."

Gavin lifts an eyebrow. "And exactly how are you planning to take down your ridonkulously powerful grandmother?"

"I can't say too much. Assume every second we're in the Compound, we're under surveillance," I say. "But I'll need all of you to do it."

I know we can do this. Every time we've teamed up, we've achieved the impossible. But hang on, why is Roxy shaking her head?

"No," she whispers.

We all stare at her, and even she looks surprised the word came out. "I mean . . . I know you didn't mean for any of this to happen, Serwa. But it did. And now we're stuck here until who knows when and our families have forgotten all about us! I—I'm done."

Eunju purses her lips. "Fighting a single vampire at our school was one thing, but we never signed up to join a war."

Roxy nods, encouraged by Eunju's support. "Whatever you're planning, I don't want any part in it."

My cousin's hands shake at her side, which is how I know this is hard for her to say. This is the same girl who let her former best friend, Ashley, bully her for years, yet now she's standing up for herself. I'm so proud of her that I can't even be upset that the person she's standing up to is me.

I turn to the other three. "Do you all feel this way?"

Eunju looks down, then up again with her mouth in a determined line. "Yeah."

"Yeah," Gavin echoes, awkwardly rubbing his neck.

Mateo pauses for a long time. He's always been the member of the GCC who understood me best, which is why it hurts so much when he says, "I j-just—I want to trust you again, Serwa, b-but I d-don't know how."

I take a deep breath. I count to ten until the despair and the hurt fade enough for me to say, "I understand."

"You d-do?"

"I do. You all have given up way too much. I can't ask any more of you than I already have."

If this were a movie, this would be the part where they all change their minds and say we're in this together no matter what. Then everyone would jump into the air and there'd be a freeze-frame before the end credits rolled.

But instead, we all shuffle awkwardly to different corners of the room to be alone with our thoughts. I'll miss my friends' unwavering support, but I can't force it to return. Not when I've broken every promise I've made to them, intentionally or not.

If they ever help me again, it has to be on their terms. I won't make them come with me to stop Nana Bekoe—even though the task just got monumentally more difficult if they won't help.

I press Owuo's mark through my sleeve and run my tongue over my fangs as I try to think. I push through my sadness, anger, and shock to the corner of my mind that comes alive whenever I'm faced with a challenge.

I thought I'd have a hard time finding a person to give to Owuo to fulfill my end of the bargain, but now the answer is clear. No one deserves to be trapped forever with the god of death more than Nana Bekoe.

Everyone in the Abomofuo may hate me because of what I am. My friends and I might be captives of the very organization I once would've given anything to join. But nothing can change the fact that, like every Slayer before me, I was trained to track down creatures who hurt me and my loved ones. And I *am* going to save my dad. I refuse to even consider a future in which I don't. I'm going to rescue him from Nana Bekoe, even if I have to do it all alone, and by the time my little sibling is born, my family will be happy and whole again.

The rules may have shifted, but the battle is the same. With my unique combination of divine wisdom and black magic, there's no force in the world that can stop me.

I stretch out on my beanbag chair, calm purpose filling me where minutes ago there was only despair.

I may as well enjoy the free pizza while I can, because it's time for me to plan a hunt.

Author's Note

A LOT OF ELEMENTS in Serwa's world are made up; for instance, there's no secret organization of Ghanaian monster hunters hiding around the globe (as far as I know, at least). However, one painfully true detail is witchcraft being used as an excuse to enact violence upon vulnerable people. Though less prevalent than they used to be, witch prisoner camps still exist in parts of Ghana. These camps often lack running water, food, and education. Even worse, some of the inhabitants feel they are safer there than returning to the communities that shunned them.

Though I fictionalized certain elements for the sake of the story, it is still a horrible reality for too many women in Ghana and some other parts of the world. Oftentimes, the accused are widows, mentally ill, or fall into some other marginalization that supposedly justifies the violence enacted upon them. While there are records of people of other genders dealing with similar accusations, the stigma still falls disproportionately on marginalized women.

If you're interested in learning more about this shameful practice, and more importantly, the work being done to end it, I highly recommend the book *Witchcraft, Witches, and Violence in Ghana* by Mensah Adinkrah and the documentary *The Witches of Gambaga* by director and author Yaba Badoe.

And I challenge anyone who reads this book to ask themselves exactly who gets to decide what makes another person a monster and why. Thank you for reading.

Glossary

Aba (ah-buh) the Fante version of the day name of a girl born on a Thursday. Like Roxy!

Abomofuo (ah-boh-moh-FWO) *hunters* in Twi. An organization dedicated to defending the world from the forces of black magic. Composed of Slayers (like me!), Middle Men, and Okomfo.

abosom (ah-BOH-sohm) the godly children of Nyame and Asaase Yaa, tasked to watch over the earth. Tend to be tied to physical locations, like rivers and lakes, though there are exceptions. Have enough intra-family drama to put the Kardashians to shame. Singular: **obosom** (oh-BOH-sohm)

abusua (eh-boo-soo-YAH) *family* in Twi, though it traditionally referred to a person's matrilineal line. Also the people in life most likely to tolerate your snoring.

Accra (ah-KRAH) the capital of Ghana

Acheampomaa (ah-chih-ahm-po-MAH-ah) a Ghanaian's girl's name and my middle name. Literally no one but my parents calls me that, though, and only when I've messed up, like, really bad.

Adinkra (eh-dihn-KRAH) Akan symbols used to convey complex messages. Often tied to proverbs.

adze (ah-DJEH) a vampire that can transform into a firefly and possess the human mind. Bad news.

Akan (ah-KAHN) one of the largest ethnic groups in Ghana. In fact, they've lived in the region since long before it ever WAS Ghana! Comprised of lots of different subgroups.

Akosua (ah-koh-soo-YAH) Akan-given name for a female child born on a Sunday. Like my mom!

akrafena (ah-krah-fih-NAH) a traditional Ashanti sword with a black blade and a gold hilt. Often has Adinkra carved into it. Try not to touch the pointy end because it hurts—a lot. Just . . . trust me on this one.

akwaaba (ah-KWAH-ah-bah) *welcome* in Twi

akwadaa boni (ah-kwah-DAAH boh-NIH) *troublesome child* in Twi. Often used as a term of endearment (*Most* of the time . . .).

Amankwah (ah-mahn-KWAH) a Ghanaian surname belonging to lots of perfectly nice people, and, unfortunately, my ETERNAL NEMESIS, DECLAN

Amokye (ah-moh-CHIH) the old woman who guards the river at the boundary between life and death. In dire need of a vacation. Preeeetty sure she hates me.

Anansi (ah-nahn-SEE) an Akan folkloric figure sometimes depicted as a man, sometimes depicted as a spider, always depicted as a pain in the butt. Though he wasn't traditionally worshipped as a god, he has weaseled his way into the role over the centuries, much to the irritation of his actually divine siblings. Last I heard he was hanging with some kid from Chicago. . . .

Antoa Nyamaa (ahn-toh-AH nyah-MAH-ah) goddess of justice and retribution and one of the most powerful members of the pantheon. She can play a *wicked* bass solo, though!

Asaase Yaa (ah-SAH-ah-say yah) goddess of the earth and wife of Nyame. Her sacred day is Thursday. These days she seems to be more interested in upping her follower count than all that hippie-dippie forest stuff, though.

Asaman (ah-SAH-mahn) *ghost* in Twi

Asamando (ah-SAH-man-do) the realm of ghosts, aka the underworld. Home to the spirits of the ancestors and also some pretty great parties. Fun place to visit—as long as you're okay with never coming back.

Awurama (ah-woo-rah-MAH) literally means *Lady Ama*. A variation of the Akan day name Ama, given to a female child born on a Saturday. Like my dad's mother!

ayie (eh-yee-AY) a traditional Akan funeral. In the old times, used to last a whole week. Can actually be pretty upbeat. Remember those dancing Ghanaian pallbearers who went viral? That's what an ayie is like.

Bekoe (beh-KWAI) a Ghanaian name composed of *be* (came) and *koe* (to fight), so loosely translating to *Fighter* or *Warrior*. Often given to a child born during wartime, which might explain why Nana Bekoe is the way she is. . . .

Bia (bee-YUH) god of the bush and twin brother of Tano. Usually chill, until someone brings up that time his twin screwed him over. Then he gets *intense*.

Biri (bee-RIH) *dizzy* in Twi

Boahinmaa (bo-ah-hin-MAH-AH) a Ghanaian girl's name meaning *She who has left her people*

Boateng (bo-ah-TING) an Akan surname coming from the Twi words *boa* (help) and *tene* (to straighten/make upright), so it loosely translates to *helper*. There's lots of Boatengs running around Ghana, but I highly doubt I'm related to them all.

bofrot (BOH-froat) a West African dessert of fried dough rolled into balls and sometimes powdered with sugar. Also called buffloaf. I once ate thirteen in a single sitting. . . . World's most delicious mistake.

bonsam (bohn-SAHM) creatures of black magic with hooks for feet. They hang in trees waiting to drop down on unsuspecting victims.

Daa (da-ah) an affectionate way to refer to an older male, like a father or grandfather.

day name a name given to an Akan child based on the day of the week on which they're born. There's lots of variations among the different tribes. However, not everyone goes by their day name.

djembe (djehm-BAY) **drum** a drum from West Africa made of a wooden body and an animal-skin head. Playing one well is a very impressive skill that I very much do not have.

dua (doo-ooh-YAH) *tree* in Twi

Ɛ (eh) a vowel in the Akan alphabet. Pronounced similarly to the first syllable in *elephant*.

Effi (eh-FEE) a Ghanaian girl's name.

efunu adaka (eh-foo-NOO eh-dah-KAH) *corpse boxes* in Ga. Usually referred to as fantasy coffins. These coffins often take the shape of something that mattered to the deceased in life, and they can get pretty whimsical! (Who wouldn't want to be buried in a giant chicken?)

egusi (eh-goo-SEE) **stew** a traditional West African dish made with spinach and melon seeds. There are variations across the region, but it's an undisputed fact that the Ghanaian version is the best one. Don't try to fight me on this. You'll lose.

Esum (eh-SOOHM) *darkness* in Twi, and one of the three celestial children of Nyame

Fante (fahn-TEE) one of the subgroups of the Akan people,

mainly located in the central and coastal regions of Ghana.
My uncle Patrick and cousin Roxy come from this tribe!

Ga (gah) an ethnic group of Ghana, Togo, and Benin

Ghana (GAH-nuh) a West African nation sandwiched between
Ivory Coast and Togo. It was once known as the British colony
Gold Coast. Though they share the same name, the current
country Ghana and the ancient empire Ghana were in two
different locations!

Gollywood (GOH-lee-wood) a nickname for the film industry
in Ghana. Imagine your favorite soap opera cranked up to a
million. Their films are a lot like that. It's amazing.

-hene (heh-neh) a suffix added to a title to indicate leadership.
Okomfohene = leader of the Okomfo. Asantehene = chief of
the Ashanti people. You get the idea.

honam (hoh-NAHM) a person's body

jollof (joh-LOHF) a West African dish of rice cooked in a
tomato stew, often garnished with meat, vegetables, and/or
seafood. It is an indisputable fact that the Ghanaian version is
the best kind. No, YOU'RE biased!!!

kente (kehn-TAY) a Ghanaian textile cloth woven with silk
and cotton. It can be done in lots of different colors, but the
orange, black, and green combo is the most famous. Traditionally it was only worn by royalty; nowadays anyone can wear
it. (And look good while doing it, too!)

Kodwo (koh-JOH) an Akan day name for a boy born on a Monday. This is also Declan's day name. Apologies to everyone he shares it with.

Kumasi (kooh-mah-SIH) second-largest city in Ghana and former capital of the Ashanti Empire. Literally means *Under the Kum Tree*. Birthplace to lots of cool people, including some author who wrote a YA book about two teens trying to kill each other.

Kwabena (kwah-BEH-nah) Akan day name for a male child born on a Tuesday. Like my dad!

Kwaku (kway-KOO) an Akan day name for a boy born on a Wednesday. Fun fact, this is actually Anansi's first name!

Kwasi Benefo (kway-SEE beh-neh-FOH) a folkloric figure famous for being the only human to have ever entered Asamando and lived to tell the tale. His first name, Kwasi, is the Akan day name for a boy born on a Sunday. You'd think after his first couple of wives died he would've given up, but that's a romantic for you.

mako (meh-KOH) a hot-pepper sauce made with tomatoes, onion, and peppers. VERY! SPICY!!!

medaase (meh-DA-ah-si) *thank you* in Twi

medaase paa (meh-DA-ah-si pah) *thank you very much* in Twi

mmoatia (moh-AY-tee-UH) forest spirits specializing in healing magic. All Slayers are partnered with one upon passing their Initiation Test. They come in three kinds: red, black, and white. One single mmoatia is technically an **aboatia**, but people use the terms interchangeably these days. All are extremely old and strangely obsessed with reality TV.

Nana (nah-NUH) a term given to a distinguished figure or elder, like a chief, priest, or god. Can also be a given name, like Nana Bekoe.

nokware (noh-KWAH-rih) *truth* in Twi. Something, apparently, *some* members of my family aren't very good at . . .

Nsamanfo (en-SAH-mahn-foh) the ancestors. They live down in Asamando, where I assume they're having the time of their afterlives.

Nsiah (en-see-AH) a Ghanaian name meaning *sixthborn*

nwoma (en-WOH-muh) *book* in Twi. The *Nwoma* is a book containing all the wisdom passed down from the Abomofuo of old. When kids misbehave, they are forced to write lines from it.

nya abotare (nyah ah-bo-tah-REH) *be patient* in Twi. Often said by a stressed-out parent trying to tame a rowdy child (not that I have experience with that or anything . . .).

Nyame (nyah-MIH) most powerful god in the Akan pantheon. Also known as Onyame and Onyankopon, among other names. Created the world. Represented by the Adinkra gye nyame. Lives in the sky and never answers anyone's texts, much to his wife's and kids' chagrin.

Ɔ (OH) a vowel in the Akan alphabet. Pronounced similarly to the first syllable in *umbrella*.

obayifo (oh-bay-YEE-foh) a witch who controls black magic. Literally translates to *child snatcher*. Some suck human blood; others don't.

obeah (oh-bay-YUH) a system of spiritual practices from the West Indies. There are theories that they derive from the Akan belief in the obayifo, though there is debate among scholars on the main origin.

Okomfo (oh-kohm-FOH) traditional priests working in service to the gods. They run the Abomofuo, overseeing the network of Middle Men, and the training and selection of all Slayers. Probably the grumpiest group of old people you'll ever meet.

Okomfohene (oh-kohm-FOH-heh-neh) leader of the Okomfo

okra (awh-KRAH) a soul. Not to be confused with the food, though the latter is delicious.

Oseiwa (oh-seh-WAH) female form of the name Osei and the traditional form of the name Serwa. Means *noble one*. I might be biased, but I like my spelling better.

Osrane (oh-soo-rah-NIH) *the moon* in Twi, and one of the three celestial children of Nyame. Sometimes also referred to as **Osram.**

Osu (oh-SOO) a neighborhood in Accra that borders the Atlantic Ocean

outdooring a traditional Ghanaian naming ceremony for infants. It usually took place on the eighth day after a baby was born and their parents took them "outdoors" for the first time. These parties can get pretty wild, even though no one ever remembers their own.

Owia (eh-ree-YUH) *the sun* in Twi, and one of the three celestial children of Nyame

red red a traditional Ghanaian stew made with tomato, palm oil, and cowpeas

sasabonsam (sah-sah-bohn-SAHM) bigger, uglier cousin of the bonsam. Known for being bright pink.

Serwa (sehr-WAH) an alternate form of the name Oseiwa, which itself is the female form of the name Osei, meaning *noble one*. Sometimes also spelled Serwaa or Serwah, but I like my spelling best.

shito (shih-taw) a hot pepper sauce made with dried fish and prawns. It is VERY. SPICY. You have been warned!

sunsum (soon-soom) a person's breath of life, spirit, or shadow. Also called **honhom** in some dialects.

Takoradi (tah-koh-rah-DEE) one half of the twin cities of Sekondi-Takoradi in southwestern Ghana

Tano (tah-NOH) god of war and the twin brother of Bia. Will do anything—and I mean *anything*—to win a fight. Kind of a jerk, but in an entertaining way.

Tegare (teh-gah-RIH) god of hunters and the patron deity of the Abomofuo. Probably the most reasonable of all the Abosom (which isn't saying much, since their idea of "reason" is very different from ours).

twe wo hɔ (cheuh woh houh) *back up* in Twi. Great to yell when people are all up in your space.

Twi (chwee) a dialect of the Akan language spoken by millions of people in Ghana and around the world. Not to be confused with the first syllable in *Twitter* or *Twilight* (Though the latter is my favorite vampire movie, and I'm not ashamed to admit it!).

waakye (wah-ah-CHEH) a Ghanaian dish made of rice and black-eyed peas boiled in sorghum leaves. Really good with eggs and shito!

Yeni aseda (yeh-NEE ah-sih-DAH) an idiom meaning *There are no thanks between u*s. Aka *No need to thank me.* Say this after paying for someone's lunch if you want them to love you forever.

Adinkra Dictionary

abode santann (ah-boh-dih-YEH sahn-TAHN)
- The all-seeing eye
- Symbol of the Abomofuo

adwo (ah-DJOH)
- Symbol of serenity and peace
- Used to calm down a target

agyin dawuru (ah-JIHN dah-wooh-ROOH)
- Agyin's gong
- Symbol of duty and alertness
- Named after a man named Agyin, who faithfully served a past Asantehene

akoben (ah-koh-BEHN)
- The war horn
- Used as a summons/call to action

akofena (ah-koh-feh-NUH)
- Swords of war
- Courage and authority
- Also literal swords

asaase ye duru (ah-SAH-ah-say yeh droo)
- Literally *The Earth has weight*
- Symbol of providence and Asaase Yaa, aka Mother Earth

asawa (as-SAH-wah)
- The sweet berry
- Symbol of sweetness and pleasure
- Used to create a pleasant, euphoric sensation

denkyem (DEHN-chehm)
- The crocodile
- Symbol of adaptability and cleverness
- Used to make something switch forms

dwennimmen (djwahn-nih-MAYN)
- The ram's horn
- Represents strength, humility, and concealment
- Used to hide/deflect attention from something

eban (eh-BAHN)
- Fence
- Creates barriers

epa (eh-PAH)
- The handcuffs
- Represents bondage, law and order, and slavery
- Creates a chain

fafanto (fah-fahn-TOH)
- *Butterfly* in Twi
- Symbol of gentleness and fragility
- Used to make a target brittle and frail

fihankra (fih-hahn-KRAH)
- From the words *fie* (house) and *hankra* (compound)
- Symbol of security
- Used to conceal or secure a target

funtunfunefu-denkyemfunefu (foohn-toohn-fooh-neh-FOOH-dehn-chem-fooh-neh-FOOH)
- Derived from a proverb about two crocodiles who must learn to work together because they share the same stomach
- Symbol of cooperation
- Rarely used in combat

gye nyame (jih nyah-MIH)
- Literally means *except Nyame*
- Symbol of Nyame
- From the proverb: "Abodee santan yi firi tete; obi nte ase a onim n'ahyase, na obi ntena ase nkosi n'awie, gye Nyame." *This Great Panorama of creation dates back to time immemorial; no one lives who saw its beginning and no one will live to see its end, except Nyame.*

hwe mu dua (shweh moo doo-YAH)
- The measuring stick
- Symbol of quality, perfection, and excellence
- Used to improve an object's innate qualities

hye wo nhye (sheh woh en-SHEH)

- Symbol of permanence and endurance
- Used to make a spell's effect permanent

mframadan (em-frahm-ah-DAHN)

- Wind house
- Symbolizes fortitude and security
- Used to strengthen an object

mpatapo (em-PAH-tah-POH)

- The reconciliation knot
- Symbolizes reconciliation, pacification, and peace
- Used to freeze/paralyze/repress a target

nkonsonkonson (en-kohn-SOHN-kohn-SOHN)

- The chain link
- Symbol of unity and brotherhood
- Used to forge connections

nkyimu (en-chih-MOO)

- Symbol of precision
- Used to increase an object's accuracy

nkyinkyin (en-CHEEN-cheen)

- Symbol of toughness and resilience
- Twisting
- Used to make a target sturdier

nsoromma (en-soh-roh-MAH)

- The star
- Symbol of faith
- Used to create light

nyame dua (nyah-MIH doo-YAH)

- Symbol of Nyame's protection
- Used as a protective ward to repel black magic

owuo atwedeɛ (oh-wooh-OH eh-cheh-dih-yeh)

- *Ladder of death* in Twi
- From the proverb "Owuo atwedee baakofoo mforo." *Death's ladder is not climbed by just one person.*
- One of the few Adinkra banned by the Abomofuo for its destructiveness

sankofa (sahn-koh-FAH)

- The bird with its head facing toward the past
- Symbol of remembrance
- Used to draw forth memories

sesa wo suban (say-SAH woh-soo-BAHN)

- Symbol of transformation, rebirth, and renewal
- Used to transform something from one state to another

Acknowledgments

IT'S ACKNOWLEDGMENTS TIME ONCE again! Normally, this is where I'd list my deep gratitude to every person involved in the making of this book, but instead, I would like to give thanks to some of the unsung heroes of my writing journey.

Thank you to every soothing email my agent sends me when I'm panicking about publishing at all hours of the day. We're five books in now, but it still feels as fun as the very first!

Thank you to my beat-up copy of *Percy Jackson and the Lightning Thief* from fifth grade. A direct cause-and-effect line can be drawn from me picking up that book to me getting to work with the incredible team at Disney Hyperion to bring Serwa's story into the world.

Thank you to the hours-long phone calls with writing friends old and new. Against all odds, we're still here! We're still writing! Who would've guessed!

Thank you to the 5,000-character long messages from my non-writer friends about the Netflix shows they're currently binging, the new coffee shop they're obsessed with, or just the usual trials-and-tribulations of surviving this eerie pandemic world. These messages remind me that Everyday Rosie is just as important as Writer Rosie.

Thank you to the stories that passed from one hand to another on their way to mine. *Serwa* would not exist without the research of so many scholars and historians intent on making sure our cultures survive despite the attempts to destroy them completely. I'll do all I can to make sure they keep moving on.

Thank you to the beat-up couch my family gathers around on every movie night/holiday/Chutes and Ladders night, where you all loudly and chaotically remind me there is life beyond the words.

And thank you to the person reading these acknowledgments—you! Without you, this story would still be a bunch of disconnected scenes in my head waiting for a home.

Praise for

Serwa Boateng's Guide to Vampire Hunting

★"This textured, richly mythological story will keep the pages turning as readers are drawn into Serwa's world. A superb, action-packed series starter."
—*Kirkus Reviews* (starred review)

★"Via Serwa's savvy narration, Brown melds Ghanian folklore, smart action, thoughtful commentary about liminal spaces, and a healthy dose of tween hijinks, making for an exhilarating introduction to Serwa Boateng's magic-filled world."
—*Publishers Weekly* (starred review)

★"Brown's middle-grade debut is an action-packed, Ghanaian-influenced contemporary fantasy that explores the bonds of family, friendship, and what happens when you don't know (or are kept from) your own history."
—*Booklist* (starred review)

"Rosie writes her characters with such lyrical power, wit, and empathy that you can't help falling in love with Serwa Boateng, her family, and her friends."
—Rick Riordan, *New York Times* best-selling author of the Percy Jackson and the Olympians series

A *Publishers Weekly* Best Book of 2022